"Kiss Me, Lauren," Demanded Nick . . .

"No," she whispered shakily. . . . "Nick, please."

"Please what?" he murmured against her throat. "Please put us both out of this misery?"

"No!"

Nick's jaw tightened. "I'm trying to get you into that bedroom so that we can ease the ache that's been building inside us for weeks. . . ."

"And then what?" Lauren demanded hotly. "I want to know the rules, dammit! Today we make love, but tomorrow we're no more than casual acquaintances, is that it?" Lauren's voice rose in mounting fury. "I'm not ready to be your Sunday-afternoon playmate. If you're bored, go play your games with someone who can handle a casual romp in bed with you."

"What the hell do you want from me?" he demanded coldly.

I want you to love me, she thought. . . .

Books by Judith McNaught

Almost Heaven
Double Standards
A Kingdom of Dreams
Once and Always
Paradise
Perfect
Something Wonderful
Tender Triumph
Until You
Whitney, My Love

Published by POCKET BOOKS

Judith McNaught

Double Standards

POCKET BOOKS

New York   London   Toronto   Sydney   Tokyo   Singapore

POCKET BOOKS, a division of Simon & Schuster Inc.
1230 Avenue of the Americas, New York, NY 10020

Copyright © 1984 by Judith McNaught

Originally published by Harlequin Enterprises Limited

ISBN: 0-671-73760-0

First Pocket Books printing January 1986

20   19   18   17   16   15   14

POCKET and colophon are registered trademarks of Simon & Schuster Inc.

Cover art by Yuan Lee

Printed in the U.S.A.

*A great love and true friends are two of life's
most precious gifts—and I have been twice blessed
for I have had both. This book is dedicated to
Kathy and Stan Zak, whose friendship I treasure.*

PHILIP WHITWORTH GLANCED UP, HIS ATTENTION drawn by the sound of swift footsteps sinking into the luxurious Oriental carpet that stretched across his presidential office. Lounging back in his maroon leather swivel chair he studied the vice-president who was striding toward him. "Well?" he said impatiently. "Have they announced who the low bidder is?"

The vice-president leaned his clenched fists on the polished surface of Philip's mahogany desk. "Sinclair was the low bidder," he spat out. "National Motors is giving him the contract to provide all the radios for the cars they manufacture, because Nick Sinclair beat our price by a lousy thirty thousand dollars." He drew in a furious breath and expelled it in a hiss. "That bastard won a fifty-million-dollar contract away from us by cutting our price a fraction of one percent!"

Only the slight hardening of Philip Whitworth's

aristocratic jawline betrayed the anger rolling inside him as he said, "That's the fourth time in a year that he's won a major contract away from us. Quite a coincidence, isn't it?"

"Coincidence!" the vice-president repeated. "It's no damn coincidence and you know it, Philip! Someone in my division is on Nick Sinclair's payroll. Some bastard must be spying on us, discovering the amount that goes into our sealed bid, then feeding the information to Sinclair so that he can undercut us by a few dollars. Only six men who work for me knew the amount we were going to bid on this job; one of those six men is our spy."

Philip leaned farther into his chair until his silvered hair touched the high leather back. "You've had security investigations made on all six of those men, and all we learned was that three of them are cheating on their wives."

"Then the investigations weren't thorough enough!" Straightening, the vice-president raked his hand through his hair, then let his arm drop. "Look Philip, I realize Sinclair is your stepson, but you're going to have to do something to stop him. He's out to destroy you."

Philip Whitworth's eyes turned icy. "I have never acknowledged him as my 'stepson,' nor does my wife acknowledge him as her son. Now, precisely what do you propose I do to stop him?"

"Put a spy of your own in his company, find out who his contact here is. I don't care what you do, but for God's sake, do *something!*"

Philip's reply was cut off by the harsh buzzing of

the intercom on his desk, and he jabbed his finger at the button. "Yes, what is it, Helen?"

"I'm sorry to interrupt you, sir," his secretary said, "but there's a Miss Lauren Danner here. She says she has an appointment with you to discuss employment."

"She does," he sighed irritably. "I agreed to interview her for a position with us. Tell her I'll see her in a few minutes." He flicked the button off and returned his attention to the vice-president, who, though preoccupied, was regarding him with curiosity.

"Since when are you conducting personnel interviews, Philip?"

"It's a courtesy interview," Philip explained with an impatient sigh. "Her father is a shirttail relative of mine, a fifth or sixth cousin, as I recall. Danner is one of those relatives my mother unearthed years ago when she was researching her book on our family tree. Every time she located a new batch of possible relatives, she invited them up here to our house for a 'nice little weekend visit' so that she could delve into their ancestry, discover if they were actually related and decide if they were worthy of mention in her book.

"Danner was a professor at a Chicago university. He couldn't come, so he sent his wife—a concert pianist—and his daughter in his place. Mrs. Danner was killed in an automobile accident a few years later, and I never heard from him after that, until last week when he called and asked me to interview his daughter, Lauren, for a job. He said there's nothing suitable for her in Fenster, Missouri, where he's living now."

"Rather presumptuous of him to call you, wasn't it?"

Philip's expression filled with bored resignation. "I'll give the girl a few minutes of my time and then send her packing. We don't have a position for anyone with a college degree in music. Even if we did, I wouldn't hire Lauren Danner. I've never met a more irritating, outrageous, ill-mannered, homely child in my life. She was about nine years old, chubby, with freckles and a mop of reddish hair that looked as if it was never properly combed. She wore hideous horn-rimmed eyeglasses, and so help me God, that child looked down her nose at *us*. . . ."

Philip Whitworth's secretary glanced at the young woman, wearing a crisp navy blue suit and white ascot-style blouse, who was seated across from her. The woman's honey-blond hair was caught up in an elegant chignon, with soft tendrils at her ears framing a face of flawless, vivid beauty. Her cheekbones were slightly high, her nose small, her chin delicately rounded, but her eyes were her most arresting feature. Beneath the arch of her brows, long curly lashes fringed eyes that were a startling, luminous turquoise blue.

"Mr. Whitworth will see you in a few minutes," the secretary said politely, careful not to stare.

Lauren Danner looked up from the magazine she was pretending to read and smiled. "Thank you," she said, then she gazed blindly down again, trying

4

to control her nervous dread of confronting Philip Whitworth face to face.

Fourteen years had not dulled the painful memory of her two days at his magnificent Grosse Pointe mansion, where the entire Whitworth family, and even the servants, had treated Lauren and her mother with insulting scorn. . . .

The phone on the secretary's desk buzzed, sending a jolt through Lauren's nervous system. How, she wondered desperately, had she landed in this impossible predicament? If she'd known in advance that her father was going to call Philip Whitworth, she could have dissuaded him. But by the time she knew anything about it, the call had been made and this interview already arranged. When she'd tried to object, her father had calmly replied that Philip Whitworth owed them a favor, and that unless Lauren could give him some logical arguments against going to Detroit, he expected her to keep the appointment he'd arranged.

Lauren laid the unread magazine in her lap and sighed. Of course, she *could* have told him how the Whitworths had acted fourteen years ago. But right now money was her father's primary concern, and the lack of it was putting lines of strain into his pallid face. Recently the Missouri taxpayers, caught in the vise grip of an economic recession, had voted down a desperately needed school-tax increase. As a result, thousands of teachers were immediately laid off, including Lauren's father. Three months later he had come home from another fruitless trip in search of a job, this time to Kansas City. He had put his briefcase down on the table and had smiled sadly at Lauren and her stepmother. "I don't think an ex-teacher could get a job as a janitor these days," he had said, looking exhausted and strangely pale. Absently he'd massaged his chest near his left arm as he had added grimly, "Which may be for the best, because I don't feel strong enough to push a broom." Without further warning, he had collapsed, the victim of a massive heart attack.

Even though her father was now recovering, that moment had changed the course of her life. . . . No, Lauren corrected herself, she had been on the verge of changing the course herself. After years of relentless study and grueling practice at the piano, after obtaining her master's degree in music, she had already decided that she lacked the driving ambition, the total dedication needed to succeed as a concert pianist. She had inherited her mother's musical talent, but not her tireless devotion to her art.

Lauren wanted more from life than her music. In a way, it had cheated her of as much as it had given her. What with going to school, studying, practicing and working to pay for her lessons and tuition, there'd never been time to relax and enjoy herself. By the time she'd turned twenty-three she'd traveled to cities all over the United States to play in competitions, but all she'd seen of the cities themselves were hotel rooms, practice rooms and auditoriums. She'd met countless men, but there was never time for more than a brief acquaintance. She'd won scholarships and prizes and awards, but there was never enough money to pay all her expenses without the added burden of a part-time job.

Still, after investing so much of her life in music, it had seemed wrong, wasteful, to throw it away for some other career. Her father's illness and the staggering bills that were accruing had forced her to make the decision she'd been postponing. In April he had lost his job, and with it his medical insurance; in July he had lost his health as well. In past years he had given her a great deal of financial help with school and lessons; now it was her turn to help him.

At the thought of this responsibility, Lauren felt as if the weight of the world was resting on her shoulders. She needed a job, she needed money, and she needed them now. She glanced around at the plush reception area she was seated in, and felt strange and disoriented as she tried to imagine herself working for a huge manufacturing corporation like this one. Not that it mattered—if the pay was high enough, she would take whatever job was offered to her. Good jobs with advancement opportunities were practically nonexistent in Fenster, Missouri, and those that were available paid pitifully low in comparison to similar jobs in huge metropolitan areas like Detroit.

The secretary hung up the phone and stood up. "Mr. Whitworth will see you now, Miss Danner."

Lauren followed her to a richly carved mahogany door. As the secretary opened it, Lauren uttered a brief, impassioned prayer that Philip Whitworth wouldn't remember her from that long-ago visit, then she stepped into his office. Years of performing in front of an audience had taught her how to conceal her turbulent nervousness, and now it enabled her to approach Philip Whitworth with an outward appearance of quiet poise as he got to his feet, an expression of astonishment on his aristocratic features.

"You probably don't remember me, Mr. Whitworth," she said, graciously extending her hand across his desk, "but I'm Lauren Danner."

Philip Whitworth's handclasp was firm, his voice tinged with dry amusement. "As a matter of fact, I remember you very well, Lauren; you were rather an . . . unforgettable . . . child."

Lauren smiled, surprised by his candid humor. "That's very kind of you. You might have said outrageous instead of unforgettable."

With that, a tentative truce was declared, and Philip Whitworth nodded toward a gold velvet chair in front of his desk. "Please sit down."

"I've brought you a résumé," Lauren said, removing an envelope from her shoulder purse as she sat down.

He opened the envelope she handed him and extracted the typewritten sheets, but his brown eyes remained riveted on her face, minutely studying each feature. "The resemblance to your mother is striking," he said after a long moment. "She was Italian, wasn't she?"

"My grandparents were born in Italy," Lauren clarified. "My mother was born here."

Philip nodded. "Your hair is much lighter, but

otherwise you look almost exactly like her." His gaze shifted to the résumé she had given him as he added dispassionately, "She was an extraordinarily beautiful woman."

Lauren leaned back in her chair, a little dazed by the unexpected direction the interview had taken. It was rather disconcerting to discover that, despite his outwardly cold, aloof attitude fourteen years before, Philip Whitworth had apparently thought Gina Danner was beautiful. And now he was telling Lauren that he thought she was, too.

While he read her résumé, Lauren let her gaze drift over the stately splendor of the immense office from which Philip Whitworth ruled his corporate empire. Then she studied him. For a man in his fifties, he was extremely attractive. Though his hair was silvering, his tanned face was relatively unlined, and there was no sign of excess weight on his tall, well-built body. Seated behind his huge, baronial desk in an impeccably tailored dark suit, he seemed surrounded by an aura of wealth and power, which Lauren reluctantly found impressive.

Seen now through the eyes of an adult, he didn't seem the cold, conceited snob she remembered. In fact, he seemed every inch a distinguished, elegant socialite. His attitude toward her was certainly courteous, and he had a sense of humor too. All things considered, Lauren couldn't help feeling that her prejudice against him all these years might have been unfair.

Philip Whitworth turned to the second page of her résumé, and Lauren caught herself up short. Exactly *why* was she having this sudden change of heart about him, she wondered uncomfortably. True, he was being cordial and kind to her now—but why wouldn't he be? She was no longer a homely little nine-year-old; she was a young woman with a face and figure that made men turn and stare.

Had she really misjudged the Whitworths all those years ago? Or was she now letting herself be influenced by Philip Whitworth's obvious wealth and smooth sophistication?

"Although your university grades are outstanding, I hope you realize that your degree in music is of no value to the business world," he said.

Lauren instantly pulled her attention to the subject at hand. "I know that. I majored in music because I love it, but I realize there's no future in it for me." With quiet dignity she briefly explained her reasons for abandoning her career as a pianist, including her father's health and her family's financial circumstances.

Philip listened attentively, then glanced again at the résumé in his hand. "I noticed that you also took several business courses in college."

When he paused expectantly, Lauren began to believe he might actually be considering her for a job. "Actually, I'm only a few courses short of qualifying for a business degree."

"And while attending college, you worked after school and during the summers as a secretary," he continued thoughtfully. "Your father didn't mention that on the telephone. Are your shorthand and typing skills as excellent as your résumé claims?"

"Yes," Lauren said, but at the mention of her secretarial background her enthusiasm began to fade.

He relaxed in his chair and, after a moment's thought, seemed to come to a decision. "I can offer you a secretarial position, Lauren, one with challenge and responsibility. I can't offer you anything more than that unless you actually get your business degree."

"But I don't *want* to be a secretary," Lauren sighed.

A wry smile twisted his lips when he saw how discouraged she looked. "You said that your primary concern right now is money—and right now there happens to be a tremendous shortage of qualified, top-notch executive secretaries. Because of this they're in demand and very highly paid. My own secretary, for example, makes almost as much money as my middle-management executives."

"But even so . . ." Lauren started to protest.

Mr. Whitworth held up a hand to silence her. "Let me finish. You've been working for the president of a small manufacturing company. In a small company, everyone knows what everyone else is doing and why they're doing it. Unfortunately, in large corporations such as this one, only high-level executives and their secretaries are aware of the overall picture. May I give you an example of what I'm trying to say?"

Lauren nodded, and he continued. "Let's say you're an accountant in our radio division, and you're asked to prepare an analysis of the cost of each radio we produce. You spend weeks preparing the report without knowing *why* you're doing it. It could be because we're thinking of closing down our radio division; it could be because we're thinking of *expanding* our radio division; or it could be because we're planning an advertising campaign to help sell *more* radios. You don't know what we're planning to do and neither does your supervisor or his supervisor. The only people who are aware of that sort of confidential information are division managers, vice-presidents, *and*," he concluded with smiling emphasis, "their secretaries! If you start out as a secretary with us, you'll get a good overview of the corporation, and you'll be able to make an informed choice about your possible future career goals."

"Is there anything else I could do in a corporation such as yours that would pay as well as being a secretary?" Lauren asked.

"No," he said with quiet firmness. "Not until you get your business degree."

Inwardly Lauren sighed, but she knew she had no choice. She had to make as much money as she possibly could.

"Don't look so glum," he said, "the work won't be boring. Why, my own secretary knows more about our future plans than most of my executives do. Executive secretaries are privy to all sorts of highly confidential information. They're—"

He broke off, staring at Lauren in stunned silence, and when he spoke again there was a triumphant, calculating quality in his voice. "Executive secretaries are privy to highly confidential information," he repeated, an unexplainable smile dawning across his aristocratic features. "A secretary!" he whispered. "They would never suspect a secretary! They wouldn't even run a security check on one. Lauren," he said softly, his brown eyes gleaming like topaz, "I am about to make you a very unusual offer. Please don't argue about it until you hear me out completely. Now, what do you know about corporate or industrial spying?"

Lauren had the queasy feeling that she was hanging over the edge of a dangerous precipice. "Enough to know that people have been sent to prison for it, and that I want absolutely nothing to do with it, Mr. Whitworth."

"Of course you don't," Philip said smoothly. "And please call me Philip; after all, we are related, and I've been calling you Lauren."

Uneasily, Lauren nodded.

"I'm not asking you to spy on another corporation, I'm asking you to spy on mine. Let me explain. In recent years, a company called Sinco has become our biggest competitor. Every time we bid on a contract, Sinco seems to know how much we're going to bid, and they bid just a fraction of a percent less. Somehow, they're finding out what we're putting into our sealed bids, then they cut the price of their bid so that it's slightly lower than ours and steal the contract from us.

"It just happened again today. There are only six men here who could have told Sinco the amount of our bid, and one of them must be a spy. I don't want to dismiss five loyal business executives just to rid myself of one greedy, treacherous man. But if Sinco continues to steal business from us this way, I'm going to have to begin laying people off," he continued. "I employ twelve thousand people, Lauren. Twelve thousand people depend on Whitworth Enterprises for their livelihoods. Twelve thousand families depend on this corporation so that they can have roofs over their heads and food on their tables. There's a chance you could help them keep their jobs and their homes. All I'm asking you to do is to apply for a secretarial position at Sinco today. God knows they'll need to increase their staff to handle the work they just stole from us. With your skills and experience, they'd probably consider you for a secretarial position with some high-level executive."

Against her better judgment, Lauren asked, "If I get the job, then what?"

"Then I'll give you the names of the six men who might possibly be the spy, and all you have to do is listen for mention of their names by anyone at Sinco."

He leaned forward in his chair and folded his hands on his desk. "It's a long shot, Lauren, but frankly, I'm desperate enough to try anything. Now, here's my part of the bargain: I was planning to offer you a secretarial position with us at a very attractive salary. . . ."

The figure he named amazed Lauren, and it showed. It was considerably more than her father had been making as a teacher. Why, if she lived frugally she could support her family and herself.

14

"I can see that you're pleased," Philip chuckled. "Wages in big cities like Detroit are very high compared to smaller places. Now, if you apply at Sinco this afternoon and they offer you a secretarial position, I want you to take it. If the salary there is lower than the one I just offered you, my company will write you a monthly check to make up the difference. If you are able to learn the name of our spy, or anything else of real value to me, I will pay you a bonus of $10,000. Six months from now, if you haven't been able to learn anything important, then you can resign from your job at Sinco and come to work as a secretary for us. As soon as you complete the courses for your business degree, I'll give you any other position here you want, providing of course that you can handle it." His brown eyes moved over her face, searching her troubled features. "Something is bothering you," he observed quietly. "What is it?"

"It *all* bothers me," Lauren admitted. "I don't like intrigue, Mr. Whitworth."

"Please call me Philip. At least do that much for me." With a tired sigh, he leaned back in his chair. "Lauren, I know I have absolutely no right to ask you to apply at Sinco. It may surprise you to learn that I'm aware of how unpleasant your visit with us fourteen years ago was. My son, Carter, was at a difficult age. My mother was obsessed with researching our family tree, and my wife and I . . . well, I'm sorry we weren't more cordial."

Under normal circumstances, Lauren would have turned him down. But her life was in a state of complete upheaval, and her financial responsibilities were staggering. She felt dazed, uncertain and incredibly burdened. "All right," she said slowly. "I'll do it."

"Good," Philip said promptly. Picking up his telephone he called Sinco's number, asked for the personnel manager, then handed Lauren the phone to make an appointment. Lauren's secret hope that Sinco might refuse to see her was instantly dashed. According to the man she spoke to, Sinco had just been awarded a large contract and was in immediate need of experienced secretaries. Since he was planning to work late that night, he instructed Lauren to come at once.

Afterward Philip stood up and put out his hand, clasping hers. "Thank you," he said simply. After a moment's thought, he added, "When you fill out their application form, give your home address in Missouri, but give them this phone number so that they can reach you at our house." He wrote a number on a note pad and tore off the sheet. "The servants answer it with a simple hello," he explained.

"No," Lauren said quickly. "I wouldn't want to impose. I . . . I'd much rather stay in a motel."

"I don't blame you for feeling that way," he replied, making Lauren feel rude and ungracious, "but I would like to make up for that other visit."

Lauren succumbed to defeat. "Are you absolutely certain that Mrs. Whitworth won't object?"

"Carol will be delighted."

When the door closed behind Lauren, Philip Whitworth picked up his telephone and dialed a number that rang in his son's private office, just across the hall. "Carter," he said. "I think we're about to drive a spike into Nick Sinclair's armor. Do you remember Lauren Danner . . . ?"

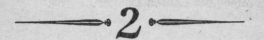

2

By the time Lauren arrived at Sinco's personnel office it was after five o'clock, and she had come to the conclusion that she couldn't possibly spy for Philip Whitworth. Just thinking of it on the way had made her heart pound and her palms perspire on the steering wheel. Even though she would like to help Philip, the intrigue and deception that would be involved petrified her. Still, she hated to admit her cowardice to him.

While she filled out the endless forms and questionnaires required by Sinco, it occurred to her that the best way out of her predicament was to honor her promise to Philip by applying for a job—and then make absolutely certain that she wasn't offered one. Accordingly, she deliberately failed her spelling, typing and shorthand tests and omitted any mention of her college degree. But her crowning achievement was the way she answered the last question on her employment application. The instructions said to list in the order of preference three positions she felt she was qualified to fill at Sinco. Lauren had written "president" for her first choice, "personnel manager" for her second, and "secretary" for her third.

The real personnel manager, Mr. Weatherby, graded her tests, and his face registered horror as he did so. He put them aside and picked up her application, and she watched his gaze glide to the bottom of the last page, where she had listed, among her three choices, Mr. Weatherby's own job. When he read that his face suffused with angry color and his nostrils flared, and Lauren had to bite her trembling lower lip to hide her laughter. Maybe she *was* cut out for intrigue and subterfuge, she thought with an inward smile as he surged to his feet and coldly informed her that she did not meet Sinco's hiring standards for *any* position.

When Lauren emerged from the building, she discovered that the dreary overcast August evening had deepened into a prematurely dark and windy night. With a convulsive shiver, she pulled her navy blue blazer closer around her.

Downtown traffic was backed up on Jefferson Avenue, a sea of white headlights and red taillights speeding past her in both directions. While Lauren waited for the light to change, fat raindrops began to spatter on the pavement around her. There was a break in traffic, and Lauren raced across the broad multi-lane boulevard, reaching the opposite curb a split second before the oncoming cars roared past her.

Breathless and damp, she glanced up at the darkened high-rise building under construction in front of her. The parking garage where she had left her car was four blocks away, but if she cut across the area surrounding the high-rise, she could save herself at least a block. A fresh blast of wind blowing off the Detroit River whipped her skirt around her legs and helped her make up her mind. Disregarding the No Trespassing sign, she ducked under the ropes surrounding the construction area.

Walking as quickly as the uneven ground would permit, Lauren glanced up at the lights scattered here and there in the otherwise dark building. It was at least eighty stories high, made entirely of mirrored glass that reflected the twinkling lights of the city. Where lights were on inside the building, the mirror surface became ordinary two-way glass, and Lauren could see boxes piled in the offices, as if the tenants were getting ready to occupy the space.

Close to the building she found she was shielded from the wind blowing off the river, so she carefully stayed within its protection. As she hurried along it occurred to her that she was a solitary female, alone in the dark in what was purported to be a crime-ridden city. The thought sent fear racing up her spine.

Heavy footsteps suddenly thudded in the dirt behind her, and Lauren's heart gave a leap of terror. She quickened her pace, and the unidentified footsteps moved more quickly too. Panicking, Lauren broke into a stumbling run. Just as she flew toward the main entrance, one of the huge glass doors swung open, and two men emerged from the shadowy building.

"Help!" she cried. "There's someone—" Her foot struck a pile of conduit that coiled around her ankle, then tightened. Lauren soared through the air, her mouth open in a silent scream, her arms flailing for balance, and landed sprawling, face down in the dirt at the men's feet.

"You damn fool!" one of the men grated in angry concern as they both squatted down on their haunches and peered anxiously at her. "What the hell do you think you're doing?"

Bracing herself on her forearms, Lauren lifted her chagrined gaze from the man's shoes to his face. "Auditioning for the circus," she told him dryly. "And for an encore, I usually fall off a bridge."

A rich chuckle sounded from the other man as he took her firmly by the shoulders and helped her to her feet. "What's your name?" he asked, and when Lauren had told him, he added worriedly, "Can you walk?"

"For miles," Lauren assured him unsteadily. Every muscle in her body was protesting, and her left ankle was throbbing painfully.

"Then I guess you can make it as far as the building so we can have a look at the damage," he said with a smile in his voice. Sliding his arm around her waist, he moved against her so that she could lean on him for support.

"Nick," the other man said sharply, "I think it would be better if I go in and call an ambulance while you stay here with Miss Danner."

"Please don't call an ambulance!" Lauren implored. "I'm more embarrassed than hurt," she added desperately, almost sagging with relief when the man called Nick began guiding her toward the dark lobby.

She briefly considered the inadvisability of going into a deserted building with two unknown men, but when they entered the lobby, the other man switched on some small spotlights high in the ceiling, and most of Lauren's doubts were dispelled: he was middle-aged, dignified and wearing a suit and tie. Even in the dim light, he seemed more like a successful business executive than a thug. Lauren glanced at Nick, whose arm was still around her. He was wearing jeans and a denim jacket. Judging from his shadowy profile, Lauren guessed him to be in his mid-thirties, and there was nothing about him, either, that struck her as being ominous.

Over his shoulder, Nick spoke to the other man. "Mike, there should be a first-aid kit in one of the maintenance rooms. Find it and bring it up."

"Right," Mike said, striding toward a glowing red Stairs sign.

Lauren glanced curiously around at the immense lobby. Everything was white travertine marble: the walls, the floors, and even the graceful pillars that soared two stories to the ceiling high above. Dozens of huge potted trees and lush green plants were lined up against one wall, apparently waiting for someone to move them to their proper positions on the vast lobby floor.

When they came to a bank of elevators set into the

far wall, Nick reached around her and pressed the elevator button. The gleaming brass doors slid open and Lauren stepped into the brightly lit elevator. "I'm taking you up to a furnished office where you can sit down and rest until you feel steady enough to walk unaided," Nick explained.

Lauren flicked a smiling, grateful glance at him— and froze with shock. Standing beside her, his features clearly illuminated now by the improved light, was one of the most handsome men she had ever seen. Simultaneously, the elevator doors closed and Lauren jerked her gaze from his face. "Thanks," she said in an odd, croaking whisper, self-consciously pulling free of his supporting arm, "but I can stand alone."

He pressed the button for the eightieth floor, and Lauren quelled the feminine impulse to reach up and pat her hair into place—it would be too obvious, too vain. She wondered if she had a trace of lipstick left, or if her face was dirty, then she caught herself up short. For a sensible young woman, she was reacting very foolishly to what was, after all, nothing more than an attractive male face.

Had he really been that handsome, she wondered. She decided to look at him again, but discreetly this time. Very casually, she raised her eyes to the light above the doors, which flashed the number of the passing floors. Cautiously, she let her gaze slide sideways. . . . Nick was watching the flashing numbers, his head tipped slightly back, his face in profile.

Besides being even more handsome than she had thought, he was at least six feet three inches tall, broad shouldered and athletically muscular. His thick dark hair was coffee brown, beautifully cut and styled. Masculine strength was carved into every feature of his proud profile, from the straight dark brows to the arrogant jut of his chin and jaw. His mouth was firm, but sensually molded.

Lauren was still studying the mobile line of his lips when they quirked suddenly, as if amusement was lurking there. Her gaze shot up, and to her utter horror she discovered that his gray eyes had shifted to her.

Caught in the act of staring at him and practically drooling over him, Lauren said the first thing that came to mind. "I—I'm afraid of elevators," she improvised madly. "I try to concentrate on something else to, er, keep my mind off the height."

"That's very clever," he remarked, but his teasing tone made it obvious he was applauding not her sensible solution to her alleged fear of elevators, but rather her ingenuity in inventing such a plausible lie.

Lauren was torn between laughing at his dry observation and blushing because she hadn't fooled him in the least. She did neither, and instead carefully kept her eyes on the elevator doors until they opened on the eighteenth floor.

"Wait here while I turn on the lights," Nick said. A few seconds later panels of ceiling lights flickered on, illuminating the entire floor, the left half of which appeared to be an immense reception area and four very large walnut-paneled offices. Nick put his hand beneath her elbow, and Lauren's feet sank into the emerald green carpeting as he guided her around the elevator wall to the opposite side.

This half of the floor contained another even larger reception area, with a circular receptionist's desk in the center. Lauren glimpsed a beautiful office opening off the right of the reception area. It was already equipped with built-in filing cabinets and a gleaming wood-and-chrome secretarial desk. Mentally she compared it to her own steel desk at her old part-time job. That one had been in the middle of a cluttered three-person office. It was hard to believe that so much spacious luxury was here for the benefit of a mere secretary.

When she voiced that thought aloud, Nick gave her a derisive look. "Skilled professional secretaries take great pride in being just that, and the salaries they're getting are soaring every year."

"I happen to *be* a secretary," Lauren told him as they walked across the reception area toward a pair of eight-foot-high rosewood doors. "I was across the street applying for a job at Sinco just before I, ah, met you." Nick threw open both doors, then stood back for Lauren to precede him while he studied her limping walk.

Lauren was so acutely aware of his penetrating silver gaze on her legs that her knees wobbled, and she was halfway across the room before she actually looked at her surroundings. What she saw stopped her short. "Good Lord!" she breathed. "What *is* this, anyway?"

"This," Nick said with a smile at her awestruck

expression, "is the president's office. It's one of the few offices that's completely finished."

Speechless, Lauren let her admiring gaze wander over the gigantic office. The long wall in front of her was glass from floor to ceiling, providing an uninterrupted view of nighttime Detroit in all its fantastic, glittering splendor as it fanned out for endless miles in the distance below. The three remaining walls were paneled in satiny rosewood.

Acres of thick cream carpeting covered the floor, and a splendid rosewood desk was off to her far right, facing the room. Six chrome chairs upholstered in moss green were strategically placed before the desk, while on the opposite side of the office, three long, deeply tufted moss green sofas formed a wide U around an immense glass-topped coffee table, its base an enormous piece of highly polished driftwood. "It's absolutely breathtaking," she said softly.

"I'll fix something for us to drink while Mike is getting the first-aid kit," Nick said.

Lauren turned, watching bemusedly as he walked over to a blank rosewood wall and pressed it with his fingertips. A huge panel glided silently aside, revealing a gorgeous mirrored bar lit by tiny concealed spotlights above it. Glass shelves held rows of Waterford crystal glasses and decanters.

When Lauren didn't reply to his offer of a drink, he glanced over his shoulder at her. She lifted her blue eyes from the recessed bar to his face and saw the expression he was trying to hide. Obviously, he was vastly amused by her thunderstruck reaction to this opulence, and the knowledge made her suddenly realize something she had heretofore overlooked; while *she* was acutely aware of his male attraction, *he* seemed completely oblivious to her as a female.

After six years of enduring men's gaping admiration, their leers and stares, she had finally met a man whom she desperately wanted to impress, and nothing was happening. Absolutely nothing. A little puzzled and definitely disappointed, Lauren tried to shrug the matter aside. Beauty was said to be in the eyes of the beholder, and apparently Nick's eyes beheld nothing of interest when he looked at her. That wouldn't have been so awful if only he didn't find her so damned funny!

"If you'd like to clean up, there's a bathroom right there." Nick inclined his head toward the wall beside the bar.

"Where?" Lauren asked blankly, following the direction of his nod.

"Walk straight ahead, and when you get to the wall, just press it."

His lips were twitching again, and Lauren gave him an exasperated look while she did as he'd said. When her fingertips touched the smooth rosewood, a panel clicked open to reveal a spacious bathroom, and she stepped inside.

"Here's the first-aid kit," the man called Mike announced as he entered the suite just then. Lauren started to close the bathroom door but paused when she heard him add in a lowered voice, "Nick, as the corporation's attorney, I'm advising you that the girl ought to be seen by a physician tonight to prove that she isn't seriously injured. If you don't insist on it, some lawyer could claim she's been crippled by her fall and could sue the company for millions."

"Stop making such a big issue out of it," she heard Nick reply. "She's just a nice wide-eyed kid who got the hell scared out of her in a nasty fall. An ambulance ride would terrify her."

"All right," Mike sighed. "I'm late for a meeting in Troy, and I've got to leave. But for God's sake, don't offer her anything alcoholic to drink. Her parents could sue you for trying to seduce a minor, and—"

Feeling both puzzled and insulted at being called a wide-eyed frightened kid, Lauren quietly closed the door. Frowning, she turned to the mirror above the sink, then stifled a shriek of horrified laughter. Her face was covered with wide streaks of dirt and grime; her neat chignon was half undone, dangling crazily askew at her nape; wisps of hair were sticking out like scraggly spikes all over her head; and her suit jacket was hanging drunkenly off her left shoulder.

She looked, she thought with a hysterical giggle, exactly like a caricature of herself—like a funny, hopelessly dirty urchin in disheveled clothing.

And for some reason, it suddenly became imperative that she look vastly different when she walked out of this bathroom. Hastily she began stripping off her soiled navy jacket, gleefully anticipating the shock that was in store for Nick when she was cleaned up and presentable.

If her pulse quickened with excitement while she scrubbed her face and hands, she told herself it was only because she was looking forward to having the last laugh on him, and *not* because she longed for him to think she was attractive. But she had to hurry; if she spent too much time in here her transformation wouldn't be nearly so effective.

She pulled off her sheer tights, grimacing at the sight of the gaping holes in her knees, and lathered more soap onto the washcloth provided. Once she was reasonably clean, she dumped the contents of her shoulder bag onto the vanity and opened the package of spare tights she happened to be carrying with her. After smoothing them on, she pulled the pins out of her dark honey blond hair and began vigorously brushing it, tugging the brush through the tangled strands with ruthless haste. When she was finished, it fell in a soft, shining mass that curled artlessly at her shoulders and back. Swiftly she applied peach lipstick, a touch of blusher, then stuffed everything into her purse and stepped from the mirror to survey her appearance. Her color was high and her eyes were sparkling with lively anticipation. Her ascot-style white blouse was a little prim, but it flattered the graceful line of her throat and emphasized the curves of her breasts. Satisfied, she turned away from the mirror, picked up her jacket and purse and stepped out of the bathroom, closing the rosewood panel with a soft click.

Nick was standing at the mirrored bar, his back to her. Without turning he said, "I had to make a phone call, but I'll have these drinks ready in a moment. Did you find everything you needed in there?"

"Yes, I did, thank you," Lauren said, putting down her purse and jacket. Quietly she stood beside the long sofa, watching his swift, economical movements as he took two crystal glasses down from the shelf and pulled a tray of ice cubes from the compact refrigerator-freezer recessed into the bar. He had removed his denim jacket and tossed it over one of the chairs. With each movement of his arms, the thin fabric of his blue knit shirt tautened, emphasizing his broad, muscular shoulders and tapered back. Lauren let her gaze drift down the clean line of his narrow hips and long legs, outlined by the comfortably snug jeans he wore. When he spoke, Lauren started guiltily, her gaze flying to the back of his dark head.

"I'm afraid this bar isn't stocked with soft drinks or lemonade, Lauren, so I've fixed you a glass of tonic with ice."

Lauren suppressed a chuckle at the mention of lemonade and demurely clasped her hands behind her back. Suspense and anticipation built inside her as he replaced the stopper in a crystal whiskey decanter, picked up a glass in each hand and turned.

He took two steps toward her and stopped cold.

His brows drew together as his narrowed gray eyes slid over the luxurious tumble of burnished honey gold hair that framed her face and fell in glorious abandon over her shoulders and back. His stunned gaze shifted to her face, noting her vivid turquoise eyes sparkling with humor beneath thick, curly lashes, her pert nose, finely sculpted cheeks and soft lips. Then it drifted downward over her full breasts, trim waist and long shapely legs.

Lauren had hoped to make him notice her as a woman, and he was certainly noticing her. Now she rather hoped he would say something nice. But he didn't.

Without a word he turned on his heel, strode over to the bar and dumped the contents of one of the glasses into the stainless steel bar sink. "What are you doing?" Lauren asked.

His voice was filled with amused irony. "Adding some gin to your tonic."

Lauren burst out laughing, and he glanced over his shoulder at her, a wry smile twisting his lips. "Just out of curiosity, how old are you?"

"Twenty-three."

"And you were applying for a secretarial position at Sinco—before you threw yourself at our feet tonight?" he prompted, adding a modest amount of gin to her tonic.

"Yes."

He carried her glass to her and nodded toward the sofa. "Sit down—you shouldn't be standing on that ankle."

"It doesn't hurt, honestly," she protested, but she obediently sat down.

Nick remained standing in front of her, regarding her curiously. "Did Sinco offer you a position?"

He was so tall that Lauren had to tip her head back in order to meet his gaze. "No."

"I'd like to have a look at your ankle," he said.

31

Putting his drink on the glass coffee table, he crouched down and began unbuckling the thin strap of her sandal. The mere brush of his fingers against her ankle sent amazing jolts of electricity shooting up her leg, and she stiffened with the unexpected shock.

Fortunately, he seemed not to notice as his strong fingers carefully explored her calf, moving slowly down toward her ankle. "Are you a good secretary?"

"My former employer thought I was."

With his head still bent, he said, "Good secretaries are always in demand. Sinco's personnel office will probably call you eventually and offer you a job."

. "I doubt it," Lauren said with an irrepressible smile. "I'm afraid Mr. Weatherby, the personnel manager, doesn't think I'm very bright," she explained.

Nick's head jerked up, his gaze moving with frank, masculine appreciation over her vivid features. "Lauren, I think you're as bright as a shiny new penny. Weatherby must be blind."

"Of course he is!" she teased, "Or else he'd never wear a houndstooth jacket with a paisley tie."

Nick grinned. "Does he really?"

Lauren nodded, and for her the companionable moment became strangely charged with an unexplainable, deepening awareness. Now, as she smiled at him, she saw more than just an extremely handsome male. She saw a mild cynicism in his eyes that was tempered with warmth and humor; the hard-bitten experience that was stamped on his strongly chiseled face. To Lauren it made him even more attractive. There was no denying the power of his sexual magnetism, either. It emanated from every rugged, self-assured inch of his body, pulling her to him.

"It doesn't feel swollen," he commented, bending his head toward her ankle again. "Does it hurt at all?"

"Very little. Not nearly as much as my dignity."

"In that case, by tomorrow your ankle *and* your dignity will probably be fine."

Still crouching, he cupped her heel in his left hand and reached over to pick up her sandal with his right. Just as he was about to slip the sandal onto her foot, he glanced up at her and his lazy smile sent Lauren's pulse racing as he asked, "Isn't there some fairy tale about a man who searches for the woman whose foot fits into a glass slipper?"

She nodded, her eyes bright. "Cinderella."

"What happens to me if this slipper fits?"

"I turn you into a handsome frog," she quipped.

He laughed, a rich, wonderful sound as their gazes held, and something flickered in the silver depths of his eyes—a brief flame of sexual attraction that he abruptly doused. The companionable bantering was over. He buckled her sandal, then stood up. Picking up his drink, he drained it quickly and set the glass down on the coffee table. It was, Lauren sensed, an unwelcome signal that their time together was at an end. She watched him lean over, pick up the telephone on the far side of the coffee table and punch a four-digit number. "George," he said into the phone, "This is Nick Sinclair. The young lady you were chasing as a trespasser has recovered from her fall. Would you bring the security car around to the front of the building and drive her to wherever she left her car? Right, I'll meet you down in front in five minutes."

Lauren's heart sank. Five minutes. And Nick wasn't even going to be the one who drove her to her car! She had an awful feeling that he wasn't going to ask how he could get in touch with her, either. That thought was so depressing that it totally eclipsed her embarrassment at having discovered that she had been fleeing from a security guard tonight. "Do you work for the company that built this high-rise?" she asked, trying to postpone their parting and discover something about him.

Nick glanced almost impatiently at his watch. "Yes, I do."

"Do you like construction work?"

"I enjoy building things," he answered briefly. "I'm an engineer."

"Will you be sent somewhere else once this building is finished?"

"I'll spend most of my time here for the next few years," he said.

Lauren stood up and picked up her jacket, her thoughts confused. Perhaps with sophisticated computers running everything from heating systems to elevators in the new high-rises, it was necessary to keep an engineer of some sort on staff. Not that it really mattered one way or another, she thought with an awful sense of foreboding. She probably wasn't going to see him again. "Well, thank you for everything. I hope the president doesn't discover that you raided his liquor cabinet."

Nick shot her a wry glance. "It's already been raided by all the janitors. It will have to be locked to stop that."

On the way down in the elevator, he seemed preoccupied and in a hurry. He probably already had a date tonight, Lauren thought glumly. With some beautiful woman—a model, at least, if she were to match his own striking good looks. Of course, he might be married—but he wasn't wearing a wedding ring, and he didn't seem like a married man.

A white car with the words Global Industries Security Division had pulled up on the packed dirt in front of the building and was waiting, a uniformed security guard at the steering wheel. Nick walked her out to the car and held the door open while she slid into the passenger seat beside the guard. Using his body to block the chilly air from her, he leaned his forearm on the roof of the car and bent his head to speak to her through the narrow opening. "I know people at Sinco; I'll give someone a call and see if they can't persuade Weatherby to change his mind."

Lauren's spirits soared at this indication that he liked her enough to try to intercede for her, but when she recalled the way she had deliberately bungled her tests, she shook her head in genuine dismay. "Don't bother. He won't change his mind—I made a terrible impression on him. But thank you for offering."

Ten minutes later Lauren paid the parking-garage attendant and pulled out onto the rainswept boulevard. Forcing her thoughts of Nick Sinclair aside, she followed the directions Philip's secretary had given her and somberly contemplated her forthcoming meeting with the Whitworth family.

In less than a half hour she was going to walk into their Grosse Pointe mansion again. Memories of her humiliating weekend at their elegant home fourteen years before invaded her mind, and she shivered with dread and embarrassment. The first day had not been bad; she had spent it virtually on her own. The awful part had begun just after lunch on the second day. Carter, the Whitworths' teenage son, had appeared in the doorway of Lauren's bedroom and announced that his mother had instructed him to get her out of the house because she was expecting some friends and didn't want them to see Lauren. For the rest of the afternoon, Carter had made her feel as miserable, insignificant and frightened as he possibly could.

Besides calling her Four Eyes because she wore glasses, he constantly referred to her father, a professor at a Chicago university, as The Schoolteacher, and her mother, a concert pianist, as The Piano Player.

While giving Lauren a tour of their formal gardens, he "accidentally" tripped her and sent her sprawling into a huge bed of thorny roses. A half hour later, after Lauren had changed her dirty, torn dress, Carter abjectly apologized and offered to show her the family dogs.

He seemed so sincere and so boyishly eager to show her his dogs that Lauren instantly decided the rosebush incident must have truly been an accident. "I have a dog at home," she had confided proudly, hurrying to keep up with him as he stalked across the lush manicured lawns toward the rear of the estate. "Her name is Fluffy, and she's white," she'd added as they came to a clipped hedge, which concealed a huge dog pen enclosed by a ten-foot-high chain-link fence. Lauren beamed at the two Doberman pinschers and then at Carter, who was removing the heavy padlock from the gate. "My best friend has a Doberman pinscher. He plays tag with us all the time, and he does tricks too."

"These two know some tricks of their own," Carter promised, opening the gate and stepping aside for Lauren to enter.

Lauren walked into the pen without fear. "Hi, dogs," she said softly, approaching the silent, watchful animals. As she stretched out her hand to pet them, the gate clanged shut behind her and Carter ordered sharply, "Hold, boys! Hold!"

Both dogs stiffened instantly, baring their gleaming white fangs and snarling as they advanced on a petrified Lauren. "Carter," she screamed, backing away until she was pressed against the fence, "Why are they doing that?"

"I wouldn't move if I were you," Carter mocked silkily from behind her on the other side of the fence. "If you do, they'll go for your throat and tear out your jugular vein." With that he sauntered off, whistling cheerfully.

"Don't leave me here!" Lauren screamed. "Please—don't leave me here!"

Thirty minutes later, when the gardener found her, she was screaming no more. She was whimpering hysterically, her eyes riveted on the snarling dogs.

"Get out of there!" the man ordered, flinging open the gate and striding angrily into the pen. "What's the matter with you, stirring up these damned dogs!" he snapped, catching her arm and practically dragging her out.

When he slammed the gate shut, something about his total lack of fear finally registered on Lauren, freeing her paralyzed vocal chords. "They were going to rip my throat open," she whispered hoarsely, tears racing unchecked down her cheeks.

The gardener looked at her terror-glazed blue eyes, and his voice lost some of its irritation. "They wouldn't have hurt you. Those dogs are trained to raise an alarm and to frighten off intruders, that's all. They know better than to bite anyone."

Lauren spent the rest of the afternoon sprawled across her bed contemplating a variety of bloodthirsty ways to get even with Carter, but while it was immensely satisfying to imagine him on his knees, begging for her mercy, all of the schemes she devised were highly impractical.

By the time her mother came upstairs to get her for dinner that night, Lauren was resigned to the fact that she was going to have to swallow her pride and pretend that nothing had happened. There was no point in telling her mother about Carter, because Gina Danner was an Italian American who possessed the deep, sentimental Italian devotion to family, no matter how distant and obscure that "family" relationship might be. Her mother would charitably assume that Carter had merely been playing some boyish pranks.

"Did you have a nice day, honey?" her mother asked as the two of them descended the curving staircase toward the dining room.

"It was okay," Lauren mumbled, wondering how she was going to restrain the urge to give Carter Whitworth a good swift kick.

At the bottom of the stairs, a maid announced that a Mr. Robert Danner was on the telephone. "You go on ahead," Gina told her daughter with one of her gentle smiles as she reached for the telephone on the small table at the foot of the stairs.

In the arched doorway of the dining room, Lauren hesitated. Beneath a glittering chandelier, the Whitworth family was already seated at the huge table. "I distinctly told the Danner woman to come down at eight o'clock," Carter's mother was saying to her husband. "It is now 8:02. If she doesn't have enough sense or manners to be punctual, then we'll eat without her." She nodded curtly to the butler, who immediately began ladling soup into the fragile porcelain bowls at each place.

"Philip, I've been as tolerant of this as I can be," the woman went on, "but I refuse to have any more of these trashy freeloaders as guests in my home." She turned her elegantly coiffured blond head to the older woman seated to her left. "Mother Whitworth, this will have to stop. By now you surely have gathered enough data to complete your project."

"If I had, I wouldn't need to have these people here. I know they've been an irritating ill-bred lot and a trial for all of us, but you will have to tolerate them a while longer, Carol."

Lauren stood in the doorway, a rebellious sparkle glittering in her stormy blue eyes. It was one thing for *her* to have suffered indignities at Carter's hands, but she would not allow these horrible, vicious people to belittle her brilliant father and her beautiful talented mother!

Her mother joined her at the entrance to the dining room. "I'm sorry to have kept you waiting," she said, taking Lauren's hand. Not one of the Whitworths bothered to reply but continued eating the soup the butler had served.

Seized by a sudden inspiration, Lauren darted a swift glance at her mother, who was unfolding a linen napkin and placing it in her lap. Piously bowing her head, Lauren clasped her hands together and, in her shrill childish voice intoned, "Dear Lord, we ask your blessing on this food. We also ask your forgiveness for people who are hypocrites and who think they are better than everybody else just because they have more money. Thank you, Lord. Amen." Meticulously avoiding her mother's eyes, she calmly picked up her spoon.

The soup—at least Lauren presumed it was soup —was cold. The butler, standing off to one side, noticed her put down her spoon. "Is something wrong, miss?" he sniffed.

"My soup is cold," she explained, braving his disdainful look.

"Boy, are you stupid!" Carter smirked as Lauren picked up her small glass of milk. "This is vichyssoise, and it's supposed to be eaten cold."

The milk "slipped" from Lauren's hand, dousing Carter's place setting and lap in a cold white deluge. "Oh, I'm *so* sorry," she said, muffling a giggle as Carter and the butler both tried to mop up the mess. "It was just an accident—Carter, you know about accidents, don't you? Shall I tell everyone about the 'accidents' you had today?" Ignoring his murderous glare, she turned to his family. "Carter had lots of 'accidents' today. He 'accidentally' tripped while showing me the garden and shoved me into the roses. Then, while he was showing me the dogs, he 'accidentally' locked me in the pen and—"

"I refuse to listen to any more of your outrageous, ill-mannered accusations," Carol Whitworth snapped at Lauren, her beautiful face as cold and hard as a glacier.

Somehow Lauren had found the courage to meet her icy gray eyes without flinching. "I'm sorry, ma'am," she said with pretended meekness. "I didn't realize it was bad manners to talk about my day." With all the Whitworths still glaring at her, she picked up her spoon. "Of course," she added thoughtfully, "I didn't know it was *good* manners to call guests trashy freeloaders, either."

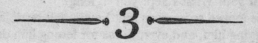

3

EXHAUSTED AND DISPIRITED, LAUREN PULLED UP IN front of the Whitworths' three-story Tudor mansion. She unlocked the trunk of her car and removed her suitcase. She had driven twelve hours straight in order to keep her appointment with Philip Whitworth that afternoon. She had been through two job interviews, fallen down in the dirt, spoiled her clothes and met the most handsome compelling man she'd ever seen. And by deliberately flunking her tests at Sinco, she had ruined her chances of working near him. . . .

Tomorrow was Friday, and she would spend it looking for an apartment. As soon as she found one, she could leave immediately for Fenster to pack her belongings. Philip had not mentioned when he wanted her to start working for his company, but she could be back here ready to report for work two weeks from Monday.

The front door was opened by a paunchy uniformed butler whom Lauren instantly recognized as one of the witnesses to her dining-room performance fourteen years before. "Good evening," he began, but Philip Whitworth interrupted him.

Striding into the vast marble foyer the executive exclaimed, "Lauren, I've been worried to death about you! What's kept you so long?"

He looked so anxious that Lauren felt terrible for worrying him, and even worse for letting him down by not trying harder to get a job at Sinco. In a few words she explained that things had "not gone very well" with her interview. Hastily she sketched in details of her fall in front of the Global Industries Building, and asked if she had time to freshen up before dinner.

Upstairs in the room the butler showed her to, she showered, brushed her hair and changed into a tailored apricot skirt and matching blouse.

Philip stood up as she approached the arched doorway of the drawing room. "You're wonderfully quick, Lauren," he said, leading her over to his wife, whose glacial personality she recalled so well. "Carol, I know you remember Lauren."

Despite her personal prejudice, Lauren had to admit that with her slim elegant figure and carefully coiffed blond hair Carol Whitworth was still a beautiful woman.

"Of course I do," Carol said with a pleasantly correct smile that didn't quite reach her gray eyes. "How are you, Lauren?"

"Obviously Lauren is very, very well, mother," Carter Whitworth remarked, grinning as he politely got to his feet. His lazy, sweeping glance covered everything from her vivid blue eyes and delicately molded features to her gracefully feminine figure.

Lauren kept her expression neutral as she was reintroduced to her childhood tormentor. Accepting the glass of sherry Carter had poured for her, she sat down on the sofa, eyeing him warily when he sat beside her instead of returning to his chair. "You've certainly changed," he said with an admiring grin.

"So have you," Lauren answered cautiously.

He draped his arm casually across the back of the sofa behind her shoulders. "We didn't get along very well, as I remember," he mused.

"No, we didn't." Lauren flicked a self-conscious glance toward Carol, who was observing her son's little flirtation, her eyes cool and inscrutable, her expression regally aloof.

"Why didn't we get along?" Carter persisted.

"I, er, don't recall."

"I do." He smiled. "I was insufferably rude and thoroughly rotten to you."

Lauren stared in amazement at his frank, rueful expression, her prejudice against him beginning to dissolve. "Yes, you were."

"And you—" he grinned "—behaved like an outrageous brat at dinner."

Lauren's eyes brightened with an answering smile as she slowly nodded her head. "Yes, I did." A tentative truce was thereby declared. Carter glanced up at the butler hovering in the doorway, then stood up and offered his hand to Lauren. "Dinner is ready. Shall we?"

They had just finished the last course when the butler appeared in the dining room. "Excuse me, but there is a telephone call for Miss Danner from a man who says he is Mr. Weatherby, with the Sinco Electronics Company."

Philip Whitworth broke into a beaming smile. "Bring the phone here to the table, Higgins."

The phone conversation was brief, with Lauren mostly listening. When she hung up, she raised amazed, laughing eyes to Philip.

"Go ahead," he said, "tell us. Carol and Carter are both aware of what you're trying to do to help me."

Lauren was a little dismayed to learn that two other people were aware of her clandestine future, but she complied. "Apparently the man who rescued me when I fell tonight had a very influential friend at Sinco. This friend called Mr. Weatherby a few minutes ago, and as a result, Mr. Weatherby has just remembered a secretarial position that he thinks is perfect for me. I'm to be interviewed for it tomorrow."

"Did he mention who'll be interviewing you?"

"I think he said the man's name was Mr. Williams."

"Jim Williams," Philip murmured softly, his smile broadening. "I'll be damned."

Shortly afterward Carter left for his own apartment, and Carol retired for the night. But Philip asked Lauren to remain in the drawing room with him. "Williams may want you to start immediately," he said when the others had gone. "We don't want any obstacles in the way of you getting that job. How soon can you go home, pack and return to work?"

"I can't go home to pack until I've found an apartment here," Lauren reminded him.

"No, of course not," he agreed. After a moment's thought he said, "You know, a few years ago I bought a condominium in Bloomfield Hills for an aunt of mine. She's been in Europe for months now and intends to stay there for another year. It would be my pleasure to have you live at her place."

"No, really, I couldn't," Lauren said quickly. "You've already done more than enough for me; I can't let you provide a place for me to live, too."

"I insist," he said with kindly firmness. "And anyway, you'll be doing me a favor, because I've had to pay the gatekeeper at the condominium complex a sizable sum every month to watch the place. This way we'll both save money."

Lauren plucked absently at the sleeve of her apricot blouse. Her father needed every penny she could send him, and as quickly as possible. If she didn't have to spend money for rent, she could send him that, too. Troubled and uncertain, she looked at Philip, but he had already extracted a pen and paper from his suit-coat pocket and was writing something down. "Here's the address and phone number of the condominium," he said, handing her the piece of paper. "When you fill out your employment papers at Sinco tomorrow, give them this information. That way, no one there will ever connect you with me."

A shiver of foreboding danced up Lauren's spine at the ominous reminder of the dual role she would be playing if she went to work for Sinco. Spying. Her mind skated away in alarm from the word. No, she wouldn't really be doing that. All she would really be doing was trying to ferret out the name of the treacherous person who was spying on Philip's company. Seen from that viewpoint, her mission became not only justified, it became positively honorable. For a moment she felt quite virtuous—until she sternly reminded herself of the *real* reason she was now so willing and eager to work for Sinco: Nick Sinclair worked right across the street, and she wanted the opportunity to be near him.

Philip's voice interrupted her thoughts. "If you're offered a secretarial position at Sinco tomorrow, accept it and leave from there for Missouri. If I don't hear from you by noon tomorrow, I'll know you got the position, and I'll arrange to have the condominium ready for you within a week."

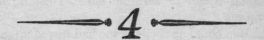

THE FOLLOWING MORNING AT ELEVEN-FIFTY, LAUREN was lucky enough to find a parking space right across from Sinco's offices, directly in front of the Global Industries Building. With a mixture of dread and anticipation, she got out of the car, smoothed her slim beige skirt, straightened the short matching military jacket and crossed the street to see Mr. Weatherby.

Despite his formal, almost ingratiating smile, Mr. Weatherby was obviously annoyed. "Really, Miss Danner," he said, ushering her into his office, "you could have saved yourself, me and several others a great deal of time and trouble if you had simply told me when you came in yesterday that you're a friend of Mr. Sinclair's."

"Did Mr. Sinclair call you and tell you I was a friend of his?" Lauren asked curiously.

"No," Mr. Weatherby said, trying hard to hide his irritation. "Mr. Sinclair called the president of our company, Mr. Sampson. Mr. Sampson called the executive vice-president, who called the vice-president of operations, who called *my* boss. And last night my boss called me at home and informed me that I had offended and misjudged Miss Danner, who happens to be extremely bright *and* a personal friend of Mr. Sinclair's. Then he hung up on me."

Lauren could not believe she had stirred up such a furor. "I'm terribly sorry to have caused you so much trouble," she said contritely. "It wasn't entirely your fault—after all, I did fail my tests."

He nodded in emphatic agreement. "I told my boss you didn't know which end of a pencil to write with, but he said *he* didn't give a damn if you typed with your toes." Heaving himself out of his chair, he said, "Now, if you'll come with me, I'll take you up to Mr. Williams's office. Mr. Williams is our executive vice-president and his secretary is moving to California. He wants to interview you for the position."

"Is Mr. Williams the executive vice-president who called the vice-president of operations, who called—" Lauren began uneasily.

"Exactly," Mr. Weatherby interrupted.

Lauren followed him, beset with the unsettling thought that even if he detested her, Mr. Williams might offer her a job because *he* had been intimidated by *his* superior. But minutes later she abandoned any such idea. James Williams, in his mid-thirties, had the brisk, authoritative air of a man who would never be *anyone's* puppet. He glanced up from the documents he was reading when Mr.

Weatherby brought Lauren into his office and nodded coolly toward the leather chair in front of his large desk. "Sit down," he said to Lauren. To Mr. Weatherby he said curtly, "Close the door behind you as you leave."

Lauren sat as she'd been told to do and waited as Jim Williams stood up and came around in front of his desk. Leaning back against it, he crossed his arms over his chest, and his penetrating gaze swept over her. "So you're Lauren Danner?" he said dispassionately.

"Yes," Lauren admitted. "I'm afraid so."

Amusement flickered across his face, momentarily softening the cool, businesslike features. "I take it from that remark that you're aware of the uproar you caused last night?"

"Yes," Lauren sighed. "In every excruciating, embarrassing detail."

"Can you *spell* 'excruciating'?"

"Yes," she said, completely taken aback.

"How fast can you type—when you aren't under testing conditions?"

Lauren flushed. "About a hundred words a minute."

"Shorthand?"

"Yes."

Without taking his eyes from her face, he reached behind him and picked up a pencil and tablet lying on his desk. Handing them to her, he said, "Take this down, please."

Lauren stared at him in amazement then recovered and began to write as he dictated swiftly: "Dear

51

Miss Danner, as my administrative assistant, you will be expected to perform a variety of secretarial duties and to function efficiently and smoothly as my personal liaison with my staff. You will, at all times, adhere precisely to company policies, regardless of your acquaintance with Nick Sinclair. In a few weeks we will be moving into the Global Building, and if you ever attempt to take advantage of your friendship with Mr. Sinclair, either by shirking your duties or ignoring the rules that apply to the rest of the staff, I will fire you on the spot and personally escort you out the front door. If, on the other hand, you show interest and initiative, I will delegate as much responsibility to you as you wish to accept and are capable of handling. If this meets with your approval, report for work here in my office at 9:00 A.M. two weeks from Monday. Any questions, Lauren?"

Lauren raised dazed eyes to him. "You mean I have the job?"

"That depends on whether you can type that memo without errors in a reasonably short time."

Lauren was too stunned by this cool, unemotional offer of a job to be nervous about transcribing her dictation. In a few minutes, she returned from the typewriter and walked hesitantly into his office. "Here's the memo, Mr. Williams."

He glanced at it and then at her. "Very efficient. How did Weatherby ever get the idea that you're a feather-brain?"

"It's the impression I gave him," Lauren said obliquely.

"Care to tell me how that happened?"

"No, not really. It was all a . . . a mis-understanding."

"Very well, we'll leave it at that. Now, is there anything else we need to discuss? Yes, of course there is—your salary."

The salary he named was $2,000 a year less than Philip had offered, but Philip had promised to make up the difference.

"Well, do you want the job?"

"Yes," Lauren said with a faint smile. "And no. I would like to work for you, because I have the feeling that I could learn a great deal. But I *don't* want the job if the only reason you're offering it to me is because of . . . of . . ."

"Nick Sinclair?"

Lauren nodded.

"Nick has nothing whatsoever to do with it. I've known him for many years, and we're good friends. Friendship, however, has no place in business matters. Nick has his job and I have mine. I do not presume to tell him how to do his, and I would not appreciate his trying to influence my choice of a secretary."

"Then why did you decide to interview me today, even though I failed my tests?"

His brown eyes twinkled. "Oh, that. Well, as a matter of fact, my former secretary, for whom I have the greatest respect, struck sparks off Weatherby from the very first. When I heard that a bright young secretarial applicant hadn't hit it off with him yesterday, I thought perhaps you might be another Theresa. You aren't, but I think you and I will work together even better, Lauren."

"Thank you, Mr. Williams. I'll see you two weeks from Monday."

"Call me Jim."

Lauren smiled, accepting his handshake. "In that case, you may call me Lauren."

"I thought I had been."

"You have."

His lips twitched. "Good for you—don't let me intimidate you."

Lauren emerged from the dim building into the dazzling sunlight of a wonderful August day. As she waited for the traffic light to change from red to green, her gaze was irresistibly drawn to the Global Industries Building across the street. Would Nick be there working, she wondered. She longed to see him.

The light changed and she crossed the wide boulevard to her car. But if Nick had wanted to see *her* again, surely he would have asked for her phone number. Perhaps he was shy. Shy! Lauren shook her head derisively as she reached for the car door handle. Nick Sinclair was not in the least shy! With his looks and lazy charm, he was probably accustomed to women who took the initiative and asked *him* out. . . .

The glass doors of the building swung open, and Lauren's heart soared as Nick himself strode into view. For a joyous moment, Lauren thought he'd seen her standing at her car and had come out to talk to her, but he turned to his right and started toward the far corner of the building.

"Nick!" she called impulsively. "Nick!"

He glanced over his shoulder, and Lauren waved at him, feeling absurdly happy when he headed toward her with those long strides of his.

"Guess where I've been?" She beamed.

There was a warm, teasing light in his gray eyes as they swept over her shining honey hair in its elegant chignon, her smart beige suit, silky blouse and chocolate brown sandals. "Modeling for a Bonwit Teller fashion show?" he ventured with a grin.

Lauren glowed at the compliment, but she hung on to her composure. "No, I've been across the street at Sinco Electronics, and they offered me a job—thanks to you."

He ignored her reference to his help. "Did you take it?"

"Did I! The money's fantastic; the man I'll be working for is terrific, and the job sounds interesting and challenging."

"You're pleased, then?"

Lauren nodded . . . then waited, hoping he would ask her out. Instead he reached down to open her car door for her. "Nick," she said before her courage could desert her. "I'm in the mood to celebrate. If you know a good place for sandwiches and a cold drink, I'll buy you lunch."

He hesitated for an unbearable moment, then a smile dawned across his tanned features. "That's the best offer I've had all day."

Rather than give her directions, Nick drove the

car. A few blocks away he turned off Jefferson and pulled into a parking lot behind what looked like a narrow, renovated three-story brick house. The sign above the back door, made of dark wood with gold letters etched deeply into it, said simply, Tony's. Inside, the house had been converted into a dimly lit, charming restaurant, with dark oaken floors, tables polished to a glossy shine and copper pots and pans hanging artistically on the rough brick walls. Sunlight illuminated the stained glass windows, and red-and-white checked tablecloths added to the warmth and charm.

A waiter stationed near the door greeted Nick with a polite, "Good morning," then showed them to the only unoccupied table in the entire place. As Nick pulled out her chair, Lauren glanced around at the other customers. She was one of the few women present, but there was certainly a mixed variety of men. Most of them were wearing suits and ties, while three others, including Nick, wore slacks with open-collared sports shirts.

An older waiter appeared at their table, greeted Nick with an affectionate pat on the shoulder, a cheery, "Good to see you again, my friend," and began to hand them huge, leather-bound menus. "We'll have the special, Tony," Nick said, and at Lauren's quizzical look, he added, "The specialty is French-dip sandwiches—is that all right with you?"

Since she had offered to buy his lunch, Lauren thought he was asking her permission to order something that cost more than a regular sandwich.

"Please have whatever you like," she insisted graciously. "We're celebrating my new job, and I can afford anything on the menu."

"How do you think you're going to like living in Detroit?" he asked when Tony, who was apparently the owner, had left. "It's bound to be a big change for a small-town girl from Missouri."

A small-town girl? Lauren was puzzled. That wasn't the impression she normally conveyed to people. "Actually, we lived in a suburb of Chicago until my mother died, when I was twelve. After that my father and I moved to Fenster, Missouri—the town where he grew up. He took a job teaching in the same school he'd attended as a boy. So you see, I'm not completely a 'small-town girl' after all."

Nick's expression didn't change. "Were you an only child?"

"Yes, but my father remarried when I was thirteen. Along with a stepmother, I also acquired a stepsister two years older than me, and a stepbrother one year older."

He must have caught the note of distaste in her voice when she mentioned her stepbrother because he said, "I thought all little girls liked the idea of having a big brother. Didn't you?"

An irrepressible smile lit Lauren's vivid face. "Oh, I liked the idea of having a big brother. Unfortunately, I didn't like Lenny at the time. We detested each other on sight. He teased me unmercifully, yanked my braids and stole money from my bedroom. I retaliated by telling everyone in town that he was gay—which no one believed because he turned out to be an absolute lecher!"

Nick chuckled, and Lauren noticed that when he smiled, his eyes crinkled at the corners. In contrast to the warm golden tan of his face, his eyes were a light metallic silver. Beneath his straight dark brows and thick spiky lashes, they glinted with humor and keen intelligence, while his firm lips promised excitingly aggressive male sensuality. Lauren felt the same delicious stirring of her senses that she had experienced the night before and cautiously lowered her gaze to the tanned column of his throat.

"What about your stepsister?" Nick asked. "What was she like?"

"Gorgeous. All she had to do was stroll down the street and the boys positively drooled over her."

"Did she try to steal your boyfriends?"

Lauren's eyes kindled with humor as she gazed at him across the narrow table. "I didn't have many boyfriends for her to steal—at least, not until I was seventeen."

One dark brow lifted in disbelief as his gaze moved over the classic perfection of her features, over her eyes like shining turquoise satin beneath their heavy fringe of curly lashes, to linger on her thick, honey-colored hair. Sunlight streaming through the stained-glass window beside their table bathed her face in a soft glow. "I find that very hard to believe," he said finally.

"I promise you, it's true," Lauren averred, dismissing his compliment with a smile. She remembered with great clarity the homely little girl she had been, and while the memories were not particularly painful, she really couldn't place much importance now on anything as unreliable as surface beauty.

Tony put two plates down on the red-checked tablecloth, each containing a crusty loaf of French bread that had been sliced lengthwise and piled high with wafer-thin rare roast beef. Beside each plate, he placed a little bowl of beef juice. "It's delicious—try it," he urged.

Lauren tasted hers and agreed. "It's wonderful," she told him.

"Good," he said, his round, mustachioed face beaming paternally at her. "Then you let Nick pay for it! He has more money than you. Nick's grandfather loaned me the money to start this place," he confided before bustling off to chastise a clumsy busboy.

They ate their meal in companionable silence interspersed with Lauren's questions about the restaurant and its owner. From what little she could gather from Nick's brief answers, his family and Tony's had been friends for three generations. At one point Nick's father had actually worked for Tony's father, yet somehow the financial situation must have reversed itself for Nick's grandfather later had enough money to lend to Tony.

The moment they were finished Tony appeared at their table to whisk away their plates. The service in the place was much too good, Lauren thought with dismay. They had only been here for thirty-five minutes, and she'd hoped to have at least an hour with Nick.

"Now, how about some dessert," Tony said, his friendly dark eyes on Lauren. "For you I have *canoli*—or some of my special spumoni. My spumoni is not what you find in stores," he told her proudly. "It is the real thing. It is ice cream of several flavors and colors, arranged in layers. Then into it I put—"

"Bits of fruit and lots of nuts," Lauren finished, smiling warmly at him. "The way my mother used to make it."

Tony's mouth dropped open, then he minutely scrutinized her face. After a long moment he nodded decisively. "You are Italian," he proclaimed with a broad smile.

"Only half Italian," Lauren corrected. "The other half is Irish."

In ten seconds Tony had pried her full name out of her, the name of her mother's family and had discovered that she was moving to Detroit where she knew no one. Lauren felt a little guilty for not mentioning Philip Whitworth, but since Nick knew people at Sinco she didn't think she should risk mentioning her connection with Philip in front of him.

She listened to Tony with a glow of happiness. It had been so long since she had lived in Chicago and visited with her Italian cousins, and it felt so good to hear that quaint familiar accent again.

"You need anything, Lauren, you come to me," Tony told her, patting her shoulder as he had Nick's.

"A beautiful young woman alone in the big city needs some family she can turn to when she needs help. Here there will always be a meal for you—a good *Italian* meal," he clarified. "Now how about my great spumoni?"

Lauren glanced at Nick and then at Tony's expectant face. "I'd love some spumoni," she announced, ignoring the groaning protest of her full stomach in the interest of prolonging their lunch.

Tony beamed, and Nick winked conspiratorially at him. "Lauren is still a growing girl, Tony."

Lauren's eyes darkened with exasperation and confusion at his words, and for a minute she idly traced a large red check on the tablecloth with her manicured fingernail. "Nick, may I ask you a question?" she said softly.

"Of course."

She folded her arms on the table and regarded him directly. "Why do you talk about me, as if I'm some naive teenager?"

Wry amusement twisted his lips. "I didn't realize I was. But I suppose it's to remind myself that you're young, that you come from a small town in Missouri and that you're probably very naive."

Lauren was amazed by his answer. "I'm a grown woman, and the fact that I grew up in a small town doesn't mean a thing!" She paused as Tony served her spumoni, but the moment he turned away she added irritably, "And I don't know what gave you the idea that I'm naive, but I'm not."

The teasing light in Nick's eyes was extinguished

as he leaned back in his chair and studied her speculatively. "You're not?"

"No, I'm not."

"In that case," he drawled smoothly, "what are your plans for this weekend?"

Lauren's heart somersaulted with delight but she asked cautiously, "What did you have in mind?"

"A party. Some friends of mine are having a party this weekend at their house near Harbor Springs. I was about to leave for their place when we met today. It's approximately a five-hour drive from here, and we'd return on Sunday."

Lauren had planned to drive directly to Fenster that afternoon. On the other hand, it only took a day to drive each way, and she could easily pack all her belongings in less than a week. She had more than two weeks before she was to start her new job, so time was no problem, and she desperately wanted to go with Nick. "Are you certain it won't inconvenience your friends if I come with you?"

"It won't inconvenience them; they were expecting me to bring someone with me."

"In that case," Lauren smiled, "I'd love to go. In fact, my suitcase is already in the trunk of the car."

Nick glanced over his shoulder and nodded at Tony, signaling for their check. The older man brought it over and placed it on the table near Nick, but Lauren deftly covered it with her hand and pulled it toward her. "I am buying lunch," she stated, carefully concealing her shock at the total on the check—rather exorbitant for the amount they had eaten. As she reached for her wallet, however,

Nick laid several bills on the table, and she watched helplessly as Tony swept them away.

Tony saw her dismay and chucked her under the chin as if she were eight years old. "You come back often, Laurie. For you I will always have an empty table and something good to eat."

"At these prices," Lauren teased him, "I'm surprised all your tables aren't empty."

Tony leaned closer confidingly. "My tables are never empty. In fact, you cannot even reserve one in advance unless your name is on my list. I will have Ricco place *your* name on our list." He lifted an imperious arm and three young, darkly handsome waiters glanced up, then came to Lauren's table. "These are my sons," Tony said, proudly introducing them. "Ricco, Dominic and Joe. Ricco, you put Laurie's name on the list."

"No, please don't bother," Lauren interjected quickly.

Tony ignored her. "A nice Italian girl like you needs a family to protect and guide her in a big city like Detroit. You come often to see us—we live on the floors above the restaurant. Ricco, Dominic," Tony ordered them sternly, "when Laurie comes, you keep an eye on her. Joe, you keep an eye on Ricco and Dominic!"

To Lauren, who had burst out laughing, Tony explained, "Joe is married."

Repressing her mirth with an effort, Lauren looked at her four appointed "guardians" with happy gratitude shining in her eyes. "Who should I keep *my* eye on?" she asked teasingly.

In perfect unison, four dark Italian faces turned accusingly to Nick, who was lounging in his chair, observing them all with an amused expression. "Lauren tells me she can take care of herself," he said imperturbably as he pushed his chair back and stood up.

Nick said he had to make a phone call, and while he did so, Lauren walked down the hall to the ladies' room. When she emerged, she recognized his broad shoulders and tapered back at a phone in the entranceway. His deep baritone voice was lowered, but one word drifted to her as clear as a bell: "Ericka."

What an odd time for him to be calling another woman, Lauren thought. Or was it? He had said that their hosts were expecting him to bring a friend, and he would have undoubtedly arranged to take someone with him long before today. He was breaking a date!

Nick slid into her sporty Pontiac Trans Am, turned on the ignition, then frowned at the generator warning light that glowed red on the dashboard. "I don't think there's anything wrong with the generator," Lauren hastily explained. "On the way up here I stopped and had a mechanic check it. He couldn't find anything wrong, so it's possible it's just a short in the warning light itself. The car is only six months old."

"Why don't we take it up north and see how it runs," Nick said after a brief pause. "That way you won't be alone on the highway en route to Missouri if the generator *does* go out."

"Wonderful," she readily agreed.

"Tell me more about your family and you," he said as they pulled out of the parking lot.

Lauren turned her face to the front, trying not to show her tension. The little web of deceit she'd woven was already growing larger and more entangled. Since Nick knew people at Sinco, and she'd deliberately omitted mentioning her college degree on her application, she was hesitant about telling him she'd been at college for the last five years. Staring out the window at the splendid glass Renaissance Center, she sighed. A person who was innately honest, she'd already lied to him about her age, because she wouldn't really be twenty-three for another three weeks. And she'd told Tony in front of him that she had no friends or relatives in Detroit. Now she was going to carefully "forget" the last five years of her life.

"Was that a tough question?" Nick joked.

His smile did crazy things to her heartbeat. She wanted to lift her hand and lay it against his hard jaw and to trace the line of those sensual lips. His shirt collar was open at the throat, and she wanted to touch the dark hairs that curled crisply just above the deep V of the third button. Even the scent of his spicy cologne was teasing her senses, inviting her closer. "There isn't much more to tell you. My stepbrother, Lenny, is twenty-four now, and he's married and starting his own family. My stepsister, Melissa, is twenty-five, and she got married in April. Her husband is a mechanic who works for the Pontiac dealer where I bought this car."

"What about your father and stepmother?"

"My father is a teacher. He's brilliant and wise. My stepmother is very sweet and completely devoted to him."

"If your father's a teacher, I'm amazed that he didn't urge you to go on to college, rather than letting you work as a secretary."

"He did," Lauren replied obliquely, vastly relieved when Nick was obliged to direct his attention to the intricacies of changing lanes and negotiating the wide curve that brought them down the entrance ramp onto Interstate 75. The expressway took them through the inner city before the scenery changed from urban factories and housing to small suburban homes, followed by a huge shopping center and far more opulent suburbs. "What about your extra clothes?" she asked suddenly. "Won't you need to pack a suitcase?"

"No. I keep some clothes at another house in Harbor Springs."

The breeze through the open car window lightly teased his thick, coffee-brown hair. Although it was cut and styled to lie flat at the sides, it was just long enough at the nape to brush his shirt collar—just long enough, Lauren reflected wistfully, for a woman's fingers to slide through it. Her fingers. Tearing her eyes from his profile, she pulled her sunglasses down onto her nose and turned her head to gaze at the passing scenery on the interstate, only dimly aware when the endless suburbs gave way to long stretches of open countryside. Nick positively radiated bold sexual expertise and confident virility. Even now she was disturbingly aware of the length of his hard, muscled thigh only inches away from hers and the way his powerful shoulders seemed to dwarf her. Everything about the way he looked, and the way he looked *at her,* warned her that he could be very dangerous to her peace of mind.

Dangerous? Agreeing to go away for the weekend with him had been completely out of character for her—as out of character and unexplainable as this deep compelling attraction she felt for him. It was also a rash, reckless thing to do, she admitted to herself. But was it dangerous? What if Nick was a demented killer who intended to murder her, mutilate her body and bury it in the woods? If he did, no one would ever know what had happened to her, because no one knew she was with him—except Tony and his sons, and Nick could simply tell them she'd gone back to Missouri. They'd believe him. Literally and figuratively, Nick could get away with murder.

Lauren stole a swift, apprehensive glance at his chiseled profile, and her features relaxed into a faint smile. Her instincts about people had never let her down before, and she knew instinctively that she was not in any physical danger.

The next three hours passed in a delightful blur. The car ate up the miles, sending a balmy breeze to touch their faces and ruffle their hair, and they talked companionably about everything and nothing.

Nick, Lauren noticed, was extremely evasive when it came to actually talking about himself, but positively insatiable when it came to probing into her background. All she learned about him was that his father had died when he was four, and that his grandparents, who had raised him, had both died a few years ago.

In the town of Grayling, which Nick said was about an hour and a half's drive from their destination of Harbor Springs, he stopped at a little grocery store. When he came out, Lauren saw that he was carrying two cans of Coke and a package of cigarettes. A few miles down the road, he pulled over at a roadside picnic table, and they both got out.

"Isn't it a gorgeous day?" Lauren tipped her head back to gaze in delight at the lacy white clouds drifting across the brilliant blue sky. She glanced at Nick and found him observing her with an indulgent expression.

Ignoring his blasé attitude she said, "At home the sky never seems to be this blue, and it's much hotter. I suppose because Missouri is so far south of here."

Nick opened both cans of Coke and handed one to her. He leaned his hip casually on the picnic table behind him, and Lauren tried to pick up their conversation where it had been interrupted a few minutes ago. "You said your father died when you were four, and your grandparents raised you—what happened to your mother?"

"Nothing happened to her," he replied. Putting a cigarette between his lips, he struck a match, cupping his hands around the flame to protect it from the breeze.

Lauren stared at the vital thickness of his dark brown hair as he bent his head to the match, then she quickly lifted her blue eyes to his. "Nick, why are you so uncommunicative about yourself?"

He squinted his eyes against the aromatic smoke drifting up from the cigarette. "Uncommunicative? I've been talking my head off for a hundred miles."

"But not about anything really personal. What happened to your mother?"

He laughed. "Has anyone ever told you that you have incredibly beautiful eyes?"

"Yes, and you're prevaricating!"

"And that you're extremely well-spoken, too?" he continued, ignoring her remark.

"Which isn't surprising because my father is an English teacher, as you've already discovered." Lauren sighed, exasperated by his deliberate evasiveness.

Nick glanced up at the sky, his gaze drifting over the trees and the deserted highway, before he finally looked at Lauren again. "I didn't realize how tense I was until three hours ago, when I finally started to relax. I needed to get away like this."

"Have you been working very hard?"

"About seventy hours a week for the past two months."

Her expressive eyes filled with sympathy, and Nick smiled at her—one of those warm, engaging smiles that quickened her heartbeat. "Did you know that you're very relaxing company?" he asked softly.

She was not particularly pleased to hear that while she found him electrifying, he found her relaxing. "Thank you—I'll try not to put you to sleep before we get to Harbor Springs."

"You can put me to sleep *after* we get there," he said suggestively.

Lauren's heart slammed into her rib cage. "What I meant was, I hope I'm not boring you."

"Believe me, you haven't bored me." His voice deepened with sensuality. "As a matter of fact, there's something I've wanted to do ever since last night, when I turned around with your glass of tonic in my hand and saw you standing there, trying very hard not to laugh at my shock."

Even in her state of heightened nervousness, Lauren knew he intended to kiss her. He took her Coke from her limp fingers and calmly put it on the picnic table beside him, then he reached out and drew her purposefully between his legs. Her hip brushed the inside of his hard thigh, sending shock waves of alarmed awareness through her entire nervous system. His hands slid up her arms to gently imprison her shoulders. In helpless anticipation she watched his firm, sensual lips slowly descend to hers.

His mouth covered hers, moving and probing in a kiss that was lazily coaxing, yet breathtakingly insistent. Lauren tried desperately to hold on to her fleeing sanity, but the moment his tongue slid against her lips she lost the battle.

With a smothered moan, she leaned into him and let him part her lips. His response was instantaneous. His arms tightened around her, imprisoning her against his chest, while his mouth opened hungrily, his tongue plunging into her mouth and stroking against hers. Something exploded inside Lauren; her body arched against him, and her hands lifted compulsively to caress his neck and slide through the soft hair at his nape as she eagerly responded to his hungry mouth.

By the time Nick finally lifted his head, Lauren felt branded by that kiss, permanently marked as his possession. Trembling with inner turmoil, she leaned her forehead against his shoulder. His warm lips drifted across her cheek to her temple, trailing downward until his teeth playfully nipped her earlobe. He chuckled huskily against her ear, "I think I owe you an apology, Lauren."

She leaned back in his arms and looked up at him. The smoky gray eyes gazing back at her were heavy-lidded and smoldering with passion, and although he was smiling, it was a wry smile of self-mockery.

"Why do you owe me an apology?"

His hand slid up and down her spine in a lazy caress. "Because despite your assurance that you aren't naive, until a few minutes ago I was worried that this weekend might be more than you could handle—and more than you bargained for."

Still dazed from their kiss, Lauren asked softly, "And *now* what do you think?"

"I think," he murmured dryly, "that this weekend might turn out to be more than *I* bargained for." He gazed into her glowing blue eyes, and his own eyes darkened with response. "I also think that if you continue to look at me like that, we're going to be about two hours late getting to Harbor Springs."

His glance flicked meaningfully to the motel across the highway but before Lauren even considered panicking, he reached up and firmly pulled her sunglasses down onto her nose. "Those eyes of yours are going to be my undoing," he said with grim humor.

Then he took her arm and led her toward the car.

Lauren collapsed into her seat, feeling as if she had just been through a cyclone. The car engine roared to life, and she forced herself to relax and think logically. She had two immediate problems facing her: the first was that it was now obvious Nick intended to take her to bed this weekend. In his mind it was already a forgone conclusion. Of course, she could simply say no when the time came, but the second problem was that she wasn't at all certain she *wanted* to say no. Never before had she been so attracted to a man, or so affected by a kiss. Never before had she so wanted a man to make love to her.

She looked at Nick's strong, capable hands on the steering wheel, then lifted her eyes to his ruggedly handsome profile. He was so attractive, so blatantly virile, that women probably took one look at him and eagerly went to bed with him without ever expecting any emotional commitment from him. Surely she herself wouldn't be such an easy conquest. Or would she?

A rueful smile touched Lauren's lips as she turned her head toward the window. Everyone always said she was so intelligent, so sensible, yet here she was, already planning to make Nick Sinclair fall in love with her . . . because she knew she was already falling in love with him.

"Lauren, this trip is getting a little lonely on my side of the car. What are you thinking about?"

Filled with thoughts of their destiny, Lauren turned to him and, smiling, slowly shook her head. "If I told you, it would scare you to death."

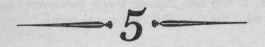

5

LAUREN'S GAZE STRAYED ADMIRINGLY OVER THE PANO-
rama of Lake Michigan's sparkling blue waves swelling and frothing with white as they tumbled lazily
onto the sandy beach. "We'll be there in a few
minutes," Nick told her as he turned off the highway
onto a well-maintained country road that wound
through towering stands of pine trees. Several minutes later he turned left onto an unmarked blacktop
driveway. For at least a mile the smooth private
drive meandered gracefully between stately moun-
tain-ash trees, their branches laden with magnificent
hanging clusters of bright orange fruit.

Lauren looked at the manicured landscape on
both sides of the drive and realized that the ordinary
lake cottage she'd originally envisioned when Nick
invited her here for the weekend was not going to be
what she would find. Nothing prepared her, however, for the sight that greeted her when they shot out
of the dappled shadows into the golden glow of the

setting sun and pulled to a stop behind a long row of expensive parked cars.

In the distance, against the backdrop of a steep bluff, sprawled an immense, modernistic three-story glass-and-stucco house. Acres of lush green lawns, dotted with colorful umbrella tables, sloped gently to a sandy beach. Waiters in light blue jackets were passing trays among what had to be at least a hundred guests, who were lounging on chaises around a gigantic kidney-shaped swimming pool, talking and laughing in animated groups on the lawn, or strolling on the beach.

Silhouetted against a pink-and-gold sky, gleaming white yachts rode languidly at anchor on the swelling water. Lauren decided they looked serenely unimpressed by a lake that was nearly a thousand feet deep in places, and unintimidated by the fact that storms could rage across its 22,000-square-mile surface, whipping it into a turbulent gray fury.

Nick got out of the car and came around to open her door. With his hand at her elbow, Lauren had no choice but to walk beside him along the winding row of racy foreign sports cars and luxurious sedans toward the throngs of guests.

At the edge of the lawn she stopped and surveyed the people with whom she was about to mingle. Besides several famous movie stars, there were other vaguely familiar faces—faces she'd seen repeatedly in magazine articles about the international jet set and the fabulously rich.

She glanced at Nick, who was slowly scanning the

crowd. He looked neither impressed nor intimidated by, this glittering assembly of the beautiful and the rich; in fact, he looked irritated. When he spoke, his voice was tinged with the same annoyance she saw in his expression. "I'm sorry, Lauren. If I'd known Tracy's 'little gathering' was going to be like this, I'd never have brought you here. It's going to be noisy, crowded and frenetic."

Although she felt rather ill at ease surrounded by such famous people, she managed an air of nonchalance and gave him a jaunty smile. "Maybe, if we're lucky, no one will realize we're here."

"Don't count on it," he warned dryly. They strolled along the perimeter of the lawn, which was bordered by dense woods. When they came to a bar that had been set up for the use of the guests, Nick stepped behind it. Rather than staring at him like a besotted idiot while he made their drinks, Lauren forced herself to turn and observe her surroundings. As her gaze moved over to a chattering group nearby, a gorgeous redhead glanced up and saw Nick.

With a smile dawning across her perfect features, the woman left her friends and hurried toward Nick and Lauren, her wide-legged lounging pants billowing softly at her ankles. "Nick, darling!" she said, laughing, her beringed hands already sliding up his arms as she leaned forward to kiss him.

Nick put the liquor bottle down and obligingly curved both his arms around her, drawing her to him to return the kiss.

76

Even after he released her, Lauren noted that the redhead kept her hands on his arms while smiling warmly into his gray eyes. "Everyone has been wondering if you were going to disappoint us and not come," she said. "But I *knew* you'd be here because the phone has been ringing off the hook with calls from your office. The servants and everyone else have been taking messages for you all afternoon. And who's this?" she asked brightly, at last taking her hands from his arms and stepping back to regard Lauren with open curiosity.

"Lauren, this is Barbara Leonardos," Nick began the introductions.

"Call me Bebe—everyone does." The woman turned back to Nick and continued, almost as if Lauren wasn't there, "I thought you were bringing Ericka."

"Really?" Nick mocked lightly. "And I thought *you* were in Rome with Alex."

"We were," Bebe admitted, "but we wanted to see you."

When she left a few moments later, Nick started to explain, "Bebe is—"

"I already know who she is," Lauren admitted softly, trying not to sound awed. Barbara Leonardos was the darling of the fashion magazines and gossip columnists, an American oil heiress who was married to a fabulously rich Greek industrialist. "I've seen her pictures in fashion magazines and newspapers dozens of times."

Nick handed Lauren the drink he had mixed for

her, picked up his own and inclined his head toward the couple who were striding quickly toward them, arm in arm. "Do you recognize either of those two?"

"No," Lauren admitted. "They don't look even slightly familiar."

Nick smiled at her. "In that case, I'll introduce you. They happen to be our host and hostess, as well as very good friends of mine."

Bracing herself for the inevitable round of introductions, Lauren studied the beautiful brunette in her thirties and the rather heavyset man beside her, who was close to sixty.

"Nick!" The woman laughed delightedly, flinging herself into Nick's arms in utter disregard of the drink he was holding and kissing him with the same intimate, enthusiastic familiarity that Bebe had. "We haven't seen you for months!" she scolded as she stepped back. "What on earth have you been doing?"

"Some of us still work for a living," Nick told her with an affectionate smile. Reaching out, he caught Lauren's arm, drawing her into the circle of comradery. "Lauren, I'd like you to meet our hosts, Tracy and George Middleton."

"Lauren, I'm so happy to meet you," Tracy said, then she demanded of Nick, "Why are you two standing way over here by yourselves? No one will even realize you're here."

"Which is precisely why I'm standing over here," Nick told her bluntly.

Tracy's breath came out in a rueful laugh. "I know I promised you this was going to be a small gathering. I swear we had no idea that nearly everyone we invited was actually going to come. You can't imagine the problem it's created up at the house."

She glanced at the purpling sky and then over her shoulder. Following her gaze, Lauren saw that nearly all the guests had begun to stroll toward the house or down to the pier, where motor launches were waiting to take them out to their yachts. Waiters had started to set up tables under a huge striped canopy, and torches were being lit around the pool. Musicians were moving their instruments onto a large portable stage that had been erected at the far end of the pool.

"Everyone is already dressing for dinner," Tracy stated. "Are you two going over to the Cove to change, or were you planning to change here?"

Lauren's mind reeled. Dressing for dinner? She had absolutely nothing that was even remotely suitable to wear if they were going to dress formally for dinner!

Ignoring Lauren's urgent grip on his forearm, Nick said, "Lauren will change here. I'll go over to the Cove, return whatever phone calls can't wait and change there."

Tracy smiled at Lauren. "The house is bursting at the seams; you and I can use our room, and George will find somewhere else to change. Shall we go?" she invited, already starting to turn away.

Nick glanced at Lauren's expression with a wry gleam of understanding. "I think there's something Lauren wants to discuss with me. You go ahead, and she'll join you."

As soon as the couple strolled out of hearing distance, Lauren said desperately, "Nick, I don't have anything suitable to wear. Surely you don't, either?"

"I have things over at the Cove, and I'll find a dress for you there too," he assured her calmly. "I'll send it over, and it will be in Tracy's room by the time you're ready to put it on."

Inside, the house was a cacophony of voices and bustling activity. Laughter and conversation drifted from twenty different rooms on three different floors, while servants hurried in every direction carrying freshly pressed clothing draped over their arms and trays of drinks in their hands.

Nick stopped one of the servants and asked for his phone messages. In an instant they were in his hand, and he turned to Lauren with a warm smile. "I'll meet you outside by the pool in about an hour. Can you manage without me for that long?"

"I'll be fine," Lauren assured him. "Take your time."

"Are you certain?"

With his compelling gray eyes searching hers, Lauren wasn't certain of her own name, but she nodded anyway. When he left, she turned to find Bebe Leonardos watching her with open curiosity. Quickly wiping the dreamy expression from her face, Lauren said, "Is there a phone I can use somewhere? I'd like to call home."

"Of course. Where's home?" Bebe inquired casually.

"Fenster, Missouri," Lauren told her, following

her into a luxurious study near the back of the house.

"Fenster?" Bebe sniffed, as if there was an offensive odor associated with the name of the town. Then she left, closing the door behind her.

The long-distance collect call to her father didn't take long because they were both acutely aware of the expense involved. But her dad laughed with pride and astonishment when he heard about her new job and salary, and he was relieved when she told him that Philip Whitworth had insisted she live in his aunt's condominium, rent free. She didn't mention her bargain with Philip because she didn't want to cause her father any anxiety. All she wanted him to know was that his financial burden was now eased.

After hanging up Lauren crossed the study and partially opened the door, pausing at the sound of a cheery female voice raised in greeting at the end of the hall. "Bebe, darling, you look marvelous; it's been ages since I've seen you. Did you know Nick Sinclair is supposed to be here this weekend?"

"He's here," Bebe answered. "I've already spoken to him."

"Thank heavens he came!" The other woman laughed. "Carlton dragged me here from a divine beach in Bermuda because he wants to talk to Nick about some business deal."

"Carlton will have to wait his turn," Bebe replied indifferently. "Nick is the reason Alex and I are here too. Alex wants to talk to him about building a chain of international hotels. He's been trying to call Nick from Rome for two weeks, but Nick hadn't returned the calls, so we flew here yesterday."

"I didn't see Ericka out there," the other woman said.

"You didn't see her because Nick didn't bring her—but just wait until you see what he brought instead." The derisive laughter in Bebe's cultured voice made Lauren stiffen, even before she added, "You won't believe it! She's about eighteen years old and straight off a farm in Missouri. Before Nick could leave her alone for an hour, he had to ask her if she would be all right by herself . . ." The voices faded as the two women moved away.

Bebe's verbal attack stunned and irritated Lauren, but she calmly pulled open the door and stepped out into the hall.

Seated at Tracy's dressing table an hour later, Lauren brushed her heavy hair until the burnished honey and gold strands framed her face and tumbled in glorious waves over her shoulders. Then she hastily applied a rosy blusher to her high cheekbones, smoothed the matching gloss over her lips and tossed the cosmetics into her purse.

By now Nick was surely down at the pool waiting for her. The thought brought a glow of sheer happiness to her turquoise eyes as she leaned closer to the mirror and carefully put on the treasured 14-karat gold earrings that had belonged to her mother.

When she finished, she stepped back to study the effect of the long, sophisticated cream jersey dress that had arrived from Nick while she was taking a bath. The soft fabric emphasized her high full breasts, and the long tight sleeves hugged her arms all the way to the wrists, where they ended in points at the backs of her hands. The gold link belt nipped in the slightly blousy waistline, so that every feminine curve Lauren possessed was beguilingly displayed, from the top of the straight neckline to the hem of the slightly full skirt where the dainty gold sandals Tracy had lent her peeped out.

"Perfect!" Tracy grinned. "Turn around so I can see the back."

Lauren obediently complied.

"How can anything that looks so demure from the front be so smashing from the back?" her hostess asked, looking at the way Lauren's trim back with its golden summer tan was exposed almost to the waistline. "Well, shall we go down?"

As the two of them walked along the balcony, Lauren could hear the sounds of the poolside revelry below floating in through the open windows. Dozens of laughing female voices blended with the deeper murmurings of males, then mingled chaotically with upbeat orchestra music.

Five seconds after they walked outdoors onto the patio, Tracy was surrounded and whisked away by a group of her friends, leaving Lauren standing alone. She craned her neck, scanning the crowd for a glimpse of Nick. She took two steps forward and immediately saw him standing amid a large group of people at the far end of the pool.

Keeping her eyes on his tall form, Lauren carefully wended her way around the obstacles of guests, waiters, torches, umbrella tables and pool. When she was closer, she could see that Nick was standing with people who were speaking animatedly to him. With his head tipped toward them, he appeared to be listening with rapt attention, yet periodically his gaze would flicker up and slide over the crowd, as if he was looking for someone.

He was looking for her, Lauren realized with an inner glow. As if he sensed her nearness, he lifted his head sharply, and his eyes met hers across the knots of humanity. With an abruptness that bordered on discourtesy, he nodded to the people who were talking to him and without a word simply strolled out of their midst.

When the last group on the patio parted to let him through, Lauren had her first full-length view of him, and her breath caught. His raven black tuxedo fit his tall, splendid frame as if it had been made specifically for him by the finest tailor. The dazzling whiteness of his frilled shirt contrasted beautifully with his bronzed face and formal black bow tie, and he wore the elegant attire with the easy assurance of a man who was thoroughly accustomed to it. Lauren felt absurdly proud of him, and she made no attempt to hide it when he finally stood in front of her. "Has anyone ever told you how beautiful you are?" she asked softly.

A slow boyish smile spread across his features. "What would you think if I told you no?"

Lauren laughed. "I'd think you were trying to appear modest."

"Then what am I supposed to do now?" he teased.

"I suppose you should try to look a little flustered and embarrassed by the flattery."

"I don't fluster or embarrass very easily."

"In that case, you could try to fluster me by telling me how *I* look," she hinted broadly. Turning slowly so that she wouldn't draw the attention of the other guests, she deliberately gave him the full shock effect of her dress. Flaring torchlight danced off the burnished honey of her hair as she completed her turn and waited while Nick's gaze moved over her glowing face, luminous blue eyes and softly full lips, then swept downward over the lush outlines of her figure.

"Well?" she teased in turn. "What do you think?"

The gray eyes that finally lifted to hers were flaming, but instead of answering, he flicked his burning gaze down her length again. He hesitated, and then said abruptly, "I think that the dress fits you perfectly."

Lauren burst out laughing. "Don't ever let anyone tell you that you have a way with flattery, because you don't."

"Is that right?" he mocked, his eyes challenging. "In that case, I'll tell you *exactly* what I think: I think that you're exquisitely lovely, and that you have the fascinating ability to look like an extremely sexy, sophisticated young woman and an utterly angelic girl at one and the same time. And I wish to hell that we weren't trapped here with a hundred other people for the next few hours, because whenever I look at you I become . . . uncomfortably eager

. . . to find out how you're going to feel in my arms tonight."

Lauren's fair complexion bloomed with color. She wasn't *that* angelic, and she understood what he meant by the phrase "uncomfortably eager." Her gaze slid away from his mocking gray eyes, and she looked at the guests, at the yachts lit up like brilliant white Christmas trees—at *anything* except Nick's tall, hard body. Why had he been so blunt? Maybe he suspected that she'd never slept with anyone before, and he was deliberately trying to panic her into admitting it. Would it even matter to him that she was a virgin?

Judging by his frank attitude toward sex; there probably wasn't anything he hadn't done or didn't know. Where women were concerned, she doubted if there was a single fiber of innocence left in Nick's entire aggressively virile body. Even so, Lauren had the feeling that he wouldn't want to seduce and bed a virgin. Of course, this particular virgin wanted very much to be "seduced" by him, but not quite so soon, and not with so little effort on his part, either. She should make him wait until he genuinely cared for her. She should, but she wasn't certain she was going to do it.

Firmly, taking her chin between his thumb and forefinger, Nick turned her face up to his, forcing her to look into his teasing gray eyes. "If I'm so beautiful, why won't you look at me?"

"That was a silly thing for me to tell you," Lauren apologized with quiet dignity, "and . . ."

"It was definitely a gross exaggeration—" he

smiled, taking his hand away from her chin "—but I liked it. And, in case you're interested," he added, his voice turning husky, "no one has ever told me that before." He glanced up as someone called his name, then pretended he hadn't heard. Putting his hand beneath her elbow he steered her toward the striped tent on the lawn, where waiters were serving hot and cold hors d'oeuvres. "Let's get something for you to eat and drink."

In the ensuing five minutes, six other people called his name. The next time it happened he said irritably, "As much as I'd like to spend the evening alone with you, we're going to have to socialize. I can't keep pretending I'm blind and deaf much longer."

"I understand," Lauren said sympathetically. "They're very rich and very spoiled, and because you work for them they think they own you."

His dark brows drew together in surprise. "What makes you think I work for them?"

"I accidentally overheard Bebe Leonardos tell someone that her husband came here from Rome because he wants to talk to you about building international hotels. And the other woman said that *her* husband, whose name is Carlton, is here to talk to you about some kind of business too."

Nick threw an annoyed look over the entire crowd, as if each person there constituted a personal threat to his peace. "I came up here because I've been working myself into the ground for two months, and I wanted to relax for a weekend," he said angrily.

"If you really don't want to talk to anyone about

business, there's no reason why you have to do it."

"When people have come thousands of miles to talk to you, they can be damned persistent," he responded, glancing at the other guests again. "And unless I miss my guess, there are at least four other men who have come here to do exactly that."

"Just leave them to me," Lauren said with a bewitching smile. "I'll hold them off."

"You will?" He grinned. "And just how will you do that?"

Beneath their luxuriant russet lashes, Lauren's blue eyes were twinkling. "The moment anyone starts talking to you about business, I'll interrupt and pretend to distract you."

Nick's gaze dropped to her lips. "That shouldn't be difficult—you always distract me."

And for the next three hours, Lauren did precisely as she'd promised. With a tactical brilliance that would have done credit to Napoleon Bonaparte, she smoothly extricated Nick from at least a dozen business conversations. The moment the discussion began to get too deeply involved, she interrupted to sweetly remind him that he had promised to get her a drink, take her for a walk, show her the grounds or whatever ploy occurred to her at the moment.

And Nick let her do it, observing her highly effective tactics with a mixture of frank admiration and veiled amusement. With his drink in his left hand and his right arm around her waist, he kept her by his side, shamelessly using her as a voluntary shield. But as the evening progressed and the liquor flowed, conversations became louder, the laughter more hilarious, the jokes more bawdy. And the men who wanted to detain Nick became more persistent.

"Do you really need to walk out a cramp in your leg?" Nick asked in a teasing whisper as they strolled away from a florid-faced yachtsman who wanted Nick to tell him everything he knew about some oil company in Oklahoma.

Lauren was sipping her third glass of a delicious after-dinner drink that had the taste and consistency of a chocolate malt, but that she was beginning to realize was far more potent than she had imagined. "Of course not—my legs are perfect," she announced gaily, turning to watch six exuberant people playing doubles tennis on a single court. One of the women, a French movie star, had removed her skirt and was clad in a sequined top, lacy black underpants that peeked from under the edge of it and high heels.

Nick took Lauren's empty glass from her hand and put it down on an umbrella table beside his. "Shall we walk down to the beach?"

A party was in progress on one of the brightly lit yachts. They stood together on the beach, listening to the music and laughter, watching the shaft of moonlight streaming across the lake. "Dance with me," Nick said, and Lauren walked obediently into his arms, loving the feel of them sliding around her.

Laying her cheek against the smooth fabric of his black jacket, she moved with him in time to the orchestra's love song, vibrantly aware of his legs shifting intimately between hers.

Since she'd gotten up that morning she'd been through a session with Mr. Weatherby, an interview with Jim Williams, lunch with Nick, a long drive and now this party where she had drunk more than she ever had before in her life. In one day she'd experienced tension, excitement, hope and passion, and now she was spending the weekend with the man of her dreams. The emotional merry-go-round she'd been on had taken its full toll; she felt deliciously exhausted and more than a little giddy.

Her thoughts floated to the French movie star, and she laughed softly. "If I was that woman playing tennis, I'd have left my skirt on, and taken my shoes off. And do you know why?"

"So that you could play better?" Nick murmured distractedly, nuzzling aside the wavy silken hair that fell over her temple.

"Nope, I don't even know how to play tennis." Abruptly lifting her face to his, Lauren breezily confided, "The reason I'd keep my skirt on is because I'm modest. Or am I inhibited? Well, anyway, I'm one of the two." She laid her cheek against the solid muscles of his chest again. Nick chuckled against her hair, and his hand splayed low against her bared spine, pressing her closer to his hard body.

"Actually," she continued dreamily, "I'm not modest or inhibited. What I am is the confused product of a semipuritanical upbringing and a liberal education. Which means that I think it's wrong for me to do anything, but I think it's perfectly all right for other people to do whatever they want. Does that make sense?"

Nick ignored her question and asked one of his own instead. "Lauren, by any wild chance are you getting drunk?"

"I'm not certain."

"Don't," he commanded.

Although quietly spoken, it was an order, and he meant it to be obeyed. Intending to protest his authoritative attitude, Lauren snapped her head up, but her lips instantly captured his attention. "Don't even *consider* it," he muttered harshly. Then his mouth opened over hers in a shattering kiss that sent her spiraling off into darkness where nothing existed except the sensual male lips locked fiercely, demandingly, to hers. His hand sank into the thick mass of hair at her nape, and his tongue plunged into her mouth, stroking and caressing hers, retreating to plunge again, until Lauren instinctively gave him what he wanted. Her lips softened and began to move with his, stimulating the desire already flaming between them. Against her, Lauren felt the bold evidence of his rising passion, and shudders of pleasure raced through her. Her body joined forces with his, demolishing her control. Mindlessly she arched herself upward in a fevered need to please him more, and his arm tightened across her hips, pulling her even closer to his rigid thighs.

He dragged his mouth roughly across her cheek,

and even his whisper was hoarse with desire. "Lady, you don't kiss like any puritan," he said, and pressed his lips to hers again.

Slowly the pressure of his mouth gentled and then was gone. Shivering with excitement and fear, Lauren weakly leaned her forehead against his shoulder. She was sinking into this abyss of desire too fast, and too deeply, to get free. His next words confirmed it. "Let's go to the Cove."

"Nick, I . . ."

His hands slid up her arms to her shoulders, then tightened, moving her an inch away. "Look at me," he said gently.

Lauren raised her dazed blue eyes to his silvery gaze.

"I want you, Lauren."

The quiet, straightforward statement sent fire racing through her entire body. "I know," she whispered unsteadily. "And I'm glad you do."

His eyes smiled his warm approval of her candor, and he laid his hand against her cheek, moving it caressingly over her temple to the to the back of her head. "And . . . ?" he prompted.

Lauren swallowed, unable to tear her gaze from his or to lie to him. "And I want you," she admitted shakily.

His fingers slid into her heavy hair, pulling her head nearer to his descending mouth. "In that case," he murmured thickly, "why are we standing out here?"

"Hey, Nick!" A friendly voice boomed out from a few feet away. "Is that you?"

Lauren jerked away as if she'd been caught in some unspeakable act, then almost burst out laughing when Nick pulled her back and said smoothly, "Sinclair left hours ago."

"No, did he? Wonder why?" the man asked, stepping closer and peering suspiciously through the darkness at them.

"He obviously had something better to do," Nick drawled.

"So I see," the man agreed good-naturedly. Having now identified his prey, he showed absolutely no inclination to take the rude hint and go away. Wearing a sociable smile on his jowly face, he sauntered out of the shadows, a stout, swarthy man who instantly reminded Lauren of a teddy bear. His tuxedo jacket was hanging open, his frilled evening shirt was unbuttoned at the collar and his formal bow tie was dangling loosely around his neck. He looked . . . lovable, Lauren decided, as Nick introduced the man as Dave Numbers.

"How do you do, Mr. Numbers," she said politely.

"I'm doing pretty well, young lady," he replied with an affable grin. Turning to Nick he said, "There's a hell of a blackjack game going on aboard Middleton's yacht. Bebe Leonardos just dropped $25,000. Tracy Middleton is shooting craps at $3,000 a throw, and George was dealt four of a kind in two different hands. The odds against that happening once are 4,000 to one. The odds against that happening twice must be roughly . . ."

Keeping a courteous smile on her face, Lauren

rested her head against Nick's chest, moving closer to him for warmth, while she pretended to listen to Dave Numbers summing up the results of the gambling in progress. She was not only cold, she was getting sleepy, and Nick's hand moving up and down her back in a lazy caress was having an almost hypnotic effect on her. She stifled a yawn, and then another one, and a few minutes later her eyelids drooped closed.

"I'm putting your young lady to sleep, Nick," Numbers apologized in the middle of quoting the odds on a forth-coming football game.

Lauren straightened self-consciously and tried to put a bright smile on her sleepy face, which Nick observed with a gleam of humor. "I think," he said, "that Lauren is ready for bed."

The older man glanced at her, then winked at Nick. "Lucky you." With a brief wave, he turned and strolled off toward the house.

Wrapping his arms around her, Nick hugged her tightly to his muscular chest and buried his face in her fragrant hair. "Am I, Lauren?"

Lauren snuggled closer into the warmth of his arms. "Are you what?" she murmured.

"Going to be lucky tonight?"

"No," Lauren sleepily replied.

"I thought not," he chuckled against her hair. Leaning back he looked down at her sleepy face and wryly shook his head. "Come on—you're already half asleep." He put his arm around her shoulders and started walking her back to the house.

"I like Mr. Numbers," she commented.

Nick's sidelong look was filled with amusement. "Actually, his name happens to be Mason. Numbers is a nickname."

"He's a mathematical wizard," Lauren remarked admiringly. "And he's very nice. He's friendly, and he's—"

"A bookie," Nick provided.

"He's a *what?*" Lauren almost stumbled in her surprise.

Despite the lateness of the hour, the house was lit up and the party was at a fever pitch. "Don't these people ever sleep?" Lauren asked when Nick opened the front door, and the noisy laughter exploded around them.

"Not if they can help it," he answered, casually surveying the scene. He asked a servant which room Lauren had been given, then led her up the staircase. "I'm going to stay at the Cove tonight. We'll spend the day there tomorrow—alone." He opened the door to Lauren's room and added, "The keys to your car are with the butler. All you have to do is turn north out of the driveway and come two miles to the first road on the left. The Cove is at the end of that road, and it's the only house there—you can't miss it. I'll expect you at eleven."

His arrogant assumption that she would be perfectly willing to come to the Cove—and do anything else he wanted—filled Lauren with exasperated amusement. "Shouldn't you ask if I *want* to be alone with you there?"

He chucked her under the chin. "You do." Grinning at her as if she were an entertaining nine-year-old, he mocked lightly, "If you don't, you can always turn south out of the driveway and head for Missouri." Curving his arms around her he claimed her lips in a long, smoldering kiss. "I'll see you at eleven."

Rankled, Lauren contradicted flippantly, "Unless I decide to leave for Missouri."

When he left, she sank down onto the bed, an unwilling smile trembling on her lips. How could any one man be so outrageously self-confident, so arrogant—and so utterly wonderful? She had been too busy with school, her job and her music to ever become deeply involved with a man, but she was a grown woman. She knew what she wanted, and she wanted Nick. He was everything a man should be—strong, gentle, intelligent, wise—and he had a sense of humor. He was handsome and sexy. . . .

Picking up her pillow, Lauren happily wrapped her arms around it and hugged it to her chest, rubbing her cheek against the white material as if it was his shirt. He was playing a game with desire, but she wanted to make him care for her too—she wanted to win *him.* If she was going to make him care for her, if she was ever going to be special to him, she had to be different from the other women he'd known.

Lauren flopped down on her back and gazed at the ceiling. He was entirely too sure of her, she decided. For example, he was perfectly confident that she would come to the Cove. A good dose of uncertainty might throw him off balance and help her cause. Therefore, she would be just late enough to make him think she *wasn't* coming. Eleven-thirty would be perfect—by then he would have decided she wasn't coming, but he wouldn't have left yet to go anywhere else.

With the pillow still wrapped in her arms and the smile still on her lips, Lauren fell asleep. She slept with the inner peace and profound joy of a woman who knows she has found the man whose destiny lies with hers.

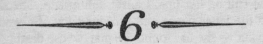

6

IN ACCORDANCE WITH HER PLAN TO ARRIVE AT THE Cove a bit late, Lauren asked the butler for the keys to her car and walked out onto the drive at eleven-twenty, only to find that there were at least six cars blocking hers.

By the time the owners had been identified, the keys found and the cars moved, it was eleven forty-five, and Lauren was a little frantic. Her hands clenched the steering wheel as she swung her car out onto the main road. What if he had decided not to wait?

Exactly two miles from the Middletons' she saw a blacktop driveway on the left with a small wooden sign that read The Cove, and she turned in to it, racing up the steep winding incline, sending startled rabbits and squirrels into the dense forest as she drove by.

An L-shaped house loomed into view at the end of the driveway, a spectacular structure of glass and rough-sawn cedar that looked as if it belonged on a cliff overlooking the Pacific Ocean. Lauren braked the car to a jarring stop beside the house, grabbed her purse and hurried up the wide flagstone walk to the front door.

She rang the bell and waited, then she rang it again and waited even longer. But when she pressed it the third time, she already knew that no one was going to answer. No one was there.

Turning, Lauren gazed despondently at the small manicured lawn. There was no point in going around to the back because the house was perched on the very edge of a bluff, with nothing behind it but a sheer drop of a hundred feet down to the water and a cedar deck that was breathtakingly suspended in midair.

Nick hadn't been willing to wait very long for her, she thought bitterly. When she didn't arrive on time he must have thought that she'd left for Missouri. He didn't have a car of his own, so he must have gone off somewhere with the owner of this magnificent home.

She started walking back down the path, feeling very stupid and very much like crying. She couldn't just sit down on the doorstoop and hope Nick eventually came back there to sleep that night, and she couldn't return to the Middletons', since she was there as his guest. She should have known better than to try to play games with a man who was obviously a master at them. Because of her scheming, she was going to end up spending this glorious day driving back to Missouri after all.

Swallowing the lump in her throat, Lauren opened

the car door and put her purse on the passenger seat. As she paused to look once more at the wild beauty of her surroundings, her gaze locked onto some steps carved into the rocky bluff just beside her, and she heard a strange metallic sound coming from far below. The steps obviously led down through the trees to the beach—and someone was down there. With her heart slamming into her ribs she hurried down the steep steps.

On the bottom step she stopped, paralyzed with joy and relief at the sight of Nick's lithe, familiar form. Clad only in a pair of brief white tennis shorts, he was crouched down, working on the motor of a small boat that had been pulled up onto the narrow crescent of sandy beach. For a long moment Lauren simply watched him, her eyes delighting in the sheer male beauty of his wide shoulders, muscular arms and tapered back, gleaming like oiled bronze in the sun.

As she stood there, he stopped working on the motor and looked down at his wristwatch. His arm dropped, and he slowly turned his head to stare at something on his right. He was so perfectly still that Lauren finally tore her eyes from his profile and followed his gaze. When she saw what he had done, tenderness vibrated through her entire body. He had spread blankets on the sand and placed a huge beach umbrella behind to screen them from the sun. A linen tablecloth had been carefully set with china, crystal goblets and silver. Three wicker picnic baskets were off to one side, and a bottle of wine was protruding from the open lid of one of them.

He must have made half a dozen trips up and down those steep steps, Lauren realized. Considering that a few minutes before she'd thought he didn't even care enough about her to wait until she got here, this evidence of how much he actually did care was doubly touching.

Not *that* touching, she hastily reminded herself, trying unsuccessfully to banish her smile. After all, what she was really looking at was the carefully prepared scene of her very own seduction. . . . *Attempted seduction,* she corrected, with an inward grin.

Smoothing down the bright green V-necked velour top that matched her shorts, she decided she would say something witty by way of greeting. And Nick would, of course, be very casual and pretend he hadn't even noticed that she was late. With that scenario in mind she stepped forward. Unfortunately, she couldn't think of anything witty to say. "Hi," she called out cheerfully.

In his crouching position, Nick slowly pivoted around, the wrench still in his hand. He draped his arm across his bent knees and stared at her with cool, inscrutable gray eyes. "You're late," he said.

That was so far from what she'd envisioned that Lauren had to gulp back a stunned giggle as she walked over to him. "Did you think I wasn't coming?" she inquired innocently.

His dark brows lifted sardonically. "Wasn't that what I was supposed to think?"

It wasn't a question, it was a cool accusation, and Lauren's first impulse was to deny it. Instead she nodded her head, an irrepressible smile teasing her lips. "Yes," she admitted softly, watching his chilly gray eyes turn warm with fascinated interest. "Were you disappointed?" Instantly she regretted the question, because she knew Nick would now retaliate by saying something cutting.

"Very disappointed," he admitted quietly.

A treacherous heat was seeping through Lauren's nervous system as she gazed into those mesmerizing gray eyes, and as Nick put the wrench down and slowly stood up, she cautiously backed away a step.

"Lauren?"

She swallowed. "Yes?"

"Would you like to eat first?"

"First," she whispered hoarsely. "Before what?"

"Before we go sailing," he replied, studying her with puzzlement.

"Oh, *sailing!*" Her breath came out in a laugh. "Yes, thank you, I would like to eat first. And I'd love to go sailing."

7

LAUREN HAD NEVER KNOWN A MORE GLORIOUS DAY than this. In the two hours since they sailed away from the Cove, a warm comradery had sprung up between them—a companionship that was made up of spontaneous comments and shared laughter, punctuated with long relaxed silences.

The brilliant blue sky was decorated with puffy white clouds, and the wind caught the sail, sending the boat shooting soundlessly through the water. She watched a sea gull screeching overhead, then glanced at Nick, who was seated at the tiller, facing her. He smiled and Lauren smiled back, then she lifted her face to the sky again, basking in the sun's golden warmth and in the knowledge that Nick's lazy, admiring gaze was on her.

"We could drop anchor here and do some sun-bathing and some fishing. Would you like that?" Nick said.

"I'd love it." Lauren watched him roll to his feet and begin taking in the sail.

"We should get some bass and blue gill for our dinner," he said a few minutes later as he rigged two fishing poles. "There's great salmon fishing here, but we'd need downriggers, and we'd have to troll."

Lauren had fished with her father many times from the banks of Missouri's verdant creeks and rivers, but she'd never fished from a boat. She didn't have the faintest idea what a downrigger was or what trolling was either, but intended to find out. If the man she loved liked to fish from boats, she would learn to like it too.

"I've got one," Nick called a half hour later as his line played out with a whir.

Lauren dropped her rod and went racing toward his end of the boat, unthinkingly shouting directions: "Set the hook! Keep your rod tip up. Don't let the line go slack. He's running—loosen the drag."

"Lord, are you bossy!" Nick grinned, and she realized with a rueful smile that he was handling the fish with expertise. A few minutes later he leaned over the side of the boat and scooped the big perch into a long-handled net. Like a proud little boy who was showing off his trophy to someone special, Nick held up his flapping fish for Lauren to properly admire. "Well, what do you think?"

One look at that boyish expression on his ruggedly chiseled features, and the love that had budded inside Lauren burst into full bloom. *You're wonderful*, she thought. "He's wonderful," she said.

And in that outwardly casual moment, Lauren made the most momentous decision of her life. Nick already owned her heart; tonight it was right that he have her body too.

The sun was setting in a blaze of crimson when Nick let out the sail and they started back to the Cove. Lauren again felt his gaze on her as he sat at the tiller, facing her in the waning light. It was getting chilly, and she drew her legs up against her chest, wrapping her arms around them. The question of how they were going to spend the night had been completely resolved in her mind, but it bothered her that she was about to take such an irrevocable step with a man whom she adored, but about whom she knew so very little.

"What are you thinking about?" Nick asked quietly.

"I was thinking that I know very little about you."

"What would you like to know?"

It was the opening Lauren desperately wanted. "Well, for a start, how do you happen to know Tracy Middleton and the crowd at her party?"

As if he was delaying his answer, Nick took a cigarette from the package in his pocket and put it between his lips. He lit a match and cupped his hands over the flame, lighting it. "Tracy and I grew up next door to each other," he said, extinguishing the match with a deft shake of his wrist. "Near where Tony's restaurant is now."

Lauren was astounded. Tony's restaurant was in what was today a fashionably renovated downtown neighborhood. But fifteen or twenty years ago, when

Nick and Tracy were growing up there, it couldn't have been very nice at all.

Nick watched the play of emotions across her features and apparently guessed the direction of her thoughts. "Tracy married George, who is nearly twice her age, in order to escape from the old neighborhood."

Cautiously, Lauren approached the topic that Nick had avoided earlier and that interested her the most. "Nick, you said your father died when you were four, and that your grandparents raised you. But what happened to your mother?"

"Nothing happened to her. She went back to live with her parents the day after my father's funeral."

Oddly, it was his complete indifference that alerted Lauren and made her study him sharply. His handsome face was composed, a neutral mask. Too composed, too unemotional, she thought. She didn't want to pry, but she was falling in love with this compelling, enigmatic, passionate man, and she desperately needed to understand him. Hesitantly she said, "Your mother didn't take you with her?"

The curtness of Nick's tone warned her that he was not pleased with the direction of the conversation, but he answered, "My mother was a wealthy, pampered Grosse Pointe debutante who met my father when he went to her family's house to repair some electrical wiring. Six weeks later she jilted her bland but wealthy fiancé, and she married my proud but penniless father instead. Apparently she regretted it almost immediately. My father insisted that she live on what he could make, and she hated him for that. Even after his business was doing better, she despised her life, and she despised him."

"Then why didn't she leave him?"

"According to my grandfather," Nick responded dryly, "there was one area where she found my father irresistible."

"Do you resemble your father?" Lauren asked impulsively.

"Almost exactly, I'm told. Why?"

"No reason," Lauren said. But she had a rueful feeling that she understood exactly how irresistible Nick's father must have been to his mother. "Go on with the story, please."

"There isn't much else to tell. The day after my father's funeral, she announced that she wanted to forget the squalid life she'd led, and she moved back to her parents' house in Grosse Pointe. Apparently I was part of what she wanted to forget, because she left me behind with my grandparents. Three months later she married her former fiancé and within a year she had another son—my half brother."

"But she did come to visit you, didn't she?"

"No."

Lauren was horrified at the idea of a mother abandoning her child and then living in luxury only a few miles away from him. Grosse Pointe was where the Whitworths lived, too, and it wasn't far from the neighborhood where Nick had grown up. "You mean you never saw her again after that?"

"I saw her occasionally, but only accidentally.

One night she pulled into the gas station where I was working."

"What did she say?" Lauren breathed.

"She told me to check the oil," Nick replied imperturbably.

Despite his outward attitude of total indifference, Lauren couldn't believe that as a younger man he'd been so invulnerable. Surely having his own mother treat him as if he didn't exist must have hurt him terribly. "Is that all she said?" she asked tightly.

Unaware that Lauren was not sharing his ironic humor in the story, he said, "No—I think she asked me to check the air in her tires too."

Lauren had kept her voice neutral, but inwardly she felt ill. Tears stung her eyes, and she turned her face up to the purpling sky to hide them, pretending to watch the lacy clouds drifting over the moon.

"Lauren?" His voice sounded curt.

"Hmmmm?" she asked, staring steadfastly at the moon.

Leaning forward, he caught her chin and turned her face toward his. He looked at her brimming eyes in stunned disbelief. "You're crying!" he said incredulously.

Lauren waved a dismissing hand at him. "Don't pay any attention to that—I cry at movies too."

Nick burst out laughing and pulled her onto his lap. Lauren felt strangely maternal as she put her arm around him and soothingly stroked his thick dark hair. "I suppose," she said in a shaky voice, "that when you were growing up, your brother got all sorts of things that you could only dream of having. New cars and everything."

Tipping her chin up, he smiled into her somber blue eyes. "I had wonderful grandparents, and I promise you that I don't have any emotional scars from what happened with my mother."

"Of course you do—anyone would! She walked out on you, then practically before your eyes lavished her attention on her next son. . . ."

"Stop it," he teased, "or you'll have *me* in tears."

With quiet gravity Lauren said, "I was crying for the boy you were then, not for the man you are now. Despite everything that happened—no, because of it—you became a strong, independent man. Actually, the one to pity is your half brother."

Nick chuckled. "You're right—he's an ass."

Lauren ignored his humor. "What I meant was that you've succeeded on your own, without wealthy parents to help you. That makes you a bigger man than your half brother."

"Is *that* why I'm bigger?" he joked. "I always thought it was in my genes. You see, my father and grandfather were both tall. . . ."

"Nick, I'm trying to be serious!"

"Sorry."

"When you were young, you must have dreamed of becoming as rich and successful as your mother's husband and her son."

"Richer," Nick confirmed. "And more successful."

"So you went to college and got your engineering

degree," Lauren concluded. "Then what did you do?"

"I wanted to start my own business, but I didn't have enough money."

"That's a shame," Lauren said sympathetically.

"That's also enough of my life history for now," he finished evasively. "We're almost home."

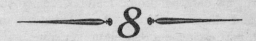

8

THE WARM CLOSENESS THAT HAD DEVELOPED BETWEEN them as they sailed back was still enfolding them as they dined by lantern light on the cedar deck suspended out beyond the bluff.

"Don't bother," Nick said quietly when Lauren stood with the intention of clearing the china and crystal from the table. "The housekeeper will take care of it in the morning." He picked up a bottle of Grand Marnier and poured some liqueur into two fragile glasses. He handed her one, then leaned back in his chair. Raising his glass to his lips, he contemplated her over the rim.

Lauren rolled the stem of her glass between her fingers, trying to ignore the atmosphere of expectation that was hanging over them. Her time was running out; Nick had satisfied their physical hunger, and now he was lazily preparing to satisfy their sexual hunger. She could see it in the way his possessive gaze lingered on her delicate features as she sat across from him, and in his warmly intimate smile when he spoke to her.

She raised her glass and took a fortifying swallow of the orange-and-cognac drink. Any moment he would stand up and take her inside. She glanced up as he lit a cigarette. In the flickering glow of the lantern, his dark handsome features seemed shadowy and almost predatory. A chill that was part fright, part excitement danced up her spine.

"Are you cold?" he asked softly.

Lauren quickly shook her head, afraid that he would immediately suggest they go in. Then she realized he must have seen her shiver, and she added, "I mean I was a little chilly just then, but it's so lovely out here I can't bear to go in yet."

Several minutes later Nick stubbed out his cigarette and moved his chair back from the table. Lauren's heart lurched. She drained her glass and held it toward him. "I'd like a little more."

She saw a flicker of surprise in his expression, but he obligingly poured more Grand Marnier into both their glasses, then he lazed back in his chair again, openly watching her.

Lauren was too jumpy to either meet his gaze or endure it. She stood up, smiled shakily and walked over to the edge of the deck, gazing across the black lake at the lights twinkling in the hills. She wanted to please him always, and in all ways, but what if she failed tonight? Nick was so alarmingly virile and blatantly experienced that her virginity and inexperience might seem like a nuisance to him.

Nick's chair scraped against the wooden deck, and Lauren heard him approach, stopping right behind her. He put his hands on her shoulders and she jumped. "You're cold," he murmured, drawing her back against his chest and wrapping his arms around her for warmth. "Is that better?" he asked, his lips against her hair.

The imprint of his legs and thighs pressing against her seemed to rob Lauren of the power of speech. She nodded, and then she trembled uncontrollably.

"You're shivering." His hands shifted to her waist and he turned her with gentle insistence toward the house. "Let's go inside where it's warm."

Lauren was so nervous that she didn't realize the sliding glass doors Nick led her to were not the ones that opened into the living room until she stepped inside and found herself in a luxurious bedroom decorated in shades of caramel, white and brown. She stopped in her tracks, her eyes on the huge king-size bed across the room. She heard Nick close the glass door with a final, deathlike thud, and her whole body tensed.

His arm slid around her waist from behind, drawing her rigid form against him. With his other hand he brushed away her heavy silken hair, exposing her neck. Lauren's breathing became shallow and rapid as his lips touched her nape, then drifted tantalizingly toward her ear, while his hands began moving lazily over her midriff, sliding upward.

"Nick," Lauren protested inanely, "I—I'm not at all tired yet."

"Good," he whispered, while his tongue sensuously traced the folds of her ear. "Because it's going to be hours before I let you go to sleep."

"What I meant was—" Lauren gasped as his tongue plunged deeply into her ear, sending warmth spreading through her limbs. Weakly, she leaned back against him and felt the bold evidence of his rising passion pressing against her. "What I meant," she clarified shakily, "was that I'm not ready for . . . for bed yet."

His deep voice acted on Lauren like an aphrodisiac. "I've waited an eternity for you, Lauren. Don't ask me to wait any longer."

The meaning Lauren read into those words banished her last doubts about how deeply he really felt about her, and about the rightness of what she was doing. She made no move to stop him when his hands slipped under her velour top, but when he removed it and turned her in his arms to face him, her heart was racing like a mad thing.

"Look at me," Nick coaxed softly.

Lauren tried to lift her eyes to his and couldn't. She swallowed convulsively.

Sliding both hands into the sides of her hair, Nick turned her face up to his, his mesmerizing gray eyes gazing deeply into hers. "We're going to do this together," he said quietly. Taking her hand, he placed it against the front of his shirt. "Unbutton my shirt," he urged gently. Somewhere in the chaotic turbulence that was her mind, Lauren realized that Nick apparently thought she was hesitating because her other less experienced lovers hadn't taught her the proper preliminaries for lovemaking, and that he was now trying to coach her.

Lauren's curly lashes flickered down, casting shadows on her flushed cheeks as she did his bidding with fingers made clumsy by a mixture of panic and joy. He deftly unhooked her lacy bra, and she slowly undid each of his buttons, unknowingly heightening his excitement by her slowness.

Her fingers moved of their own volition, pushing his shirt open, exposing his bronzed, muscular chest. He was so beautiful, and he was hers to touch, Lauren thought, so intoxicated with the knowledge that she scarcely noticed when he slipped her bra off her arms.

"Touch me," Nick ordered hoarsely.

She required no more urging and no more instruction. Guided by love and instinct, she slid her hands sensuously through the dark hairs of his chest, and leaned forward to kiss his hard, muscular flesh. A shudder ran the length of his body at the first brush of her lips, and his free hand sank into the soft hair at her nape, tilting her face up to his. For a moment he just gazed at her, his eyes smoldering with the desire he was holding back, and then he bent his head.

His lips were warm and exquisitely gentle at first, tasting and shaping hers. And then they slowly parted, and his tongue began to explore her mouth with a languorous hunger that drove Lauren mad with pleasure.

She arched against him, her hands gliding over his bare chest, and he lifted his head. His flaming gray eyes burned into hers, seeing his own desire reflected in their blue depths. He drew a labored breath, visibly trying to slow his passion, and lost the battle. "God, I want you!" he said fiercely, and his demanding lips crushed down on hers, his tongue parting her lips and driving into her mouth in a kiss that sent fire exploding through her body.

Lauren moaned, molding herself to his hardened thighs, and his hands moved over her, sliding up the sides of her breasts, her back, then lower, forcing her hips tighter to the throbbing heat of his swollen manhood.

The world tilted as he swept her up into his arms, his mouth devouring hers while he moved her onto the bed, following her down and covering her with his body.

His hands cupped her naked breasts, arousing her nipples into aching tightness before his lips closed on them. His lips came back to hers, and he opened her mouth hungrily with his own, his knowledgeable hands exploring and exciting and tormenting her, bathing her senses in a kaleidoscope of fiercely erotic pleasures that sent hot need pulsing through every nerve in Lauren's throbbing body.

He shifted on top of her, and something wild and fierce stirred deep within her, ready to welcome him. But the moment his knee wedged its way between her legs to spread them apart, Lauren's entire body jerked into rigid, involuntary alarm. "Nick!" she gasped, clamping her legs together. "Nick, wait I—"

He overruled her belated refusal with two hoarse words: "Don't, Lauren."

The ache in his voice shattered her resistence, and she wrapped her arms tightly around his broad shoulders, drawing him to her as her hips lifted to greet him. Nick plunged full-length into her, burying himself into her welcoming softness with a deftness that gave Lauren only an instant of pain, a pain that was forgotten as he began to move with tormenting slowness within her.

"I've only been waiting a few days for you, but it feels like an eternity," he rasped, and began steadily increasing the tempo of his driving plunges, pushing her closer and closer to her peak, until Lauren's love and passion finally exploded into shuddering ecstasy. Nick tightened his arms around her and with one final plunge, he joined her in the wild, sweet oblivion where he had sent her. . . .

Dreamily descending from the misty euphoria where she was floating, sated and happy, Lauren slowly became conscious of the warmth emanating from Nick's body beside her, and the weight of his hand resting atop her stomach. But as she lay there, a vague uneasiness slowly crept into her fogged mind. She tried to shut it out, to keep it from disturbing the bliss of the moment, but it was too late. She remembered that Nick had been holding her tightly in his arms, his body driving into hers when he had whispered, "I've only been waiting a few days for you, but it feels like an eternity."

Lauren's boneless contentment gave way to harsh reality. She had misinterpreted what Nick had meant when he told her he'd been waiting an eternity for her. What he meant was that the few days he'd had to wait to make love to her *seemed* like an eternity. It didn't change the way she felt about him, but it made her uneasy.

Had he noticed her virginity? How would he react? What if he asked her why she had decided to make love with him? She certainly couldn't tell him the truth yet—that she was in love with him, and she wanted him to love her.

Lauren decided she would have to avoid the subject altogether. Hesitantly she opened her eyes. Nick was lying on his side, propped up on his elbow, gazing intently at her face. He looked puzzled, dubious, and distinctly amused. . . .

He had noticed. And judging from his expression, he intended to discuss it.

Lauren rolled away from him and hastily sat up, keeping her back to him. Reaching for his discarded shirt at the foot of the bed, she plunged her arms into the sleeves in an effort to cover her nakedness. "I'd love some coffee," she mumbled, seizing on that as an excuse to escape his questions. "I'll make it." She stood up and looked at him, then flushed as his warm gaze slid down her long, shapely bare legs before lifting to her face.

Never had she felt as self-conscious as she did at that moment standing there, stark naked under his voluminous shirt. "You . . . you don't mind sharing your shirt, do you?" she asked, fumbling with the buttons.

"I don't mind at all, Lauren," he solemnly replied, but with a gleam of laughter in his eyes. His amusement was so unnerving that Lauren's hands began to shake. Concentrating on rolling up the shirt cuffs, she asked, "How do you like it?"

"Exactly the way we did it."

Her gaze shot to his face and the blush on her cheeks deepened. "No," she corrected with a quick, nervous shake of her head. "I meant, how do you like your *coffee?*"

"Black."

"Do . . . do you want some?"

"Some what?" he asked suggestively, grinning wickedly at her.

"Some coffee!"

"Yes, thanks."

"For what?" she quipped jauntily, then she pivoted on her heel and hastily left before he could reply.

Despite her bravado when she'd left the bedroom, she felt precariously close to tears as she walked into the kitchen and turned on the lights. Nick was laughing at her, and she had never expected that sort of reaction from him. Had she been that inept, that amusingly inexperienced?

Behind her, she heard Nick walk into the kitchen, and she quickly busied herself spooning coffee into the percolator. "Why are these cupboards so empty? Except for what we ate tonight, there's no food."

"Because the house is being sold," Nick replied. His hands settled firmly on her waist, drawing her against him until the denim of his jeans pressed against the backs of her bare legs. "Why didn't you tell me?" he asked her quietly.

"Tell you what?" Lauren hedged.

"You know damned well what."

She stared out the window over the sink. "I forgot about it, actually."

"Wrong," Nick chuckled. "Try again."

"Because the subject never came up," she said with an indifferent shrug, "and because I didn't think you'd notice."

"The subject never came up," he said dryly, "because twenty-three-year-old virgins in this day and age are rare as hell. And twenty-three-year-old virgins who look like you, rarer still. As far as the rest—well, it was self-evident."

Lauren turned around to face him, her blue eyes searching his. "But before that . . . that point, you didn't realize that I hadn't . . . hadn't . . . before?"

"I had no idea that you were a virgin until it was too late to make any difference to either of us." Putting his arms around her, he added, "But you should have told me you were before we got into that bed."

"If I had told you, would you have changed your mind?" Lauren asked, loving the sound of his voice and the feel of his arms around her.

"No, but I would have been more gentle with you." Leaning back, he stared at her in genuine puzzlement. "Why should I have changed my mind?"

"I don't know," Lauren mumbled uneasily. "I thought you might have some, well, reservations about . . . about . . ."

"About what?" he mocked tolerantly. "About 'stealing' something that belongs to your future husband? Don't be ridiculous. He won't expect you to be a virgin; men don't prize virginity anymore. We don't want or expect a woman to be inexperienced. We're liberated too, you know. You have the same physical desires I do, Lauren, and you have the right to satisfy them with whomever you wish."

Lauren cautiously lowered her eyes to the gold medallion hanging on a long gold chain around his neck and asked, "Have you ever cared, really cared, for any of the women in your life?"

"Some of them, yes."

"And you didn't mind if they'd had sexual relationships with lots of other men?"

"Of course not."

"That seems like a very . . . coldblooded . . . attitude."

His lids flickered down, his glance lingering on the tantalizing mounds of her breasts. "If I've given you the impression that I'm coldblooded, I think it's time we go back into that bedroom."

Lauren wondered if he was deliberately misinterpreting her use of the word because he wanted to avoid the issue. If he had really cared for those other women, shouldn't he have felt more possessive about them? If he really cared for *her*, shouldn't he be pleased that he was the only man she'd let make love to her? Lauren raised her troubled blue eyes to his. "Nick?"

He looked down at the delicate young beauty in his arms. Her face was framed in tousled waves of burnished honey, her mouth was soft and generous, and her full breasts were pressed enticingly against his bare chest. His arms tightened around her, and he bent his head. "What?" he murmured, but his mouth opened on hers in a deep, drugging kiss that silenced her voice.

Sometime after dawn, Lauren rolled over and saw Nick's dark head on the pillow beside her. With a dreamy smile of satisfaction, she closed her eyes and sank back into the deep slumber of blissful exhaustion. She did not awaken again until Nick put a cup of coffee on the night table beside her and sat down on the bed.

"Good morning," she said, her smile fading as she realized that he had already showered, shaved and dressed in tailored gray slacks and an open-necked gray shirt. "Is something wrong?" she asked, clutching the sheet to her breasts as she struggled up against the pillows. She felt awkward being stark naked when he was dressed, but Nick seemed unaware of her discomfort. For that matter, he seemed unaware of her nakedness.

"Lauren, I'm afraid we're going to have to cut today short. A . . . a business associate of mine phoned this morning and will be here in an hour. I'll find another ride back to the city."

Lauren was terribly disappointed, but forty minutes later, as Nick walked her out to her car, her disappointment had grown into confused alarm. Gone was her passionate, seductive lover of the night before. Today Nick was friendly but impersonal, treating her as if they'd spent a pleasant but meaningless night playing cards instead of making love. Or was this the way men always acted afterward? She was probably being oversensitive, Lauren decided, stopping at her car and turning toward him.

She hoped he would take her in his arms and kiss her goodbye. Instead he put his hands in his pockets, looked at her levelly and said, "Lauren, did you take any precautions against the possible consequences of last night?"

Pregnancy! Lauren's face felt as if it was on fire as she shook her head.

She sensed that her answer irritated him, but his voice was calmly unemotional. "If there should be any consequences, I want you to let me know. Don't try to face it alone. Will you promise to let me know?"

Lauren was too embarrassed to speak. She nodded, and he opened the car door for her. By the time she put the car into reverse, he was already striding back into the house.

Lauren glanced at the clock on the dashboard as she drove through the long stretches of Indiana farmland. "If there should be any consequences, I want you to let me know." *Let me know* . . . The last three words revolved continuously in her brain.

Yesterday, when they'd been talking about her move to Detroit, she had managed to casually impart the information that she would be back in Detroit on Friday, and that in the meantime the phone was being connected in her name. Nick could reach her on Friday simply by picking up the telephone and asking the operator for her new number, and he knew it. Why had he made it sound as if they wouldn't be talking to each other unless she needed to reach him to tell him she was pregnant?

In a way Lauren felt like something that had been used and then thrown away. They had laughed together and gotten to know each other; she felt so close to him—surely he felt close to her too. Surely he couldn't intend to just walk away and forget about her.

She loved Nick, and she knew he liked her. Perhaps he had already begun to love her. . . . Perhaps that was why he had become so withdrawn and impersonal this morning! After thirty-four years of independence, and after being shunned by his own mother, Nick wouldn't like feeling dependent on a woman for his happiness. The more he felt himself caring, the more he would probably fight it, Lauren decided.

The sky was streaked with a pink sunrise as Lauren drove across the Mississippi River into Missouri. She was weary, but optimistic. When she got back to Detroit on Friday, Nick would call her. He might even hold out until Saturday or Sunday, but surely no longer.

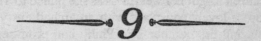

9

LAUREN'S OPTIMISM STAYED WITH HER THROUGH THE busy days of packing, and blossomed into excited anticipation on Thursday morning as she waved goodbye to her father and stepmother and started for Michigan.

With the directions Philip Whitworth had given her she had no trouble locating the elegant suburban community of Bloomfield Hills that night. She did have a little trouble believing that she was actually going to live there. One magnificent home after another flashed by. Spectacular stone-and-glass ranch houses were set well back from the tree-lined street, partially obscured by careful landscaping; splendid tudors sprawled beside immense white-pillared Georgian colonials.

It was ten o'clock at night when she pulled to a stop at the gates of a breathtakingly lovely Spanish-style condominium complex. The gatekeeper came out and peered at her through the open car window. When Lauren told him her name, he said, "Mr.

Whitworth drove in half an hour ago, miss." Then he directed Lauren to the proper street, respectfully touched his fingers to the visor of his cap, and added, "I understand you're a new resident. If I can be of help, just let me know."

Lauren forgot her weariness as she pulled to a stop before a lovely courtyard with an arched entryway displaying the number 175. Philip had promised to meet her here and show her around, and his Cadillac was parked in the driveway leading to the private garage.

"Well, what do you think?" he said a half hour later as they completed the tour of the luxurious apartment.

"I think it's wonderful," Lauren said, carrying one of her suitcases into the bedroom, where an entire mirrored wall concealed closet space. She opened a closet door and her gaze swung back to Philip. "What should I do with these clothes?" It and every closet she opened was filled to capacity with wonderful suits and dresses of linen, silk and crepe. Lauren recognized some of the designer labels, while other garments looked as if they were Paris originals. Most of the things still had tags on them and had obviously never been worn. "Your aunt certainly has very youthful tastes in clothes," Lauren commented.

"My aunt is a compulsive shopper," Philip explained disinterestedly. "I'll phone some charity and have them come over and take all this stuff."

Lauren ran her hand down a gorgeous wine velvet blazer, then she glanced at the tag hanging from the sleeve. Not only did the woman have very youthful taste in clothing, she also wore the same size Lauren did. "Philip, would you consider letting me buy some of these clothes?"

He shrugged. "Take whatever you want and give the rest away; you'll save me the trouble."

He had started down the stairs to the living room below, and Lauren turned off the lights and followed him. "But those are very expensive clothes—"

"I know what they cost," he interrupted irritably, "I paid for them. Take whatever you want—they're yours."

After helping her carry in the rest of her things from the car, he turned to leave. "By the way," he said, pausing with his hand on the doorknob. "My wife doesn't know I bought this place for my aunt. Carol feels that my relatives impose on me financially, so I've never mentioned it to her. I'd appreciate it if you wouldn't mention it either."

"No, of course I won't," Lauren promised.

After he left, she looked around at the luxurious apartment that was now her home, at the marble fireplace, valuable antiques and gracious silk-upholstered furnishings. The condominium looked as if it had been decorated for a magazine layout. A vision of the alluring clothes hanging in the upstairs closets superimposed itself in her mind. "My wife doesn't know I bought this place for my aunt; so I'd appreciate it if you wouldn't mention it. . . ."

A knowing smile slowly dawned on Lauren's face as she glanced again at the beautiful room and wryly shook her head. Not his aunt—his mistress! At some time in the recent past, Philip Whitworth must have had a mistress. Lauren shrugged the matter aside; it was none of her business.

She walked over to the telephone, sighing with relief when she heard the dial tone. The phone was working. Tomorrow was Friday, and Nick might call.

Early the next morning she sat at the kitchen table, making out her grocery list. Besides all the essentials, she needed two special items for when Nick came over: bourbon and Grand Marnier. Picking up her purse, she glanced at the telephone. The thought that he might never call her pushed forward in her mind, but she shoved it aside. Nick had wanted her very badly in Harbor Springs; he had made that obvious. If nothing else, sexual desire would bring him to her.

Two hours later she carried in the groceries she'd bought. She spent the rest of the day sorting through the clothes in the closets, trying them on and separating those that fit from those that had to be altered. Nick hadn't called by the time she went to bed, but she consoled herself with the thought that he would surely call tomorrow, which was Saturday.

She spent the next day unpacking and staying close to the phone. On Sunday she sat down at the desk and worked out a budget that would enable her to send home as much money as possible. Both Lenny and Melissa were helping too, but each of them had mortgages and other financial obligations she was free of.

The $10,000 bonus Philip had promised her was

certainly tempting. If she could only find out the name of that spy, or else learn something that would be of real value to the Whitworths' company. Lauren shied away from the latter alternative. If she gave Philip confidential information, she would be no better than the spy she was trying to unmask.

Apart from her parents' debts there were her electrical bill, phone bill, groceries. She had a car payment to make and automobile insurance. . . . There seemed to be no end to the list of obligations.

On Monday she saw some silver-gray yarn the color of Nick's eyes in a store, and she decided to buy it and knit a sweater. She told herself she would make it as a Christmas present for her stepbrother, but inside she knew she was knitting it for Nick. . . .

The following Sunday night, as she laid out the clothes she would wear for her first day at work, she told herself that *tomorrow* he would call—he would call her at her new job to wish her luck.

10

"Well, are you ready to quit?" her new boss, Jim Williams, joked at five o'clock the next afternoon. "Or do you think you want to stay on?"

Lauren sat across the desk from him, her shorthand notebook loaded with dictation. Nick hadn't called to wish her good luck on her first day, but she'd been so busy that she hadn't had much time to be miserable about it. "I think," Lauren said, laughing, "that you're like working with a whirlwind."

He grinned apologetically. "We work so well together that after you'd been here an hour, I forgot you were new."

Lauren smiled at the compliment. It was true, they did work well together.

"What do you think of the staff?" he prodded, and before Lauren could answer, he added, "It's the concensus among the men here that I have the most beautiful secretary in the corporation. I've been answering questions about you all day."

"What sort of questions?"

"About your marital status mostly—whether you're married, engaged or available." With an inquiring lift of his brows he said, "Are you available, Lauren?"

"For what?" she quipped, but she had an uneasy feeling he was indirectly asking about the status of her relationship with Nick. Standing up, she said quickly, "Do you want me to finish this dictation tonight before I leave?"

"No, tomorrow morning will be soon enough."

Had she only imagined it, or had Jim's questions been for himself rather than for the sake of general information, Lauren wondered as she cleared off her desk. Surely he couldn't be thinking of asking her out. According to what she'd been told at lunch today, three of his secretaries had made the mistake of falling for Jim's charismatic appeal, and he had promptly transferred them to other divisions.

According to the gossip, Jim was socially prominent, wealthy and infinitely eligible, but he did not believe in mixing business with pleasure. He was certainly good-looking, Lauren thought dispassionately. Tall, with thick sandy hair and warm golden brown eyes.

She glanced at the clock and hastily locked her desk. If Nick was ever going to call, he would surely do it tonight. He would call to ask her how her first day on the job had been. If he didn't call now, after two weeks and a day, he obviously had no intention of ever calling her again. She felt sick at the thought.

She drove home as quickly as the heavy traffic permitted. It was six-fifteen as she rushed into the condominium. She made herself a sandwich, snapped on the television set, then sat down on the blue-and-white striped silk sofa, staring at the phone. Willing it to ring.

At nine-thirty she went upstairs and showered, leaving the bathroom door open so that she could hear the phone in her bedroom. At ten o'clock, she climbed into bed. Nick was not going to call her. Ever.

She closed her tear-shrouded eyes, and his handsome, bronzed face was there before her. She could see the frank desire in his heavy-lidded gaze when he looked at her, could hear his smooth, deep voice saying, "I want you, Lauren."

Obviously, he did not want her anymore. Lauren turned her head on the pillow, and hot tears trickled from the corners of her eyes.

The next morning Lauren threw herself into her work with more determination than success. She made errors on the letters she typed, disconnected two of Jim's calls and mislaid an important file. At noon she went for a walk past the Global Industries Building, hoping against hope that Nick would materialize. But it proved futile, and what was worse, in doing so she sacrificed what little was left of her ravaged pride.

So much for the sexual liberation of women! she thought miserably, winding another sheet of paper into her typewriter that afternoon. She was not capable of treating sex casually. She would still feel confused and disappointed if she hadn't slept with

Nick, but at least she wouldn't feel used and discarded.

"Having a bad day?" Jim asked late that afternoon as she handed him a report she'd had to retype twice before it was correct.

"Yes, I'm sorry," Lauren said. "I don't have them often," she added, with what she hoped was a reassuring smile.

"Don't worry about it—it happens to everyone," he remarked, scrawling his initials across the bottom of the report. He glanced at his watch, then stood up. "I have to take this report over to the controller's office in the new building."

Everyone there referred to the Global Industries Building as "the new building" so there was no doubt in Lauren's mind what he meant.

"Have you seen the space we're going to occupy over there?"

Lauren felt as if her smile was plastic. "No, I haven't; all I know is that on Monday morning we're all supposed to report for work over there."

"Right," he said, shrugging into his suit jacket. "Sinco is the smallest and least profitable of the Global Industries subsidiaries, but our offices are going to be very impressive. Before you leave," he said, handing Lauren a folded sheet torn from a newspaper, "would you show this to Susan Brook in public relations and ask her if she's seen it? If she missed it, tell her she can have this copy for her file."

He turned back as he started from his office. "You'll probably be gone by the time I get back. Have a nice evening."

A few minutes later Lauren headed rather listlessly for the public relations department. She nodded and smiled at the other staff as she passed their desks, but in her mind she was seeing Nick. How was she ever going to forget the way the breeze had ruffled his dark hair when he caught that stupid fish? Or the way he looked in a tuxedo?

Fighting back her desolation, she smiled at Susan Brook as she handed her the sheet Jim had torn from the newspaper. "Jim said to ask you if you'd seen this. If not, he said you can have this copy for your file."

Susan unfolded the paper and glanced at it. "I didn't see it." Grinning, she reached into her desk and extracted a very thick folder crammed with magazines and newspaper clippings. "My favorite job is keeping his file updated," she said, laughing as she opened the folder. "Look—isn't he the most gorgeous hunk of male you've ever seen?"

Lauren's gaze slid from Susan's irrepressible smile to the coolly handsome masculine face looking back at her from the cover of *Newsday* magazine. Shock froze her entire body into rigidity as she reached compulsively for the magazine. "Take the whole file back to your desk and drool at your leisure," Susan suggested gaily, unaware of Lauren's state of alarm.

"Thank you," she answered hoarsely. She fled back to Jim's office and, closing the door behind her, sank into a chair and opened the file. Her clammy hands left fingerprints on the glossy cover of *Newsday* magazine as she traced Nick's arrogant dark brows, the faintly smiling male lips that had caressed and devoured hers. "J. Nicholas Sinclair," the caption below the picture read. "President and Founder, Global Industries." She couldn't believe what she was seeing; her mind refused to accept it.

Putting the magazine aside, Lauren slowly unfolded the page Jim had torn from the newspaper. The paper was dated two weeks ago—that would be the day after Nick had sent her home from Harbor Springs because a "business associate" was coming to see him. The headline read: "FINANCIAL EAGLES AND THEIR BUTTERFLIES GATHER FOR FIVE DAYS OF PLEASURE AT PARTY IN HARBOR SPRINGS." The entire page was devoted to the pictures of and commentary about the party. In the center of the page was a picture of Nick lounging on the cedar deck of the house at the Cove, his arm around a beautiful blonde who hadn't been at the party while Lauren was there. The caption said, "Detroit industrialist J. Nicholas Sinclair and longtime companion, Ericka Moran, shown at Miss Moran's home near Harbor Springs."

Longtime companion . . . Miss Moran's home . . .

Pain ripped through Lauren, cutting and tearing at her. Nick had taken her to his girlfriend's house and had made love to her in his girlfriend's bed! "Oh, my God," she whispered aloud, her eyes filling with scalding tears. He'd made love to her, and then he'd sent her away because his girlfriend had decided to join the group at Harbor Springs.

As if she needed to further torment herself, Lauren read every word on the page, and then she picked up the issue of *Newsday* and read the entire eight-page article. When she finished, the magazine slid from her numb fingers to the floor.

No wonder Bebe Leonardos had been so hostile! According to the magazine story, Nick and Bebe had once indulged in a widely publicized torrid affair that had lasted until he dropped Bebe for a French movie star—the same woman who had been playing tennis in her high heels that night in Harbor Springs. . . .

Hysterical laughter bubbled up inside Lauren. While she had been driving back to Missouri, he had been making love to his mistress. While she had been sitting by the phone day and night last week, knitting him a sweater, he had been attending a charity ball with Ericka in Palm Springs.

Humiliation washed over her in drowning waves and exploded through her body. Her shoulders shook with silent wrenching sobs as she folded her arms on Jim's desk and buried her face in them. She wept for her stupidity, for her shattered illusions and broken dreams. Shame sent more tears pouring from her eyes—she'd made love with a man whom she'd known for only four days—and she hadn't even known his real name! If it hadn't been for sheer good luck, she could have been pregnant right now!

She remembered the angry hurt she had felt because his mother had abandoned him as a young boy, and she cried even harder. His mother should have drowned him!

"Lauren?" Jim's voice interrupted her sobbing.

She jerked her head up just as he reached her side. "What's wrong?" he demanded in alarm.

Swallowing her misery, she dragged her gaze to his concerned face. Her luxurious lashes were spiky with tears and her blue eyes were swimming. "I thought—" she stopped to draw a tortured breath "—I thought he was an ordinary engineer who wanted to start a business of his own someday. And he let me think it!" she choked. "He let me!"

The compassion in Jim's face was more than she could bear. She stood up. "Can I get out of here without anyone seeing me? I mean, has everyone gone home?"

"Yes, but you aren't driving in this condition. I'll take you—"

"No," she said swiftly. "I'm fine, really! I can drive."

"Are you certain?"

She finally got control of her quavering voice. "Positive, I was just shocked and a little embarrassed, that's all."

Jim gestured lamely at the file. "Are you done with this?"

"I haven't read it all," she said distractedly.

He picked up the magazine from the floor, put it in the folder with the newspaper clipping and held the thick file toward her. Lauren took it automatically, and then fled. She thought she would cry again when she got to her car, but she didn't. Nor did she cry during the three hours she spent reading the file. There were no more tears left in her.

Lauren pulled into the parking lot past the sign that read, Reserved for Sinco Employees. After what she'd read the night before, the name Sinco had a new meaning: Sinclair Electronic Components. The company had been founded, according to *The Wall Street Journal*, by Matthew Sinclair and his grandson Nick twelve years before, in a garage behind what was now Tony's restaurant.

She parked her car, picked up the file on J. Nicholas Sinclair from the seat beside her and got out. Nick had built a financial empire, and now he kept it alive by employing spys among his competitors. Obviously he was as unscrupulous in his business dealings as he was in his personal life, she thought fiercely.

The women in the office smiled cheerful greetings at her, and Lauren felt guilty because she was going to play a part in destroying the company for whom they worked. No, not destroying it, she corrected herself as she put her purse in her desk. If Sinco was fit to survive, then it should be able to compete honestly for contracts. Otherwise it deserved to die before it destroyed its honest competitors, companies like Philip Whitworth's.

She paused outside Jim's office. Did he know that Sinco was paying spys? Somehow she didn't think he did. She couldn't believe that he would approve of such a thing. "Thank you for letting me take the file home," she said softly, walking into his office.

His gaze leaped from the report in his hand to her pale, composed features. "How do you feel this morning?" he asked quietly.

Self-consciously she put her hands in the deep side

pockets of her skirt. "I feel embarrassed . . . and pretty foolish."

"Without going into painful detail, could you give me some idea of what Nick did that hurt you so much? Surely you weren't crying like that just because you discovered he's wealthy and successful?"

Lauren felt a fresh stab of pain at the memory of how willingly she'd collaborated in her own seduction. But she owed Jim some sort of explanation for her hysterical behavior yesterday, and she said with a lame attempt at indifference, "Because I thought he was simply an engineer, I said and did some things that are extremely embarrassing to remember now."

"I see," Jim said calmly. "And what do you intend to do about it?"

"I intend to throw myself into my job here, and to learn everything I can," she replied with bitter honesty.

"I meant, what do you intend to do when you see Nick?"

"I never want to see him again as long as I live!" she retorted tersely.

A half smile tugged at his lips, but his voice was solemn. "Lauren, next Saturday there's a private cocktail party being given in the revolving restaurant atop the Global Industries Building. All the chief executives of our various companies are expected to attend, along with their secretaries. The purpose of the party is to bring together all of us who have worked in different buildings in the past, so that we can meet face to face. You'll have an opportunity to meet the secretaries you'll be dealing with in the future, as well as their bosses. Nick is the host."

"If you don't mind, I'd rather not go," Lauren said flatly.

"I do mind."

She was trapped. Jim wasn't the sort of boss who would allow her personal life to interfere with her job, she knew. And if she lost her job she'd never find out who Nick was paying to spy on Philip Whitworth's company.

"Sooner or later you're going to have to meet Nick face to face," Jim continued persuasively. "Wouldn't you rather have it happen on Saturday, when you're prepared for it?" When Lauren still hesitated, he said firmly, "I'll pick you up at seven-thirty."

11

LAUREN'S HAND SHOOK AS SHE APPLIED HER LIPSTICK and brushed some blusher on her cheekbones. She glanced at her watch; Jim would be there in fifteen minutes. Walking over to one of the mirrored closets, she removed a flowing chiffon cocktail dress, the one she'd finally chosen that afternoon after trying on all of her newly acquired evening dresses.

Now that she knew what an unprincipled, deceitful, arrogant bastard Nick really was, she probably wouldn't find him the slightest bit attractive, she decided, zipping up the dress and stepping into dainty sandals. Even so, her battered pride demanded that she look her best tonight.

Closing the closet, she stepped back to survey her full-length image in the mirrored doors. Panels of cream chiffon drifted into deepening shades of peach, creating a subdued rainbow effect in the full skirt, while matching panels of chiffon crisscrossed beneath her breasts and swept upward in a deeply slashed halter top that clasped behind her neck, leaving her arms, shoulders and upper back bare.

She tried to feel pleasure in her appearance but couldn't. Not when she was about to confront the man who had effortlessly seduced her and then suggested she call him if she got pregnant; a multi-millionaire whom she'd invited to lunch and assured him that they could afford anything on the menu.

Considering how low and cynical Nick was, it was amazing he hadn't actually let her pay for the expensive meal, Lauren thought, searching through her jewelry box for the precious gold earrings that had belonged to her mother.

She paused to mentally rehearse the way she was going to treat him tonight. Because of what had happened, Nick would naturally expect her to be hurt and angry, but she had no intention of letting him see that she was either. Instead she was going to convince him that their weekend in Harbor Springs had been nothing but an amusing little escapade to her, just as it had obviously been to him. Under no circumstances would she treat him coldly, because by coldness she would show him that she still cared enough to be angry. Even if it killed her, she was going to treat him with casual, detached friendliness —the same sort of impersonal friendliness she would show the gatekeeper or the janitor at work.

That should throw him off balance, Lauren decided, still searching for her mother's earrings.

But where were they, she wondered a little frantically a moment later. She couldn't have lost them— she was always so careful with them. They were the only things of her mother's she had. She had worn them to the party in Harbor Springs, she remembered . . . and the next day at the Cove. And that night in bed Nick had been kissing her ear, and he'd taken her earrings off because they were in his way. . . .

Her mother's earrings were somewhere in Nick's girlfriend's bed!

Lauren leaned her hands on the dresser, and her head fell forward as a fresh surge of anger and pain raged through her. Nick's girlfriend probably had her mother's earrings.

The doorbell pealed downstairs, and she straightened up with a jerk. Taking a deep breath she walked downstairs and opened the door.

Jim was standing in the doorway, looking every inch the impressive business executive in an attractive dark suit and tie. "Please come in," Lauren said quietly. He stepped into the foyer, and she added, "I'll just get my purse, and we can leave. Or would you like a drink first?"

When he didn't immediately answer, she turned. "Is something wrong?"

His gaze moved over her perfect features and the lustrous mass of her honey-colored hair, which spilled over her shoulders in deep, swirling waves. Appreciatively he examined her figure in the seductive chiffon, and her long, shapely legs. "Nothing that I can see," he said with a grin.

"Would you like a drink?" Lauren repeated, surprised but not insulted by his frank masculine appraisal.

"Not unless you need one to bolster your courage to face Nick."

Lauren shook her head. "I don't need courage. He means nothing to me." Jim shot her an amused look as he ushered her out to his dark green Jaguar.

"I gather you want to convince him that you no longer have any romantic interest in him, is that it?"

Lauren had the uneasy feeling that Jim was not deceived by her facade of indifference—but then he had witnessed her crying her heart out. "That's right," she admitted.

"In that case—" Jim shifted gears as they thundered onto the expressway "—I'll give you some unsolicited advice. Why don't you spend a few minutes chatting with him about the party or your new job and then, with a *very* charming smile, excuse yourself and walk over to someone else—me, if I'm close at hand, and I'll try to be."

Lauren turned toward him with a soft smile of gratitude. "Thank you," she said. Feeling calm and confident, she relaxed.

But when the elevator doors swept open at the elegant revolving restaurant on the eighty-first floor, Lauren took one look at the animated crowd milling around, and a rope of tension coiled around her chest, suffocating her. Nick was somewhere in this room.

At the bar, Jim ordered their drinks, and Lauren cautiously glanced around just as a group of people shifted to one side.

And there was Nick. . . .

He was standing across the room, his dark head

thrown back as he laughed at something being said. Lauren's heart pounded uncontrollably as her gaze took in his handsome, tanned features; the elegant ease with which he wore his impeccably tailored dark suit; the casual way he held his drink in his hand. She noticed every painfully familiar thing about him. And then she noticed the beautiful blonde who was smiling up at him, her hand resting familiarly on his sleeve.

Anguish poured through Lauren's veins like hot acid. It was Ericka Moran, the woman with Nick in the newspaper photograph. And the gorgeous cream dress she had on was the same one Nick had sent over to Lauren herself in Harbor Springs. . . .

She jerked her gaze away and started to speak to Jim, but the taut set of his jaw as he, too, saw the beautiful blond woman across the room stopped Lauren cold. On his face she saw angry desolation and helpless yearning—the same emotions she'd experienced a moment ago when she'd looked at Nick. Jim, she instantly concluded, was in love with Ericka.

"Here's your drink," he finally said, handing it to Lauren. "It's time to begin our little charade." With a grim smile he took her elbow and started to guide her toward Nick and Ericka.

Lauren drew back. "We surely don't have to rush right over to them, do we? If Nick is the host, it's his responsibility to make certain he greets everyone at his party."

Jim hesitated, then nodded. "All right, we'll make them come to us."

During the next half hour, as they circulated among the guests, Lauren became increasingly convinced that she was right about Jim and Ericka, and that her boss was trying to make both Nick and Ericka jealous. Whenever Ericka glanced in their direction, Jim would smile at Lauren or tease her about something. Lauren cooperated by trying to look as if she was having a positively wonderful time—but she did so for his sake, not for hers. In her shattered heart she knew that Nick didn't care what she did or with whom she did it.

She was sipping her second drink when Jim suddenly slipped his arm around her. She was so surprised that she overlooked the warning squeeze of his hand at her waist. "The group standing over there," he said with a deliberate smile, "is the board of directors—all wealthy, industrialists in their own right. The man on the left is Ericka's father, Horace Moran. Horace's family," he explained, "has been in oil for generations."

"How dreadfully uncomfortable for them," Lauren joked, comically batting her eyelashes to make him laugh.

Jim shot her a warning look, then he continued, "The man beside him is Crawford Jones. Crawford's family, and his wife's family, as well, are in bonds."

"I wonder why someone doesn't cut them loose?" Lauren teased.

"Because," said an achingly familiar, laughing voice right behind her, "Crawford and his wife are both ugly, and no one wants them running around loose, frightening little children."

Lauren's whole body snapped into rigidity at the sound of Nick's deep baritone, then she forced herself to turn. One look at the amusement in his gray eyes as he waited for her reaction made her pride come to her aid. Although she was crumbling into a thousand pieces inside, she managed to smile as she put her hand into his. "Hello, Nick."

His fingers closed around hers. "Hello, Lauren," he said, grinning.

She carefully pulled back her hand, then turned a bright, expectant smile on Ericka, whom Jim promptly introduced to her.

"I've been admiring your dress all evening, Lauren," Ericka said. "It's stunning."

"Thank you." Without looking at Nick, Lauren added, "I noticed your dress the moment we walked in." Then she turned to Jim. "Oh, there's Mr. Simon. He's been trying to talk to you all evening, Jim." With the last remaining ounce of her vanishing poise, Lauren raised her blue eyes to Nick's inscrutable features and said politely, "Will you excuse us, please?"

Shortly afterward Jim became absorbed in a conversation with a vice-president, so Lauren made an effort to be charming and witty and to manage on her own. She was soon surrounded by a flatteringly large cluster of interested, admiring males, and for the rest of the evening she scrupulously avoided looking in Nick's direction. Twice she accidentally turned and encountered his piercing stare, and both times she casually looked right past him, as if she was searching for someone else. But after three hours, the tension of being in the same room with him had become unbearable.

She needed some solitude, a few minutes' respite from the constant pull of his presence. She looked for Jim and saw him standing near the bar, talking to a group of men. Lauren waited until she caught his attention, then she tipped her head slightly toward the sliding glass doors that opened onto the outdoor patio portion of the restaurant. He nodded, his expression telling her that he would join her there.

Turning, she slipped out doors into the welcome quiet of the cool evening. Wrapped in the velvet blackness of the night, she walked over to the chest-high wall that surrounded the patio restaurant and gazed at the glittering panorama of lights fanning out for miles, eighty-one stories below. She had succeeded—she had managed to treat Nick with a perfect combination of impersonal friendliness and smiling disregard. No recriminations, no justifiable indignation because he hadn't called her. He must have been amazed by her attitude, Lauren thought with tired satisfaction, as she lifted her glass and sipped her drink.

Behind her, she heard the whisper of the sliding glass door opening and closing, and she resigned herself to the loss of her badly needed solitude. Jim had come out to join her. "How am I doing so far?" she asked, forcing a cheerful lightness into her voice.

"You're doing very well," Nick's lazy voice mocked. "I'm half convinced that I'm invisible."

Lauren's hand shook so violently that the ice cubes in her glass clinked together. She turned slowly, trying to gather her scattered wits. She should be unconcerned and urbane, she reminded herself, as if what had happened between them had meant no more to her than it had to him. She forced her gaze upward past his white shirt and striped tie, to his humor-filled eyes. "It's a lovely party," she commented.

"Have you missed me?"

Lauren's own eyes widened with pretended innocence. "I've been very busy."

Nick walked over to the wall, leaned his elbow on it and studied her in silence. He watched the breeze blowing her shimmering hair across her bare shoulder before he shifted his gaze back to her face. "So," he said with a smile, "you haven't missed me at all?"

"I've been busy," Lauren repeated, but her composure slipped a notch and she added, "And why should I miss you? You aren't the only willing and available man in Michigan."

His dark brow flicked upward in amused speculation. "Is that your way of telling me that after you tried sex with me, you decided you liked it and you've been . . . ah . . . adding to your experience?"

Dear God! He didn't even *care* if she'd gone to bed with other men.

"Now that you've had other men to use as a basis for comparison, how do I rate?" he teased.

"That's an adolescent question," Lauren retorted scornfully.

"You're right. Let's go." Tossing down the remainder of his drink in one swallow, he put his glass on one of the tables, took hers and put it beside his, then caught her hand. He twisted his wrist and laced his strong fingers through hers, and Lauren was so giddily aware of his warm fingers firmly clasping hers that she didn't stop to think until he had started to lead her toward an unidentified door around the corner of the building.

When he reached out to open the door, sanity returned, and she drew back. "Nick, I would like to ask you a question, and I want an honest answer." He nodded and she said, "When I left you in Harbor Springs, did you ever intend to see me again—I mean, to take me out?"

Nick looked at her levelly. "No."

She was still reeling from the blow of that one word when he reached out again to open the door. "Where are we going?"

"To my place, or yours, it doesn't matter."

"Why?" she asked obstinately.

He turned and looked at her. "For a smart girl, that's a very stupid question."

Lauren's temper exploded. "You are the most arrogant, egotistical . . . !" She stopped long enough to draw a steadying breath and said tightly, "I can't handle casual, indiscriminate sex, and what's more, I don't like people who can—people like you!"

"You liked me rather well four weeks ago," he reminded her coolly.

Her color rose and her eyes blazed. "Four weeks ago I thought you were someone special!" she shot back angrily. "Four weeks ago, I didn't know you

150

were a licentious millionaire playboy who changes beds as often as you change clothes. You're everything I despise in a man—you're unprincipled, promiscuous and morally corrupt! You're ruthless and selfish, and if I'd have known who you really were, I wouldn't have given you the time of day!"

Nick's eyes raked the tempestuous young beauty standing before him in all her scornful defiance. In a dangerously soft voice, he challenged, "But now that you do know who and what I am you don't want anything to do with me? Is that right?"

"That's right!" Lauren hissed, "And I'll—"

In one swift motion he caught her shoulders, jerked her into his arms, and captured her lips in a kiss of savage, insolent sensuality. The instant he touched her, every fiber of Lauren's being quickened with longing to know again the incredible pleasure of his hard body driving deeply into hers. Her arms went around his neck, and she arched against his hardening length. Nick groaned, gentling the kiss and deepening it hungrily. "This is insane," he muttered, his mouth tormenting hers with promises of his possession. "Anyone could walk out here and see us."

And then his mouth was gone. He let her go, and Lauren leaned weakly against the railing behind her. "Are you coming?" he asked.

She shook her head. "No, I told you—"

"Spare me your lecture on my morality," he cut her off icily. "Go find some man as naive as you are, and the two of you can fumble in the dark and learn together, if that's what you want."

Like a deep, clean cut that doesn't bleed for several moments after the wound is inflicted, Lauren was blessedly numb to the pain of his words; she felt only fury. "Wait," she said, as he pulled the door open, "your mistress, or your girlfriend, or whatever Ericka is, has my mother's earrings. I left them in her bed, in her house, with her lover. She's welcome to you—I don't want you. But I do want my mother's earrings back." The pain was beginning to seep through her like a steady ache, intensifying with each moment until her voice shook with it. "I want those earrings back. . . ."

The ceiling above Lauren's bed was a shadowy void as dismal as her heart as she went over the parting scene with Nick. He had brought Ericka to the party, but he had wanted to leave with Lauren. At least tonight he must have desired her more than he desired Ericka. Perhaps she'd been a fool not to go with him.

Furiously she rolled onto her stomach. Where was her pride and self-respect? How could she even consider having some fleeting, sordid relationship with that arrogant, unprincipled libertine? She would not think of him anymore. She would put him out of her mind. Permanently!

12

WITH THAT RESOLUTION FIRMLY IMPLANTED IN HER mind, Lauren drove to work on Monday and threw herself wholeheartedly into her job.

At noontime some of the other secretaries invited her to join them for drinks after work at a local pub, and Lauren happily agreed. When she returned from lunch, the phone on her desk was ringing. Putting down her purse, she glanced over her shoulder into Jim's empty office, then answered it. "Miss Danner?" It was Mr. Weatherby. "Please report to me in the personnel department immediately."

"We haven't much time, so I'll be brief," Mr. Weatherby said five minutes later, when Lauren was seated in his office. "To begin with, I should explain that the information contained on every employee's application for employment is automatically fed into the Global Industries computers. Then, whenever a project requires someone with specialized skills or talents, the personnel department is notified and a computer search is made. This morning the director of Global Industries personnel received a top priority call for an experienced, skilled secretary who is fluent in Italian. *You* are the computer's selection. Actually, you're the computer's second choice. The first was a woman named Lucia Palermo, who has worked on this project before, but she is on sick leave.

"You should expect to be away from your regular position every afternoon for the next three weeks. I will notify Mr. Williams of your reassignment when he returns from lunch, and I'll arrange for another secretary to work for him in the afternoons while you're working on this project."

Lauren's objections to this arbitrary reassignment tumbled out in a flow of disjointed words. "But I'm still trying to learn my present job, and Jim—Mr. Williams—isn't going to be at all pleased about—"

"Mr. Williams has no choice," he interrupted coolly. "I don't know the exact nature of the project that requires your fluency in Italian, but I do know it is top priority, confidential." He stood up. "You are to report to Mr. Sinclair's office immediately."

"Whaaat?" Lauren gasped, leaping to her feet in alarm. "Does Mr. Sinclair know I'm the one who's being assigned to him?"

Mr. Weatherby gave her a withering look. "Mr. Sinclair is in a meeting at present, and his secretary did not feel that he should be interrupted to discuss this minor substitution."

An atmosphere of suppressed excitement seemed to pervade the eightieth floor as Lauren walked across the thick, emerald green carpeting toward the circular desk in the center of Nick's private reception area. "My name is Lauren Danner," she told the receptionist, a beautiful brunette. "Mr. Sinclair requested a bilingual secretary, and I've been sent here from personnel."

The receptionist glanced over her shoulder as the doors to Nick's office opened and six men emerged. "I'll tell Mr. Sinclair that you're here," she said politely. As she reached for the telephone it began to ring, and she picked it up. With her hand over the mouthpiece, she whispered to Lauren, "Just go on in. Mr. Sinclair is expecting you."

No, Lauren thought nervously, *he's expecting Lucia Palermo.*

The tall rosewood doors to Nick's office were slightly ajar, and he was standing behind his desk, his back to her, talking to someone on the telephone. Drawing a deep breath, Lauren walked into the immense cream-carpeted suite and silently closed the doors behind her.

"Right," Nick said into the telephone after a pause. "Call the Washington office and tell our labor relations team that I want them at Global Oil in Dallas tonight."

With the phone hooked between his shoulder and his ear, he picked up a file from his desk and began reading it. He had removed his suit coat, and as he slowly flipped the pages, his white shirt stretched rippling across his broad muscled shoulders and tapered back. Lauren's hands tingled as she recalled the rippling strength of that powerful male body, the feel of his warm, tanned skin beneath her finger-tips. . . .

Tearing her gaze away, she tried to still the treacherous sensations unfurling inside her. Off to her left were the three moss green sofas that formed a wide U around an immense glass-topped coffee table. Nick had knelt there to examine her ankle the night she'd met him. . . .

"Notify the Oklahoma refinery that they may have some problems too, until this gets straightened out," Nick said calmly into the phone. There was a brief pause. "Fine. Get back to me when you've met with the labor relations team in Dallas." He hung up the phone and flipped over another page of the file he was reading.

Lauren opened her mouth to announce her presence, then stopped. She couldn't very well call him Nick, and she absolutely refused to humbly and respectfully call him "Mr. Sinclair." As she started toward his rosewood desk, she said instead, "Your receptionist told me to come in."

Nick turned abruptly. His gray eyes were unreadable as he casually tossed the file folder onto his desk, shoved his hands deeply into his pant pockets and silently contemplated her. He waited until she was standing directly across his desk from him before he said quietly, "You've chosen a poor time to apologize, Lauren. I have to leave for a luncheon appointment in five minutes."

Lauren almost choked on his outrageous presumption that *she* owed *him* an apology, but she merely favored him with an amused smile. "I hate to bruise your ego, but I didn't come up here to apologize. I came because Mr. Weatherby in personnel sent me."

Nick's jaw tightened. "Why?" he snapped.

"To help with some special project that requires an additional secretary for the next three weeks."

"Then you're wasting my time," he informed her bitingly. "In the first place, you aren't qualified or experienced enough to work at this level. In the second place, I don't want you here."

His contempt brought Lauren's simmering fury to a rolling boil, and she couldn't stop herself from goading him.

"Perfect!" she said brightly, backing away a step. "Now would you just be kind enough to call Mr. Weatherby and tell him that? I've already given him *my* reasons for not wanting to work for you, but he insisted that I come up here."

Nick jabbed at the intercom. "Get me Weatherby," he snapped, then his gaze sliced back to Lauren. "Just what 'reasons' did you give him?"

"I told him," Lauren lied wrathfully, "that you are an arrogant conceited lecher, and that I'd rather be dead than work for you."

"You told Weatherby that?" he asked in a low, threatening voice.

Lauren kept the smile fixed on her face. "Yep."

"What did Weatherby say?"

Unable to endure the icy blast of his gaze, Lauren pretended to study her manicure. "Oh, he said that a lot of women you've slept with probably feel that way about you, but that I should put company loyalty above my understandable revulsion for you."

"Lauren," Nick said silkily, "you're fired."

Inside, Lauren was a churning mass of rage and pain and fear, but she held on to her composure. With a regal inclination of her head, she said, "You know, I was positive you wouldn't want me to work for you either, and I tried to tell Mr. Weatherby that." She started toward the rosewood doors. "But he felt that when you realized I'm bilingual, you'd change your mind."

"Bilingual?" Nick scoffed contemptuously.

She turned toward him with her hand on the doorknob. "Oh, but I am. I can tell you exactly what I think of you in perfect Italian." She saw a nerve jerk in his tightly clenched jaw, and she added in a low, scathing voice, "But it's much more satisfying to say it to you in English: you're a bastard!"

Wrenching open the door, Lauren marched across the luxurious reception area. She was punching the button to summon an elevator when Nick's hand clamped over her wrist. "Get back into my office," he growled between his teeth.

"Take your hand off me!" she whispered furiously.

"There are four people watching us," he warned. "Either you walk into my office on your own, or I'll drag you in there in front of them."

"Go ahead and try it!" she raged right back at him. "I'll sue you for assault and subpoena all four of them as witnesses!"

Unexpectedly, her threat wrung a reluctant, admiring smile from him. "You have the most incredibly beautiful eyes. When you're angry, they—"

"Save it!" Lauren hissed, jerking violently at her wrist.

"I have been," he teased suggestively.

"Don't talk to me like that—I don't want any part of you!"

"Little liar. You want *every* part of me."

His mocking confidence knocked the breath, and the fight, out of Lauren. Defeated, she leaned her shoulder against the marble wall and looked at him with helpless pleading. "Nick, please let me go."

"I can't." His forehead creased into a dark frown of irritated bewilderment. "Whenever I see you, I can't seem to let you go."

"You fired me!"

He grinned. "I just rehired you."

Lauren was too weakened by the turbulence of the last few minutes to resist that devastating smile of his, and besides, she desperately needed this job. Resentfully, she shoved away from the wall and accompanied him into his secretary's office, which connected to his by a door.

"Mary," he said to the gray-haired woman whose sharp, bespectacled glance instantly lifted to him, "this is Lauren Danner. Lauren will be working on the Rossi project. While I'm at lunch, get her settled here at the spare desk and have her start translating the letter that came from Rossi this morning." He turned to Lauren with a warmly intimate smile in his eyes. "You and I are going to have a long talk when I get back."

Mary Callahan, as the nameplate on her desk proclaimed, did not seem any more enthusiastic about Lauren's presence in her office than Lauren herself was. "You're rather young, Miss Danner," Mary summarized, her pale blue gaze scraping Lauren's face and figure.

"I'm aging quickly," Lauren replied. Ignoring the older woman's piercing look, she settled into the secretarial desk opposite Mary's in the large office.

At one-thirty, Mary's telephone rang, and Lauren got up from her desk to answer it. "Mary?" a cultured female voice asked doubtfully.

"No, this is Lauren Danner," Lauren said in her best secretarial manner. "Miss Callahan is away from her office. May I take a message?"

"Oh, hello, Lauren," the voice said with friendly surprise. "This is Ericka Moran. I don't want to interrupt Nick, but would you tell him I'm arriving on the late flight from New York tomorrow? Tell him I'll go directly to the Recess Club from the airport, and I'll join him there at seven o'clock."

Lauren's astonishment that Ericka obviously remembered her was outweighed by her resentment at having to take messages from Nick's girlfriends. "He's still at lunch, but I'll give him the message," she promised briskly. She hung up the phone and it instantly rang again. This time the woman had a low, husky Southern drawl. She asked for "Nicky."

Lauren squeezed the receiver so hard that her

hand ached, but she said courteously, "I'm sorry, he isn't in at the moment. May I take a message?"

"Oh dahm," the sexy voice breathed. "This is Vicky. He didn't tell me whether the party Saturday night is formal or not, and I haven't the foggiest notion what to wear. I'll call him at home tonight."

You do that! Lauren thought, almost slamming the phone down.

But by the time Nick returned from lunch, she was calm again. For the next three weeks, she promised herself, she was going to adhere to her original plan and treat Nick with the polite friendliness she would show any of her colleagues. If he pressed her, she would merely act amused, and if that annoyed him—well, good!

The intercom on her desk buzzed. Nick's rich baritone voice sent a delicious little shiver through her, a shiver she stoically repressed. "Lauren, will you come in here please?"

He was obviously ready to have their "long talk" now. Lauren picked up his messages and walked into the office. "Yes?" she said, lifting her delicate brows in inquiry.

Nick was perched on the edge of his desk, his arms crossed over his chest. "Come here," he said quietly.

Lauren warily contemplated his relaxed stance and the lazy, caressing look in his eyes. She came forward, but stopped just out of his reach.

He said, "That's not close enough."

"It's *more* than close enough."

Amusement gleamed in his eyes, and his voice deepened coaxingly. "We need to straighten out some personal matters between us. Why don't we do it over dinner tonight?" he suggested.

Lauren courteously refused with a half truth. "I'm sorry, I already have a date."

"All right, how about tomorrow night?" he asked, holding out his hand for hers.

Lauren plunked his messages into his outstretched palm. "You already have a date—Miss Moran at seven at the Recess Club."

Nick ignored that reminder. "I'm leaving for Italy on Wednesday—"

"Have a good trip," Lauren interrupted lightly.

"I'll be back on Saturday," he continued with a trace of impatience. "We'll go—"

"Sorry," Lauren said with an amused little smile that was intended to annoy him. "I'm busy Saturday, and so are you. Vicky called to find out if the party Saturday night is formal or not." And then because she was thoroughly relishing his visible frustration, she added with a dazzling smile, "She calls you Nicky. I think that's adorable—Vicky and Nicky."

"I'll break the date," Nick stated tersely.

"But I won't break mine. Now, is there anything else?"

"Yes, dammit, there is. I hurt you and I'm sorry. . . ."

"I accept your apology," Lauren said brightly. "Anyway, the damage was only to my pride."

He studied her with narrowed eyes. "Lauren, I'm trying to apologize to you so that—"

"You already apologized," Lauren interrupted.

"So that we can go on from here," he finished implacably. After a thoughtful pause, he continued, "For both our sakes, we'll have to be discreet in order to avoid gossip within the corporation, but I think if we're reasonably cautious when we're together, we can manage."

Fury, not pleasure, tinted Lauren's smooth cheeks, but she managed to sound merely perplexed. "Manage what? A sleazy affair?"

"Lauren," Nick said in a warning voice, "I want you and I know you want me. I also know you're angry with me for initiating you sexually and then—"

"Oh, but I'm not!" Lauren protested with deceptive sweetness. "I wouldn't trade that night for the world." Taking a cautious step backward, she added lightly, "In fact, I've already decided that when I have a daughter my age, I'll give you a call. If you're still 'active' I'd like to send her to you so that you—"

One step wasn't enough. Nick lunged forward, seized her wrists, and jerked her between his legs, his muscular thighs clamped against her hips. His eyes were flaming with an alarming combination of anger and desire. "You beautiful, outrageous . . ." His mouth swooped down, seizing her lips with raw, devastating hunger and ruthless insistence.

Lauren clamped her teeth together, resisting the shattering persuasion of his kiss. With a supreme physical effort, she twisted her face from his. "Damn you, stop it!" she choked, burying her face against his chest.

His grip on her shoulders eased slightly, and when he spoke, his voice was rough with confusion. "If I could stop this, believe me, I would!" Threading his fingers through her hair, he cupped her face between his hands and forced her to look at him. "After you left Harbor Springs, I kept thinking about you. All during the meeting at lunch today I couldn't concentrate on anything but you. I *can't* stop it."

His admission shattered Lauren's resistance, subduing and seducing her in a way that no kiss could have.

Nick saw her capitulation in the trembling softness of her lips. He stared at them, the banked fires in his eyes leaping into flames as he slowly lowered his head again.

"Is this the 'top priority confidential' project that required Lauren's presence up here?" Jim's amused drawl aborted the kiss, and their heads snapped around toward Mary's office, where he was lounging in the connecting doorway.

Lauren wrenched free of Nick's arms as Jim straightened from the doorway and strolled into the office. "This makes things rather awkward for Lauren," he continued thoughtfully to Nick. "In the first place, I'm afraid Mary witnessed a bit of this scene, and since she's blindly loyal to you, she's bound to blame Lauren."

Lauren's mortified horror at Mary's having seen them was totally eclipsed by her shock over Jim's next announcement. "In the second place," he lied with a bland grin, "the date you wanted Lauren to break on Saturday happens to be with me. Since I am one of your oldest and closest friends, and since there are seven nights in a week, I don't think it's very sporting of you to try to usurp *my* night."

Nick's brows drew together in annoyance, but Jim continued imperturbably. "Since we both intend to pursue Lauren, I think we ought to establish some ground rules. Now," he mused, "is she fair game here at the office or not? I'm perfectly willing to abide by—"

Lauren finally recovered her power of speech. "I refuse to listen to another word of this," she exclaimed as she stalked toward Mary's office.

Jim stepped out of her way, but kept his challenging smile aimed directly at Nick. "As I was saying, Nick, I'm perfectly willing—"

"I sincerely hope," Nick interrupted shortly, "that you have a valid reason for this unscheduled visit of yours."

Jim relented with a chuckle. "As a matter of fact, I do. Curtis called while I was out. I think he wants to talk about a deal. . . ."

Lauren was already through the doorway of Mary's office when the name hit her. Curtis. Her palms began to perspire. Curtis was one of the six names Philip Whitworth had asked her to listen for.

Curtis wants to talk about a deal.

She sank into her chair, the blood pounding in her ears as she strained to hear more from Nick's office, but the men's voices had dropped and the furious clatter of Mary's electric typewriter made it impossible.

Curtis could be a first name rather than a last

name. Michael Curtis was the name Philip had given her, but Jim had merely mentioned Curtis. Lauren groped for the Global Industries telephone directory in the desk drawer. Two men named Curtis were listed—perhaps it was one of them. She couldn't believe Jim would act as an intermediary for the spy whose treachery was strangling Philip's company. Not Jim.

"If you don't have any work to do—" Mary Callahan's voice was like an icicle "—I'll be happy to give you some of mine."

Lauren flushed and doggedly resumed her work.

Nick was in meetings for the rest of the day, and at five o'clock Lauren breathed a sigh of relief. Back downstairs on Sinco's floor, the sounds of raised voices and closing drawers heralded the end of another workday. Lauren nodded absently at the women who reminded her to join them at the pub. Her eyes were on Jim as he came striding around the corner to her desk.

"Want to talk?" he asked, inclining his head toward his office.

"Well?" he teased when Lauren was seated in the leather chair in front of his desk. "Go ahead—we've certainly passed the point where we need to maintain any sort of formality between us."

Lauren nervously pushed her hair back off her forehead. "What made you stand there and . . . and listen to everything? What made you say the things you did about us—you and me?"

Jim leaned back in his chair, a wry grin tugging at his lips. "When I came back from lunch and found

166

out you'd been reassigned to Nick, I went up to be certain that you were doing all right. Mary told me that you'd just gone into Nick's office, so I opened the door and looked in to see if you needed rescuing. There you were—smiling angelically at him while you gave him messages from other women and turned down his offer of an 'affair.'"

Resting his head against the back of his chair, Jim closed his eyes and laughed. "Oh Lauren, you were magnificent! I was just about to leave when you pushed him too far and told him you'd call him when your daughter was of age, so that he could, er, initiate her, as I gather he initiated you?"

He opened one eye, saw Lauren's scarlet cheeks and waved a dismissing hand. "Anyway, you seemed to be resisting Nick's physical retaliation well enough. I had just decided to leave when Nick put on the pressure and told you he couldn't concentrate on anything but you. You swallowed the line and started to sink, so I stepped in to give you time to recover."

"Why?" Lauren persisted.

He hesitated for a suspiciously long time. "I suppose because I saw you crying over him, and because I don't want you to get hurt. For one thing, if you do get hurt, you'll resign, and I happen to like having you around." His brown eyes warmed with admiration as he studied her. "Not only are you extremely decorative, young lady, but you're witty, intelligent and capable."

Lauren acknowledged the compliment with a smile, but she wouldn't let the matter drop. He had explained why he'd interrupted, but not why he'd deliberately made Nick think there was something between Lauren and him. "And," she speculated boldly, "if Nick thinks *you're* interested in me, I'll become even more of a challenge. If that happens, he'll spend more time and effort pursuing me, won't he?" Before Jim could reply, Lauren finished smoothly, "And if he's busy chasing me, he won't have much time to devote to Ericka Moran, will he?"

Jim's eyes narrowed. "Nick, Ericka and I went to college together. We've been friends for years."

"Close friends?" Lauren prodded.

He shot her a piercing look, then dismissed the matter with a shrug. "Ericka and I were engaged, but that was over years ago." He gave a devilish grin. "Maybe I ought to do exactly what I told Nick I was going to do and pursue you myself."

Lauren smiled. "I have a feeling you're as jaded and cynical as he is." He looked so stung that she added teasingly, "Well, you are—but still very attractive, for all that."

"Thanks," he said dryly.

"Were you and Nick fraternity brothers?" she asked, helplessly longing to learn more about Nick.

"Nope, Nick was at college on a scholarship. He couldn't have afforded to belong to my fraternity. Don't look sorry for him, you lovely idiot. He didn't have money, but he had brains—he's a brilliant engineer. He also had the girls, including several *I* wanted."

"I wasn't feeling sorry for him," Lauren denied, standing up to leave.

"By the way—" Jim stopped her "—I spoke with Mary and set her straight about who was seduced by whom a few weeks ago."

Lauren sighed defeatedly. "I wish you hadn't. . . ."

"Be damned glad I did. Mary worked for Nick's grandfather, and she's known Nick since he was a baby. She's fiercely loyal to him. She's also a staunch moralist with a particular dislike for aggressive young women who pursue Nick. She'd have made your life a living hell."

"If she's such a staunch moralist," Lauren said mutinously, "I can't imagine how she can possibly work for Nick."

Jim winked. "Nick and I are great favorites of hers. She's convinced that the two of us aren't beyond redemption."

Lauren stopped in the doorway and turned. "Jim," she said awkwardly. "Was I the only reason you came upstairs? I mean, did you make up that excuse about Curtis wanting to talk about a deal?"

Jim's brown eyes leveled curiously on her. "No, that was the truth. But it was just an excuse." He chuckled as he opened his briefcase and began shoving papers into it. "As Nick rather bluntly informed me when you left, the Curtis matter wasn't urgent enough to justify my coming up there and interrupting him. Why do you ask about Curtis?" he added.

Lauren's blood ran cold. She felt transparent and obvious. "No reason, I just wondered."

He picked up his briefcase. "Come on, I'll walk you outside."

They crossed the marble lobby together, and Jim pulled open one of the heavy glass doors for Lauren to precede him. The first thing she saw when she stepped into the sunlight was Nick striding quickly toward a long, sleek silver limousine waiting for him at the curb.

As Nick turned to slide into the back seat, he glanced toward the building and saw them. His gaze sliced over Jim before settling on Lauren. His gray eyes smiled a promise at her—and a warning: tomorrow he would not be so easily put off.

*

"Where to, Mr. Sinclair?" the chauffeur asked as Nick settled back into the luxurious automobile.

"Metro Airport." He turned his head to watch Lauren cross the wide boulevard with Jim. With sheer aesthetic appreciation he contemplated the gentle sway of her hips. There was a quiet poise, a pride, in her bearing that lent grace to her movements.

The chauffeur saw a break in the traffic, and the limousine surged into the flow of rush-hour automobiles. Now that he thought about it, Nick realized that everything about Lauren appealed to him. In the time he had known her, she had amused him, infuriated him and sexually excited him. She was laughter and sensuality, gentleness and defiance all wrapped up in an extremely alluring package.

Leaning back against the soft seat, Nick considered the affair he was planning to have with her. It was insanity to get involved with one of his employees; if he'd known it was going to happen, he'd have gotten her a job in one of his friends' companies. But it was too late now. He wanted her.

He had wanted her since that first night, when he had turned around to hand her a glass of tonic and had found not a disheveled teenager but an exquisitely beautiful woman. Nick smiled, remembering the expression on her face when she'd observed his shock. She had anticipated his surprise, and she had openly relished every instant of it.

He had decided that night to keep her at a distance. She was too young for him . . . he hadn't liked the unexplainable surge of desire he'd experienced when she laughingly warned him if her "slipper" fit, she was going to turn him into a handsome frog. If his desire hadn't overridden his reason when he'd taken her to Tony's for lunch, he'd never have invited her to Harbor Springs. But he had taken her there.

And she had been a virgin. . . .

Nick's conscience pricked him, and he sighed irritably. Hell, if he hadn't made love to her another man would have, and soon. Jim Williams wanted her. So did a dozen others, he thought, remembering the calculating, avidly admiring way that many of his executives had watched her at the party on Saturday.

A vision of Lauren standing outside on the balcony that night drifted across Nick's mind. "Four weeks ago, I thought you were someone special!" she'd burst out, looking like an angry angel. "Four weeks ago, I didn't know that you were unprincipled, promiscuous and morally corrupt!" She certainly knew how to express her opinions, he thought wryly.

Every instinct he possessed warned him that an affair with Lauren would complicate his life. Already she had gotten under his skin. He should have stuck to his decision to avoid all further contact with her, the decision he'd made when he sent her away from Harbor Springs. He would have stuck to it if he hadn't seen her at the party Saturday night, looking so sexy and glamorous in that damned provocative dress.

She had wanted him that night even though she'd denied it. And she'd wanted him today in his office too. One of the first things he was going to teach that lovely, exasperating beauty was to accept her own sexuality and to admit her desires. Then he was going to bathe her senses in every exquisite sensation a man could give a woman in bed. He would teach her to please him too. He remembered her sweet, inexperienced attempts at doing so when he'd made love to her in Harbor Springs, and a stirring hardness instantly tightened his loins. The effect she had on him was incredible, he thought grimly as he shifted position.

What if she couldn't cope emotionally with an affair? What if she fell apart when it was over? He didn't want to hurt her.

Nick reached down and opened his briefcase, extracting the contracts for the land acquisition he was about to negotiate with the men who were flying in to meet with him. It was too late to worry about the possible consequences; he wanted her too badly —and she wanted him.

13

At one o'clock the next afternoon, Lauren went up to the eightieth floor and was informed by Mary that Mr. Sinclair wanted to see her immediately. Fighting down her nervous tension, Lauren smoothed her hair, which was held in a loose knot at her nape, and walked into his office. "You wanted to see me?" she said politely.

Nick tossed the documents he was reading down on his desk, leaned back in his chair and lazily surveyed her. "You were wearing your hair up like that the day we left for Harbor Springs," he said, his deep voice pitched seductively low. "I like it."

"In that case," Lauren said lightly, "I'll start wearing it down."

He grinned. "So that's the way we're going to play it, is it?"

"Play what?"

"This little game we started yesterday."

"I am not playing your game," she said with quiet firmness. "I do not want the prize." But she did. She wanted him forever, for herself. And she despised herself for that same stupid weakness.

Nick observed her troubled expression with a feeling of satisfaction and nodded toward the chair in front of his desk. "Sit down. I was just about to review a file I had sent up."

Relieved that he was ready to get to work, Lauren sat down, but her breath caught in her chest when he picked up the file and opened it. CONFIDENTIAL —PERSONNEL FILE was stamped across the front, and beneath it was a typed label that read, LAUREN E. DANNER/EMPLOYEE NO. 98753.

A flush tinted her delicately molded cheekbones as she remembered deliberately failing her tests and listing president as her first preference for a job. Nick would see that and—

"Hmmm," he said, "Lauren *Elizabeth* Danner. Elizabeth is a beautiful name and so is Lauren. They suit you."

Unable to endure the sweet torment of having him flirt with her, Lauren said repressively, "I was named after two maiden aunts. One of them had a squint and the other had warts."

Nick ignored that and continued aloud. "Color of eyes, blue." He regarded her over the top of the file, his gray eyes intimate and teasing. "They are definitely blue. A man could lose himself in those eyes of yours—they're gorgeous."

"My right eye used to wobble unless I wore my glasses," Lauren informed him blithely. "They had to operate on it."

"A little girl with wobbly blue eyes and glasses on

her nose," he reflected with a slow grin. "I'll bet you were cute."

"I looked studious, not cute."

Nick's lips twitched as if he knew exactly what she was trying to do. He turned over the application, and Lauren watched him scanning it, his gaze nearing the bottom where she had listed her job preferences. She knew the exact instant he spotted what she had written. "What the . . . !" he said, astonished, and then he burst out laughing. "Weatherby and I are going to have to be careful. Which of our jobs do you want the most?"

"Neither," Lauren said shortly. "I did that because on my way to the interview at Sinco, I decided I didn't want to work there after all."

"So you purposely flunked your tests, is that it?"

"That's it."

"Lauren . . ." he began in a soft seductive voice that instantly put her on her guard.

"I've had the dubious pleasure of reading through *your* file," Lauren cut in coolly. "Your public-relations file," she clarified, at his stunned look. "I know all about Bebe Leonardos and the French movie star. I even saw the picture of you that was taken with Ericka Moran the day after you sent me away because a 'business acquaintance' was coming to see you."

"And," he concluded evenly, "you were hurt."

"I was disgusted," Lauren shot back, refusing to admit to any of the anguish she'd felt. She caught hold of her temper and said with a measure of her former calm, "Now can we please get down to work?"

A moment later Nick was called into a meeting that lasted the rest of the afternoon, so Lauren was left in peace. A peace that was disturbed by Mary Callahan's frequent thoughtful glances.

At ten o'clock the next morning, Jim, looking harried, appeared at Lauren's desk. "Nick just called. He wants you up there right now, and he's going to need you for the rest of the day." Sighing, he gestured toward the report she'd been preparing for him. "Go ahead. I'll finish that."

Mary was gone when Lauren arrived, but Nick was seated at his desk, his suit coat and tie removed, his dark head bent as he concentrated on the notes he was writing. His shirtsleeves were rolled up on his tanned forearms and his collar was unbuttoned. Lauren's gaze drifted to the tanned column of his throat. Not so long ago, she remembered, she had pressed her lips to the hollow there where his pulse beat. . . .

She looked at his beautifully styled dark hair and the ruggedly chiseled angles of his jaw and cheek. He was the handsomest, most compelling man she had ever seen, she thought with a pang of longing. But when she spoke, her voice was calmly detached. "Jim said you needed me up here right away. What do you want me to do for you?"

Nick turned and looked at her, a smile sweeping across his features. "Now there's a question," he teased.

She pointedly ignored his sexual innuendo. "I understand that you have an urgent task for me."

"I do."

"What is it?"

"I want you to go to the coffee shop and get me something to eat."

"That—" Lauren choked. "That's your idea of urgent?"

"Very urgent," Nick replied imperturbably. "I happen to be starved."

Lauren clenched her hands into fists. "To you I may merely be some frivolous, amusing sexual object, but downstairs I have an important job to do, and Jim needs me."

"*I* need you, honey. I've been here since—"

"Don't you dare call me honey!" she burst out, reeling with unwanted joy at the casual endearment.

"Why not?" he cajoled, a smile lighting his face. "You're sweet."

"You won't think so if you call me honey again," Lauren promised.

His brows drew together at her tone, and Lauren had to remind herself that he was still her boss. "Oh all right!" she capitulated ungraciously. "What do you eat for breakfast?"

"Irritating secretaries," he mocked.

Lauren stalked back to her temporary office and discovered that Mary had returned. "You won't need money, Lauren," the woman said. "We have an account set up at the coffee shop."

Two things hit Lauren at once: the first was that

Mary had just called her Lauren instead of her usual frosty Miss Danner. And the second was that she was smiling—and what a smile Mary Callahan had! It seemed to glow from inside her, lighting her face and softening her austere features in a way that made her seem absolutely lovely.

Lauren found herself returning that contagious smile. "What does he eat for breakfast?" she sighed.

Mary's eyes twinkled. "Irritating secretaries."

As if to atone for sending her on such an unimportant errand, Nick thanked her for the sweet rolls she brought him and gallantly insisted on pouring her a cup of coffee.

"I'll fix it myself, but thank you anyway," Lauren said firmly. To her sublime discomfort, Nick strolled over to the bar and casually leaned against it, watching her add cream and sugar.

When she reached out to pick up her cup, he put his hand on her arm. "Lauren," he said quietly, "I'm sorry I hurt you. Believe me, I never intended to do that."

"There's no need for you to keep apologizing," she replied, carefully pulling her arm away. "Let's just forget the whole thing happened." She picked up her cup and started toward her desk.

"By the way," he said casually, "I'm leaving for Italy tonight. But beginning on Monday, I'll need you up here in the mornings too."

"For how long?" Lauren asked, appalled.

He grinned. "For as long as it takes me to win this game of ours."

With those words the gauntlet was tossed, and the battle of wills that ensued promptly wore Lauren to a frazzle.

She had scarcely put down her coffee cup when Nick buzzed her on the intercom and asked her to come into his office and take a letter to Rossi, the Italian inventor. "And bring your coffee," he invited.

In the middle of his rapid-fire dictation he said softly, without pausing, "When the sun is on your hair, it shines like spun gold," and launched back into his letter. Lauren, who had inadvertently taken half of the compliment down in shorthand, gave him a killing glance, and he chuckled.

At one o'clock he asked her to sit in on a meeting in his office and take notes. In the middle of the meeting, she glanced up to find his heavy-lidded gaze on her crossed legs. Her whole body turned warm, and she uncrossed her legs. Nick looked into her eyes and smiled knowingly.

When the meeting adjourned Lauren stood to leave, but Nick stopped her. "Have you finished typing your Italian translation of that list of questions I dictated, so that Rossi will understand what I want to know?" Flicking a charmingly apologetic smile in her direction, he added, "I hate to rush you, honey, but I have to take it with me to Casano."

Why, Lauren wondered resentfully, did her stupid heart turn over when he called her honey? "It's ready," she answered.

"Good. And have you figured out from the work

you've been doing what the Rossi project is all about?"

She shook her head. "No, not really. It's all too technical. I know Rossi is a chemist who lives in Casano and that he's invented something you're interested in. And I know you're considering financing his research as well as producing his product in the future."

"I should have explained it to you before. It would have made your work up here more enjoyable," he said, changing unexpectedly from seducer to considerate boss. "Rossi has developed a chemical that appears to make certain synthetic materials, including nylon, completely waterproof, fireproof, weatherproof and soil-proof, without changing the appearance or texture of the original substance. Carpeting and clothing made of these synthetics would be virtually impossible to wear out or ruin."

He was treating her like a business associate, and Lauren relaxed in his company for the first time since their weekend together. "But does the chemical really work, without changing or harming anything?"

"Damned if I know," Nick admitted wryly. "But I intend to find out on this trip. So far all I've seen are demonstrations. I need a sample to bring back with me for testing in a legitimate lab, but Rossi is paranoid about secrecy. He says *he's* testing *me*."

Lauren wrinkled her nose. "He sounds a little crazy."

"He's eccentric as hell," Nick sighed. "He lives in

a little cottage in Casano, a tiny Italian fishing village. He keeps dogs to protect him, but his laboratory is in a shed a half mile away, protected by nothing."

"At least you've seen demonstrations."

"Demonstrations don't mean much without thorough testing. For example, his chemical may make something waterproof—but what will happen if milk is spilled on it? Or a soft drink?"

"But what if it's everything he says it is?" she asked.

"In that case I'll put together a consortium—an alliance between Global Industries and two other cooperating corporations—and we'll present the world with Rossi's discovery."

"He's probably afraid that if he gives you a sample to test, someone at the lab will analyze it and learn what chemicals he's using. Then they could steal his discovery."

"You're right," he replied with a grin. Without warning, he put his arm around her and tipped her chin with his free hand. "I'll bring you a present from Italy. What would you like?"

"My mother's earrings," Lauren said flatly. With a sharp jerk backward, she freed herself from his arms, then she turned on her heel and marched into Mary's office. Nick's throaty chuckle followed her.

As he watched her walk away, Nick felt a strange, unfamiliar emotion budding deep inside him, a tenderness that made him feel vulnerable. The sight of her pleased him, her smile warmed him and touching her sent desire exploding through his system. She had poise and a natural, artless sophistication. In comparison to the other women in his life, Lauren was a tender innocent—and yet she had the courage to openly defy him and the strength to resist the pressure he was putting on her.

His smile faded. He was pressuring her, and he had never done that to a woman in his life. He was stalking her, backing her into corners, and he was disgusted with himself for it. And yet he couldn't stop. . . . He felt more for her than desire; he genuinely liked her. He admired her courage and her stubbornness, and even her idealism.

That unnamed and unwanted emotion stirred inside him again, and Nick mentally cast it aside. He wanted her because she was a beautiful enigma. He liked her and he desired her. Nothing more.

At 4:55 a joint conference call that Nick had scheduled came through from California, Oklahoma and Texas. When Mary told him it was ready, Nick asked her to send Lauren in to take notes.

"He's putting it on the speaker phone," Mary explained. "He'll only need you to take down any figures that are discussed."

The call was already under way when Lauren walked into his office. Nick gestured toward his chair and got up so that she could sit at his desk and take notes. Two minutes after Lauren sat down, he leaned over her from behind, braced his hands on the desk on either side of her and brushed his lips across her hair.

Lauren's self-control snapped. "Damn you, stop it!" she burst out.

"What?" "What?" "What?" three masculine voices chorused.

Nick leaned toward the speaker and drawled, "My secretary thinks you're talking too fast, and she'd like you to stop it so she can catch up."

"Well, all she had to do was ask," one offended male replied.

"I hope you're satisfied!" Lauren whispered furiously.

"I'm not," Nick chuckled in her ear. "But I'm going to be."

Fully intending to leave him to take his own notes, Lauren slammed her notebook closed and and tried to shove her chair back. Nick's body blocked the chair. She twisted her head around to say something scathing, and his lips captured hers in a kiss that forced her head against the back of the chair, tripled her pulse rate and robbed her of thought. When he took his mouth away, she was too shaken to do anything except stare at him.

"What do you think, Nick?" a voice asked over the speaker.

"I think it gets better every time," he answered huskily.

When the call was finally over, Nick pressed a button on his desk, and Lauren saw the door leading into Mary's office swing shut electronically. He grasped her arms and drew her out of the chair, turning her toward him. His mouth came closer to hers, and Lauren felt herself being helplessly drawn into his magnetic spell. "Don't!" she pleaded. "Please don't do this to me."

His hands tightened on her arms. "Why can't you just admit you want me and enjoy the consequences?"

"All right," she said wretchedly, "You win. I want you . . . I admit it." She saw the gleam of triumph in his eyes, and her chin lifted. "When I was eight years old, I also wanted a monkey I saw in a pet store."

The triumph faded. "And?" he sighed irritably, letting go of her.

"And unfortunately I got him," Lauren said. "Daisy bit me, and I had to have twelve stitches in my leg."

Nick looked as if he was torn between laughter and anger. "I imagine he bit you for naming him Daisy."

Lauren ignored his mockery. "And when I was thirteen, I wanted sisters and brothers. My father obliged me by remarrying, and I got a stepsister who stole my clothes and my boyfriends, and a stepbrother who stole my allowances."

"What the hell does that have to do with us?"

"Everything!" She raised her hands in a gesture of appeal, then dropped them in defeat. "I'm trying to explain that I want you, but that I'm not going to let you hurt me again."

"I won't hurt you."

"Oh, yes you will!" she said, fiercely fighting back tears. "You won't mean to, but you will. You already have. When I left you up north, you went off to Palm Springs with one of your bed partners. Do you know what I was doing while you were there?"

Nick shoved his hands in his pockets, his expression guarded. "No. What were you doing?"

"I," Lauren said on a note of hysterical, choking laughter, "was sitting by the telephone waiting for you to call and knitting you a gray sweater to match your eyes." She looked at him, her eyes pleading with him to understand. "If we have an affair, you won't be emotionally involved, but I will. I can't detach my emotions from my body, hop into bed and have a wonderful time, and then forget about it. I'd want you to care, and I'd care. I'd be jealous if I thought you were with another woman. And if I *knew* you were, I'd be hurt and furious."

If he had mocked her or tried to persuade her, she would have burst into tears. But he did neither and she gained strength from that. She even managed a sad smile. "If we had an affair, when it was over you'd want us to be friends, wouldn't you? You'd expect it."

"Naturally."

"Then since our 'affair' is over, can we be friends now?" Her voice shook as she added, "I—I would really like to think of you as my friend."

Nick nodded, but he didn't speak. He simply stood looking at her, his gray eyes enigmatic.

Afterward, Lauren walked to her car, congratulating herself on the maturity with which she'd handled the situation. She had been honest and direct; she'd withstood temptation and upheld her principles. She had done the "right" thing, and she was a stronger, better person for it.

She folded her arms on the steering wheel and burst into tears.

14

LAUREN SPENT THE REST OF THE WEEK WORKING LIKE A
fiend at the office. At home she alternately thought
about Nick and worried about her father's financial
situation. The hospital was demanding half of the fee
at once. The only thing she could think of doing was
to sell her mother's splendid grand piano, but the
thought broke her heart. It was her piano too, and
here in Michigan she missed it. She missed being
able to play, to work out her frustrations and
disappointments at the keyboard as she used to do.
On the other hand, her father was far from being
well, and if he needed to go to the hospital again, she
couldn't risk having him turned away because his last
bill wasn't paid.

Late Friday afternoon, Susan Brook stopped her
in the public relations department. "Jim's birthday is
next week, on Thursday," she told Lauren. "It's sort
of a custom here to bring a cake for your boss." With
an irrepressible grin she added, "Cake and coffee is
a terrific excuse to quit working fifteen minutes
early."

"I'll bring a cake," Lauren quickly assured her. She glanced at her watch, said good-night to Susan and quickened her pace toward her desk. Philip Whitworth had called and invited her over for dinner that night, and she didn't want to be late.

On the way to her apartment to change her clothes, Lauren considered telling Philip about the Curtis deal. She felt uneasy about it, however. Before she interfered with anyone's reputation and job, she ought to be certain of what she actually knew. It occurred to her that Philip might consider news of the Rossi project "valuable information," and that he might pay her the $10,000 he'd offered, but her conscience screamed at her for even contemplating the thought. She decided to write to the hospital and offer $3,000. She might be able to borrow that much from a bank.

Over dinner later Philip asked her if she liked her job at Sinco. When Lauren replied that she did, he said, "Have you heard mentioned any of the names I gave you?"

She hesitated. "No, I haven't."

Philip sighed with disappointment. "The most important contracts we've ever considered bidding on have deadlines only a few weeks from now. Before then I've got to know who's leaking the information to Sinco. I *need* those contracts."

Lauren immediately felt guilty for not telling him about Curtis or Rossi. More than ever she felt confused, torn between her loyalty to Philip and her desire to do the right thing.

"I told you Lauren wouldn't be able to help," Carter put in.

Lauren didn't know how she'd ever let herself get into this mess. In her own defense, she said, "It's too soon to know, actually. I've been reassigned to work on a special project on the eightieth floor, so I haven't been working full time for Sinco until yesterday, when Nick—Mr. Sinclair—flew to Italy."

Nick's name sent a bolt of electricity through the entire room, and all three Whitworths stiffened perceptibly.

Carter's eyes gleamed with excitement. "Lauren, you're fantastic! How did you manage to get yourself assigned to him? Hell, you'll have access to all sorts of confidential—"

"I didn't manage anything," Lauren interrupted. "I'm there because I happened to put down on my application that I speak Italian, and he needed a temporary secretary who was fluent in it to work on a special project."

"What kind of project?" Philip and Carter demanded in unison.

Lauren glanced uneasily at Carol, who was watching her intently over the rim of her glass. Then she looked at the two men. "Philip, you promised when I agreed to work for Sinco that all you would ask me to do was tell you if I overheard one of those six names. Please don't ask me about anything else. If I tell you, I'll be no better than the person who's spying on you."

"You're right of course, my dear," he instantly agreed.

But an hour later, when Lauren had left, Philip turned to his son. "She said Sinclair flew to Italy yesterday. Call that pilot friend of yours and find out if he can get access to his flight plan. I want to know exactly where in Italy he went."

"Do you really think it's that important?"

Philip studied the brandy in his glass. "Lauren obviously thinks it's very important. If she didn't, she would have told us about it without a qualm." After a pause he said, "If we can trace him, I want you to send a team of investigators over there to pick up his trail. I have a hunch he's working on something big."

Lauren glanced at the small thermometer outside the window of her bedroom as she pulled on a buttercup yellow sweater and slacks. Despite the sunny autumn Sunday afternoon, despite her luxuriously furnished apartment, she felt lonely and isolated. Shopping for Jim's birthday present would give her something to do, she decided. She was debating what to buy him when the sudden shrill ring of her doorbell interrupted her thoughts.

When she opened the door she stared in amazement at the man whose tall frame seemed to fill the doorway. Dressed in an open-collared cream shirt with a rust-colored suede jacket hooked negligently over his shoulder, Nick looked so unbearably handsome that Lauren could have cried. She forced herself to sound composed and only mildly curious. "Hi. What are you doing here?"

He frowned. "Damned if I know."

Unable to suppress her smile she said, "The usual excuse is that you happened to be in the neighborhood and decided to drop by."

"Now why didn't I think of that?" Nick mocked dryly. "Well, are you going to invite me in?"

"I don't know," she said honestly. "Should I?"

His gaze traveled down the entire length of her body, lifted to her lips and finally her eyes. "I wouldn't if I were you."

Breathless from his frankly sensual glance, Lauren was nevertheless determined to abide by her decision to avoid all personal involvement with him. And judging from the way he had just looked at her, his reason for being here was very, very personal. Reluctantly she made her decision. "In that case, I'll follow your advice. Goodbye, Nick," she said, starting to close the door. "And thank you for stopping by."

He accepted her decision with a slight inclination of his head, and Lauren made herself finish closing the door. She forced herself to walk away on legs that felt like lead, reminding herself at the same time how insane it would be to let him near her. But halfway across the living room she lost the internal battle. Pivoting on her heel, she raced for the door, yanked it open and hurtled straight into Nick's chest. He was lounging with one hand braced high against the doorframe, gazing down at her flushed face with a knowing, satisfied grin.

"Hello, Lauren. I happened to be in the neighborhood and decided to drop by."

"What do you want, Nick?" she sighed, her blue eyes searching his.

"You."

Resolutely she started to close the door again, but his hand shot out to stop her. "Do you really want me to go?"

"I told you on Wednesday that what I *want* has nothing to do with it. What matters is what's best for me, and—"

He interrupted her with a boyish grin. "I promise I'll never wear your clothes, and I won't steal your allowances or your boyfriends either." Lauren couldn't help starting to smile as he finished, "And if you swear never to call me Nicky again, I won't bite you."

She stepped aside and let him in, then took his jacket and hung it in the closet. When she turned, Nick was leaning against the closed front door, his arms crossed over his chest. "On second thought," he grinned, "I take part of that back. I'd love to bite you."

"Pervert!" she returned teasingly, her heart thumping so much with excitement that she hardly knew what she was saying.

"Come here and I'll show you just how perverted I can be," he invited smoothly.

Lauren took a cautious step backward. "Absolutely not. Would you like some coffee or a Coke?"

"Either would be fine."

"I'll make some coffee."

"Kiss me first."

Lauren shot him a look over her shoulder and walked into the kitchen. As she made the coffee, she was acutely conscious that he was standing in the kitchen doorway, watching her.

"Do I pay you enough to afford this apartment?" he asked casually.

"No. There's a burglary problem here, so in return for watching the place, I get to live here free." She heard him start toward her, and she hastily turned to the table and put out cups and saucers. When she straightened, she knew he was standing right behind her, but she had no choice except to turn around and face him.

"Have you missed me?" he asked.

"What do you think?" she evaded smoothly—but not smoothly enough, because he chuckled.

"Good. How much?"

"Is your ego in need of bolstering today?" she countered lightly.

"Yep."

"Really, why?"

"Because I got shot down by a beautiful twenty-three-year-old, and I can't seem to get her out of my mind."

"That's too bad," Lauren said, trying unsuccessfully to hide the joy in her voice.

"Isn't it," he mocked. "She's like a thorn in my side, a blister on my heel. She has the eyes of an angel, a body that drugs my mind, the vocabulary of an English professor and a tongue like a scalpel."

"Thanks, I think."

His hands glided up her arms, then curved around her shoulders, tightening as he drew her to within a few inches of his chest. "And," he added, "I like her."

His mouth was making a deliberately slow descent, and Lauren waited helplessly for the physical impact of his lips covering hers. Instead he bypassed her lips and began to explore the creamy skin of her neck and shoulder, his warm mouth nuzzling the sensitive area, then slowly wandering upward along her neck toward her ear. With the kitchen table behind her and Nick's body in front, Lauren was incapable of doing anything except standing there, a mass of quivering sensations. His mouth left a burning trail of kisses up to her temple, then slowly began to drift toward her lips. A fraction of an inch above hers he stopped and repeated his earlier command. "Kiss me, Lauren."

"No," she whispered shakily.

He shrugged and began leisurely kissing her other cheek, stopping to linger sensuously at her ear, his tongue tracing every curve and hollow. He nipped her earlobe, and Lauren lurched forward in a startled movement that jolted their bodies together. A current leaped between them, and they both stiffened with the delicious shock of it. "God!" Nick muttered under his breath, and his lips began to trail down her neck to her shoulder.

"Nick, please," Lauren whispered weakly.

"Please what?" he murmured against her throat. "Please put us both out of this misery?"

"No!"

"No?" he repeated silkily, raising his head. "You don't want me to kiss you, and undress you, and make love to you?" His lips were tantalizingly close, and Lauren was almost faint with the desire to feel them crushing down on hers. Instead he bent his head and lightly brushed his mouth over hers, first in one direction, then the other. "Please kiss me," he coaxed huskily. "I dream about the way you kissed me in Harbor Springs, about how sweet and warm you felt in my arms. . . ."

With a silent moan of surrender, Lauren slid her hands up his muscular chest and kissed him. She felt the tremor that ran through his body, the gasp of his breath against her lips in the instant before his arms closed around her, and his mouth opened passionately over hers.

Desire was racing through her like a wild fury by the time he finally dragged his mouth from hers. "Where's the bedroom?" he whispered hoarsely.

Lauren pulled back in his arms and lifted her eyes to his. His face was dark with passion, and demand was blazing in his gray eyes. She remembered the last time she had looked into those insistent eyes and had yielded to his fiery passion. Memories flashed through her mind in chilling sequence: he had made love to her in Harbor Springs, had held her and caressed her as if he couldn't get enough of her, and then he had coolly sent her home. She had learned to her own shame and anguish that he was completely capable of making tender, passionate, shattering love to a woman for the sheer physical pleasure of it—without feeling the slightest emotional involvement with her.

He wanted her more now than he had in Harbor Springs—Lauren knew that. She could feel it. She was also half convinced that he felt more for her than just desire, but then she'd foolishly believed that in Harbor Springs too. This time she wanted to be certain. Her pride would not permit her to let him use her again.

"Nick," she said nervously, "I think it would be better if we got to know each other first."

"We already know each other," he reminded her. "Intimately."

"But I mean . . . I would like us to know each other better before we . . . before we start anything."

"We've already started something, Lauren," he said with a hint of impatience in his voice. "And I want to finish it. So do you."

"No, I—" She gasped as his hands cupped the thrusting roundness of her breasts and his thumbs began circling the hardened buds of her nipples.

"I can feel how badly you want me," he told her. His hands swept around her grasping her hips, holding her tightly against him and making her forcefully aware of his hardened manhood thrusting against her. "And you can feel how much I want you. Now, what else do we need to know about each other? What else matters?"

"What else matters?" Lauren hissed, pulling free of his arms. "How can you ask me that? I told you I couldn't handle a casual, unemotional affair with you. What are you trying to do to me?"

Nick's jaw tightened. "I'm trying to get you into that bedroom so that we can ease the ache that's been building inside us for weeks. I want to make love to you all day until we're both too weak to move. Or, if you prefer it more blunt than that, I want to—"

"And then what?" Lauren demanded hotly. "I want to know the rules, dammit! Today we make love, but tomorrow we're no more than casual acquaintances, is that it? Tomorrow you can make love to another woman if you want to, and I'm not supposed to care—right? And tomorrow I can let another man make love to me, and *you* won't care—is *that* right?"

"Yes," he snapped.

Lauren had her answer—he didn't care about her any more now than he had before. He merely wanted her more. Tiredly she said, "Coffee is ready."

"*I'm* ready," he said crudely.

"Well, I'm not!" Lauren stormed in mounting fury. "I'm not ready to be your Sunday-afternoon playmate. If you're bored, go play your games with someone who can handle a casual romp in bed with you."

"What the hell do you want from me?" he demanded coldly.

I want you to love me, she thought. "I don't want anything from you," she said. "Just go away, leave me alone."

Nick's insolent eyes raked over her. "Before I go, I want to give you a piece of advice," he said icily. "Grow up!"

Lauren felt as if he had slapped her. Infuriated past reason, she struck back at his ego. "You're absolutely right!" she blazed. "That's what I should do. Beginning today I'm going to grow up and start practicing what *you* preach! I'm going to sleep with any man who appeals to me. But not with you. You're much too old and too cynical for my taste. Now get out of here!"

Nick pulled a small velvet box from his pocket and slapped it onto the kitchen table. "I owed you a pair of earrings," he said, already striding out of the kitchen.

Lauren heard the front door slam behind him, and with trembling fingers she picked up the little box and opened it. She expected to find her mother's small golden hoops, but instead there was a pair of glowing pearls in a setting so fragile that the pearls appeared to be two large, luminous raindrops suspended in thin air. Lauren snapped the box shut. Which of his girlfriends had lost those in his bed, she wondered in angry loathing. Or were they her "present" from Italy?

She marched upstairs to get her purse and a warmer sweater to cover her shoulders. She would go shopping for Jim's birthday gift exactly as she'd planned, and she would put the last hour out of her thoughts—permanently. Nick Sinclair was not going to haunt her anymore. She would erase him from her mind. She jerked open her bottom drawer and stood looking down at the beautiful silver gray sweater she'd knitted for that . . . that bastard!

Lauren removed it from the drawer. Jim was almost exactly Nick's size, and he would probably like it very much. She would give it to him, she decided, ignoring the sharp stab of anguish that shot through her.

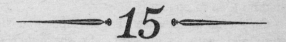

15

LAUREN WALKED INTO THE OFFICE THE NEXT MORNING wearing a chic burgundy suede suit and a determinedly bright smile. Jim took one look at her and grinned. "Lauren, you're gorgeous—but aren't you supposed to be upstairs?"

"Not anymore," she replied, handing him his mail. She had assumed that because their "game" was over, Nick would no longer want her upstairs in the mornings.

She was wrong. Five minutes later, as they were discussing a report Lauren was working on, the phone on Jim's desk rang. "It's Nick," he said, passing the receiver to her.

Nick's voice was like a whip crack. "Get up here! I said I wanted you here all day and I meant it. Now move!"

He hung up on her, and Lauren looked at the receiver as if it had just bitten her. She hadn't expected Nick to sound like that. She'd never heard anybody sound like that. "I—I think I'd better go upstairs," she said, hastily standing up.

Jim's face was a study in incredulity. "I wonder what the hell has gotten under his skin?"

"I think I have." She saw the thoughtful smile that slowly spread across Jim's attractive face, but she had no time to ponder it.

Only a few minutes later Lauren tapped on Nick's door and, with an outward calm she didn't feel, walked into his office. She waited a full two minutes for him to acknowledge her, but after having practically shouted at her to get up there, he continued writing, ignoring her presence. With an irritated shrug she finally went over to his desk and held the little velvet jeweler's box toward him.

"These are not my mother's earrings, and I don't want them," she told his granite profile. "My mother's earrings were ordinary gold hoops, not pearls. They weren't worth a fraction of what these are; their only value was sentimental. But to me they're priceless. They *mean something* to me, and I want them back. Are you capable of understanding that?"

"Perfectly capable," he replied icily, without looking up. He reached out and buzzed for Mary to come in. "However, yours are lost. Since I couldn't get them back for you, I gave you something that had sentimental value to me. Those earrings belonged to my grandmother."

Lauren's stomach knotted sickly, and the resentment left her voice as she said quietly, "I still can't accept them."

"Then leave them there." He nodded curtly toward the corner of his desk.

Lauren put the box down and went back to her temporary office. Mary followed her a minute later, closed the door to Nick's office behind her and came over to Lauren's desk. Smiling kindly, she relayed the instructions Nick had obviously just given. "Sometime during the next few days he's expecting a call from Signor Rossi. He wants you to be available to act as translator whenever the man decides to call. In the meantime, I would be very grateful for your help with some of my work. If you still have time to spare, you could bring some of Jim's work up here to do."

During the next three days, Lauren saw sides of Nick that she had only imagined existed. Gone was the teasing man who had held and kissed and pursued her so relentlessly. In his place was a powerful, dynamic businessman who treated her with a brisk, aloof formality that thoroughly intimidated her. When he wasn't on the phone or in meetings, he was dictating or working at his desk. He arrived before she did in the morning and was still there when she left at night. Acting as his auxiliary secretary, she grew petrified of displeasing him in any way. She had the feeling he was merely waiting for her to make a mistake so that he would have a legitimate reason to fire her.

On Wednesday, Lauren made the mistake she'd been dreading: she left an entire paragraph out of a detailed contract Nick had dictated to her. The moment his summons snapped over the intercom she knew her time had come, and she walked into his office with limbs shaking and hands perspiring. But instead of flaying her alive, which she could see was what he wanted to do, he pointed out the error and shoved the contracts toward her. "Do it again," he snapped, "and this time get it right."

She relaxed slightly after that. If Nick hadn't fired her for that blunder, he obviously wasn't looking for an excuse to get rid of her. He must need her at hand for that call from Rossi no matter how poorly she performed.

"I'm Vicky Stewart," a breathy voice announced to Lauren at noon that same day. Lauren looked up to see an incredibly glamorous brunette standing in front of her.

"I happened to be downtown and decided to stop by and see if Nicky—Mr. Sinclair—is free for lunch," she informed Lauren. "Don't bother announcing me, I'll just go in."

A few minutes later, Vicky and Nick strolled out of his office together, heading toward the elevators. Nick's hand was resting familiarly at the small of her back, and he was grinning at whatever she was telling him.

Lauren swung back around to her typewriter. She hated Vicky Stewart's drawl; she hated the possessive way she looked at Nick; she hated the woman's breathless laugh. In fact, she loathed everything about her and she knew exactly why—Lauren was hopelessly, completely, irrevocably in love with Nick Sinclair.

She adored everything about him, from the aura of power and authority that surrounded him, to the energetic confidence in his long strides, to the way he looked when he was deep in thought. She loved the way he wore his expensive clothes, the way he absently rolled his gold pen in his hand when he was listening to someone on the telephone. He was, she decided with an aching sense of tormented hopelessness, the most forceful, compelling, dynamic man in the world. And he had never seemed further beyond her reach.

"Don't worry too much, my dear," Mary Callahan said, getting up to leave for lunch. "There have been many Vicky Stewarts in his life in the past. They don't last long."

The reassurance only made Lauren feel worse. She'd suspected that Mary not only knew everything that had happened between Nick and herself in the past, but that she also knew exactly how Lauren felt about Nick now. "I don't care what he does!" she said with angry pride.

"Is that right?" Mary retorted with a smile, and left for lunch.

Nick didn't return until afternoon, and Lauren wondered furiously whose bed they had gone to—his or Vicky's.

By the time she left the office, she was so overwrought with jealousy and so filled with self-loathing for loving such an unprincipled libertine that she had a splitting headache. At home she wandered aimlessly around the elegant living room.

Being near Nick was hurting her more every day. She had to leave Sinco—she couldn't bear to be so close to him, to love him as she did and have to watch him with other women. To have him look at her as if she was a piece of office equipment whose presence offended him but whom he was obliged out of necessity to have nearby.

Lauren had a sudden wild longing to tell both Nick Sinclair and Philip Whitworth to go to hell, to pack up and go home to her parents, her friends. But of course she couldn't do that. They needed . . .

Abruptly she stopped pacing, her mind seizing on a solution that should have occurred to her before. There were other large corporations in Detroit that needed good secretaries and that paid high salaries for them. When she bought the ingredients for Jim's birthday cake that night she would also buy a newspaper. Beginning immediately she would start looking for another job.

In the meantime, she would phone Jonathan Van Slyke, whom she had studied under for the past year, and offer to let him buy her grand piano. He had wanted it the moment he'd laid eyes on it.

Despite the dull ache she felt at the prospect of selling it, Lauren felt peaceful for the first time in weeks. She would find an inexpensive little apartment and move out of this place. Until then she would do the best job she could at Sinco—and if she happened to hear one of the names Philip had given her, she would forget it just as soon as she heard it. Philip was going to have to do his own dirty work. She could not and would not betray Nick.

16

LAUREN WALKED ACROSS THE MARBLE LOBBY THE NEXT morning, carefully balancing the box with Jim's birthday cake inside it as well as a gaily wrapped package that held the gray sweater. She felt relaxed and lighthearted, and she smiled as an elderly man wearing a brown suit stepped back in the elevator to give her more room.

The elevator stopped on the thirtieth floor, and the doors opened. Lauren noted that directly across the hall was an office door bearing a nameplate that read, Global Industries Security Division.

"Excuse me," the man in the brown suit said. "This is my floor."

Lauren shifted to one side, and he maneuvered past her. She watched him walk across the hall to the security office.

The security divisions' primary function was to protect Global Industries' manufacturing facilities, particularly those outlying facilities throughout the country where actual research was under way, or where government contracts were involved. However, here at headquarters the security division mostly processed paperwork from the field. As director in Detroit Jack Collins felt rather bored, but his failing health and advancing age had forced him to leave the field and accept this desk job.

His assistant, an over-eager, round-faced young man named Rudy, was sitting with his feet propped up on his desk when Jack walked into the office. "What's up?" the younger man asked, hastily sitting up straight.

"Probably nothing." Jack slid his briefcase onto the desk and removed a file that was labelled "SE-CURITY INVESTIGATION REPORT/LAUREN E. DANNER/EMPLOYEE NO. 98753." Jack didn't particularly like Rudy, but part of his job before he retired was to train him. Reluctantly he explained, "I just got the report from an investigation we ran on a secretary in the building."

"A secretary?" Rudy sounded disappointed. "I didn't think we ran security checks on secretaries."

"Normally we don't. In this case she was assigned to a top priority, confidential project, and the computer automatically reclassified her and issued a security clearance request."

"So what's the problem?"

"The problem is that when the investigators in Missouri checked with her former employer, he said that she worked for him part-time for five years while she went to college. Not full time, as Weatherby at Sinco assumed."

"So she lied on her application, right?" Rudy asked, becoming interested.

"Yes, but not about that. She didn't actually say she worked there full-time. The thing is, she lied and said she had never attended college. The Missouri investigators checked with the university, and she not only graduated, she also got a Master's degree."

"Why would she say she hadn't gone to college if she had?"

"That's one of the things that bothers me a little. I could understand if she said she'd gone to college when she actually hadn't. I'd presume she must have figured that a college degree would help her get hired."

"What are the other things that bother you?"

Jack glanced up at Rudy's rotund face, his avid eyes, and shrugged. "Nothing," he lied. "I just want to check her out for my own peace of mind. I have to go into the hospital for some tests this weekend, but on Monday I'll start working on it."

"How about letting me check her out while you're in the hospital?"

"If they decide to keep me in for more tests, I'll call you and tell you how to handle it."

"It's my birthday," Jim announced as Lauren walked into his office. "Normally a secretary brings a cake for her boss, but I don't suppose you've been here long enough to know that." He sounded a little doleful.

Lauren started to laugh. She hadn't realized how much her promise to Philip Whitworth had burdened her until now. Suddenly the weight of it was gone. "Not only did I bake you a cake, I have a present for you too," she informed him gaily. "One I made myself."

Jim unwrapped the package she handed him, and he was boyishly delighted with the sweater. "You shouldn't have—" he grinned, holding it up "—but I'm glad you did."

"It was to say happy birthday and thank you for helping me with . . . things," she finished lamely.

"Speaking of 'things,' Mary tells me that Nick is like a keg of dynamite ready to explode at the first spark. She says you're bearing up under the strain marvelously. You've won her wholehearted approval," he added quietly.

"I like her too," Lauren said, her eyes clouding at the mention of Nick.

Jim waited until she had left to go upstairs, then he picked up his telephone and punched four numbers. "Mary, what's the atmosphere like up there this morning?"

"Positively explosive," she chuckled.

"Is Nick going to be in the office this afternoon?"

"Yes, why?"

"Because I've decided to light a match under him and see what happens."

"Jimmy, don't!" she said in a low, sharp voice.

"See you a little before five, beautiful," he laughed, ignoring her warning.

When Lauren returned from lunch there were two dozen breathtakingly gorgeous red roses in a vase on her desk. She removed the card from its envelope and stared at it in blank amazement. On it was written "Thank you, sweetheart," followed by the initial J.

When Lauren looked up, Nick was standing in the doorway, his shoulder casually propped against the frame. But there was nothing casual about the rigid set of his jaw or the freezing look in his gray eyes. "From a secret admirer?" he asked sarcastically.

It was the first personal comment he had addressed to her in four days. "Not a secret admirer exactly," she hedged.

"Who is he?"

Lauren tensed. He seemed so angry she didn't think it would be wise to mention Jim's name. "I'm not absolutely certain."

"You aren't absolutely certain?" he bit out. "How many men with the initial J are you seeing? How many of them think you're worth more than a hundred dollars in roses as a way of saying thank you?"

"A hundred dollars?" Lauren repeated, so appalled at the expense that she completely overlooked the fact that Nick had obviously opened the envelope and read the card.

"You must be getting better at it," he mocked crudely.

Inwardly Lauren flinched, but she lifted her chin. "I have much better teachers now!"

With an icy glance that raked her from head to toe, Nick turned on his heel and strode back into his office. For the rest of the day he left her completely alone.

At five minutes to five, Jim walked into Mary's office, wearing his gray sweater and balancing four pieces of birthday cake on two plates. He put the plates down on Mary's empty desk and glanced at the doorway to Nick's office. "Where's Mary?" he asked.

"She left almost an hour ago," Lauren said. "She said to tell you that the nearest fire extinguisher is beside the elevators—whatever that means. I'll be right back. I have to take these letters in to Nick."

As she got up and started around the desk, she was looking down at the letters in her hand, and what happened next stunned her into immobility. "I miss you, darling," Jim said, quickly pulling her into his arms.

A moment later he released her so suddenly that Lauren staggered back a step. "Nick!" he said. "Look at the sweater Lauren gave me for my birthday. She made it herself. And I brought you a piece of my birthday cake—she made that too." Seemingly oblivious to Nick's thunderous countenance, he grinned and added, "I have to get back downstairs." To Lauren he said, "I'll see you later, love." And then he walked out.

In a state of shock, Lauren stared at his retreating back. She was still staring after him when Nick spun her around to face him. "You vindictive little bitch, you gave him my sweater! What else has he gotten that belongs to me?"

"What else?" Lauren repeated, her voice rising. "What are you talking about?"

His hands tightened. "Your delectible body, my sweet. That's what I'm talking about."

Lauren's amazement gave way to comprehension and then to fury. "How dare you call me names, you hypocrite!" she exploded, too incensed to be afraid. "Ever since I've known you, you've been telling me that there's nothing promiscuous about a woman satisfying her sexual desires with any man she pleases. And now—" she literally choked on her wrath "—and now, when you think I've done it, you call me a dirty name. You of all people—you, the United States contender for the bedroom Olympics!"

Nick let go of her as if she had burned him. In a low, dangerously controlled voice he said, "Get out of here, Lauren."

When she'd left, he walked over to the bar and poured himself a stiff bourbon, while fury and anguish twisted through him like a hundred snakes.

Lauren had a lover. Lauren probably had several lovers.

Regret shot through him like acid. She was no longer a starry-eyed little fool who thought people should be in love before they made love. That beautiful body of hers had been thoroughly explored by others. His mind instantly conjured up tormenting pictures of Lauren lying naked in Jim's arms.

He tossed down his drink and poured himself another to blot out the pain, the images. Carrying it over to the sofa, he sat down and propped his feet up on the table.

The liquor slowly began to work its numbing magic, and his rage subsided. In its place was nothing, only an aching emptiness.

"What possessed you?" Lauren demanded of Jim the next morning.

He grinned. "Call it an uncontrollable impulse."

"I call it insanity!" she burst out. "You can't imagine how furious he was. He called me names! I—I think he's insane."

"He is," Jim agreed with complacent satisfaction. "He's insane about you. Mary thinks so too."

Lauren rolled her eyes. "You're *all* insane. I have to work up there with him. How am I going to do that?"

Jim chuckled. "Very, very cautiously," he advised.

Within an hour Lauren knew exactly what Jim meant, and during the days that ensued she began to feel as if she were walking on a tightrope. Nick began to work at a demonic pace that kept everyone, from his top executives to the lowest mailboys, rushing frantically to keep up with him and trying to avoid the lash of his temper.

If he was satisfied with someone's efforts, he was coolly courteous. But if he wasn't satisfied—and he usually wasn't—he tore into the offender with an icy savagery that chilled Lauren's blood. With democratic impartiality he spread his displeasure from switchboard operators to vice-presidents, ripping into them with a caustic sarcasm that made the vice-presidents perspire and the switchboard operators cry. High-powered executives walked confidently into his office, only to slink out a few minutes later and exchange warning glances with auditors who in turn soon scurried out, clutching their ledger sheets and computer printouts protectively to their chests.

By Wednesday of the following week the atmosphere on the eightieth floor had deteriorated to a strained, crackling panic that stretched its tentacles from division to division, from floor to floor. No one laughed on the elevators or gossiped at the copy machines anymore. Only Mary Callahan seemed serenely impervious to the mounting tension. In fact, it seemed to Lauren that she grew more elated with every harrowing hour that passed. But then Mary escaped the cutting edge of Nick's tongue, while Lauren herself did not.

To Mary Nick was always courteous, and to Vicky Stewart, who called him at least three times a day, he was positively charming. No matter how busy he was, or what he was doing at the time, he always had time for Vicky. And whenever she called he would pick up the phone and lean back in his chair. From her desk Lauren could hear the lazy, seductive huskiness that vibrated in his deep voice when he spoke to the other woman, and her heart twisted every time.

That Wednesday evening Nick was scheduled to leave for Chicago, and Lauren was eager to see him go. After so many days of tension, of being treated as if the sight of her revolted him, she felt her composure crumbling, and she restrained her temper and tears by nothing but sheer force of will.

At four o'clock, two hours before his departure time, Nick called Lauren into the conference room to help Mary take notes during a meeting of the financial staff. The meeting was under way, and Lauren's attention was riveted on her shorthand notebook, her pen flying across the pages, when Nick's voice slashed into the proceedings. "Anderson!" he snapped murderously, "if you can tear your attention from Miss Danner's bust, the rest of us will be able to finish this meeting." Lauren flushed a vivid pink, but the elderly Anderson turned a purple hue that might be indicative of an impending stroke.

As soon as the last staff member had filed out of the conference room, Lauren ignored Mary's warning look and turned furiously on Nick. "I hope you're satisfied!" she hissed furiously. "You not only humiliated me, you nearly gave that poor old man a heart attack. What do you plan to do for an encore?"

"Fire the first woman who opens her mouth," Nick retorted coldly. He walked around her and strode out of the conference room.

Outraged past all reason, Lauren started after him, but Mary stopped her. "Don't argue with him," she said, gazing after Nick with a beatific smile on her face. She looked as if she had just witnessed a miracle. "In his present mood he'd fire you, and he'd regret that for the rest of his life."

When Lauren hesitated, she added kindly, "He

isn't coming back from Chicago until Friday night, which gives us two days to recuperate. Tomorrow we'll have a long lunch out of the building—maybe at Tony's. We've earned it."

Without Nick's electric vitality, the executive suite seemed hauntingly empty the next morning. Lauren told herself it was blissfully peaceful and that she liked it this way, but she really didn't.

At noon she and Mary drove to Tony's, where Lauren had phoned for a reservation. A headwaiter wearing the usual formal black was stationed at the entrance to the dining rooms, but Tony saw them and hurried over. Lauren stepped back in surprise as he caught Mary in a bear hug that nearly swept her off her sensibly shod feet. "I liked it better when you worked for Nick's papa and grandpapa in the garage behind us," he was saying. "In the old days, I at least got to see you and Nick."

He turned to Lauren with a beaming smile. "So, my little Laurie, now you know Nick *and* Mary *and* me. You are becoming one of the family."

He showed them to their table, then grinned at Lauren. "Ricco will take care of you," he said. "Ricco thinks you are beautiful—he blushes when your name is mentioned."

Ricco took their order and blushed when he put a glass of wine in front of Lauren. Mary's eyes twinkled, but when he left she looked directly at Lauren and said without preamble, "Would you like to talk about Nick?"

Lauren choked on her wine. "Please, let's not ruin a lovely lunch. I already know more than enough about him."

"What, for example?" Mary persisted gently.

"I know that he's an egotistical, arrogant, bad-tempered, dictatorial tyrant!"

"And you love him." It wasn't a question, it was a statement.

"Yes," Lauren said angrily.

Mary was struggling obviously to hide her amusement at Lauren's tone. "I was certain that you did. I also suspect that he loves you."

Trying to suppress the anguished hope that flared in her heart, Lauren turned her face to the stained-glass window near their table. "What makes you think so?"

"To begin with, he isn't treating you the way he normally treats the women in his life."

"I know that. He's nice to the others," Lauren said bitterly.

"Exactly!" Mary agreed. "He's always treated his women with an attitude of amused indulgence . . . of tolerant indifference. While an affair lasts he's attentive and charming. When a woman begins to bore him he courteously but firmly dismisses her from his life. Not once to my knowledge has any woman touched an emotion in him deeper than affection or desire. I've seen them try in the most inventive ways to make him jealous, yet he has reacted with nothing stronger than amusement, or occasionally exasperation. Which brings us to you."

Lauren blushed at being correctly categorized with the other women Nick had taken to bed, but she knew it was useless to deny it.

"You," Mary continued quietly, "have evoked genuine anger in him. He is furious with you and with himself. Yet he doesn't dismiss you from his life; he doesn't even send you downstairs. Doesn't it seem odd to you that he won't let you work for Jim, and simply have you come upstairs to act as translator when Rossi's call finally comes through?"

"I think he's keeping me up there for revenge," Lauren said grimly.

"I think he is too. Perhaps he's trying to get back at you for what you're making him feel. Or possibly he's trying to find fault with you, so that he won't feel the way he does any longer. I don't know. Nick is a complex man. Jim, Ericka and I are all very close to him, and yet he keeps each one of us at a slight distance. There's a part of himself that he will not share with others, not even us. . . . Why do you look so strange?" Mary interrupted herself to ask.

Lauren sighed. "If you're matchmaking, and I think you are, you have the wrong woman. You should be talking to Ericka, not me."

"Don't be silly—"

"Did you see the newspaper article about the party in Harbor Springs a few weeks ago?" Lauren's embarrassed gaze drifted away from Mary's face as she added, "I was in Harbor Springs with Nick, and he sent me home because Ericka was coming. He called her a 'business acquaintance.'"

"Well, she is!" Mary said, reaching across the table and giving Lauren's hand a squeeze. "They're close friends, and they're business acquaintances—and that's *all* they are. Nick is on the board of directors of her father's corporation, and her father is on Global's board of directors. Ericka was buying the house at the Cove from Nick. She's always loved it, and she probably went up there to close the deal."

Lauren's heart soared with sudden relief and happiness, even though her mind warned her that her situation with Nick was still hopeless. At least he hadn't taken her to his girlfriend's bed in his girlfriend's house! She waited while Ricco served them their food, then she asked, "How long have you known Nick?"

"Forever," Mary said. "I went to work as a bookkeeper for his father and grandfather when I was twenty-four. Nick was four years old. His father died six months after that."

"What was he like when he was little?" Lauren felt helplessly eager to learn everything she could about the powerful, enigmatic man who owned her heart and didn't seem to want it.

Mary smiled reminiscently. "We called him Nicky then. He was the most charming little dark-haired devil you've ever seen—proud like his father and stubborn occasionally. He was sturdy, cheerful and bright—exactly the sort of little boy that any mother would be proud to have. Except his own," she added, her face sobering.

"What about his mother?" Lauren persisted, remembering how reluctant Nick had been to talk about her in Harbor Springs. "He didn't say much about her."

"I'm amazed that he spoke of her at all. He *never* talks about her." Mary's glance strayed slightly as she thought back to the past. "She was an extraordinarily beautiful woman, as well as being rich, spoiled, pampered and moody. She was like a Christmas-tree ornament—beautiful to look at, but brittle and empty inside. Nicky adored her, despite all her faults.

"Right after Nicky's father died, she walked out, leaving Nicky with his grandparents. For months after she left the house, he watched out the window, waiting for her to come back. He understood that his father was dead and couldn't come back to him, but he refused to believe that his mother wasn't coming back either. He never asked about her, he just *waited* for her. I mistakenly thought his grandparents wouldn't let her come, and frankly, I blamed them for that—unfairly, as it turned out.

"And then one day, about two months before Christmas, Nicky stopped waiting at the window and suddenly became a whirlwind of activity. By then his father had been dead for nearly a year. His mother had remarried, and she'd just had a baby boy, though none of us knew about the baby. Anyway, Nicky became a bundle of energy; he did every chore he could think of that would earn him a nickel for doing it. He saved up all his money, and about two weeks before the holidays talked me into taking him shopping for 'an extraspecial present.'

"I thought he was searching for a gift for his grandmother, because he dragged me in and out of a dozen stores looking for something that was 'just perfect for a lady.' Not until late in the afternoon did I discover that he wanted to buy a Christmas present for his mother.

"In the bargain section of a huge downtown department store, Nicky finally found his 'extra-special present'—a lovely little enameled pillbox marked down to a fraction of what it should have cost. Nicky was ecstatic, and his enthusiasm was contagious. In five minutes he'd charmed the sales-clerk into gift wrapping it, and *me* into taking him over to his mother's house so that he could present her with the gift."

Mary glanced at Lauren with tear-brightened eyes. "He . . . he intended to *bribe* his mother into coming back to him, only I didn't realize it." She swallowed and then continued, "Nicky and I took the bus to Grosse Pointe, and he was so nervous he could hardly sit still. He kept making me check to see if his hair and clothes were tidy. 'Do I look all right, Mary?' he kept asking me again and again.

"We found the house without any trouble—a palatial estate that was beautifully decorated for the holidays. I started to ring the doorbell, but Nicky put his hand on my arm. I looked down at him, and I have never seen a child look so desperate. 'Mary,' he said, 'are you *sure* I look okay to see her?' "

Mary turned her face toward the restaurant window and her voice shook. "He looked so vulnerable, and he was such a handsome little boy. I honestly believed that if his mother saw him, she'd realize that he needed her, and she'd at least visit him from time to time. Anyway, a butler let us in, and Nicky and I were shown into a beautiful drawing room with an enormous Christmas tree that looked as if it had been decorated for the window of a department store. But Nicky didn't notice that. All he saw was the shiny red bicycle with the big bow on it that was beside the tree, and his face positively lit up. 'See,' he said to me, 'I knew she didn't forget me. She's just been waiting until *I* came to see *her*.' He reached out to touch the bicycle, and the maid who was dusting the room almost snapped his head off. The bicycle, she told him, was for the baby. Nicky pulled his hand away from it as if he'd been burned.

"When his mother finally came downstairs, her first words to her own son were, 'What do you want, Nicholas?' Nicky gave her the present and explained that he'd chosen it for her himself. When she started to put it under the tree, he insisted that she open it right then. . . ."

Mary had to wipe her eyes as she finished, "His mother opened the package, glanced at the dainty little pillbox and said, 'I don't take pills, Nicholas— you know that.' She handed it to the maid who was dusting the room, and said, 'Mrs. Edwards takes pills, however. I'm sure she'll put it to good use.' Nicky watched his gift go into the maid's pocket, and then he said very politely, 'Merry Christmas, Mrs. Edwards.' He looked at his mother and said, 'Mary and I have to go now.'

"He didn't say anything else until we got to our bus stop. I was fighting back tears the whole way, but Nicky's face was . . . expressionless. At the bus stop, he turned to me and pulled his hand out of mine. In a solemn little voice he said, 'I don't need her anymore, Mary. I'm all grown up now. I don't need anybody anymore.'" Mary's voice quavered. "It was the last time he ever let me hold his hand."

After a moment of painful silence, Mary went on, "From that day forward, to the best of my knowledge, Nick has never bought a gift for a woman—other than his grandmother and me. According to what Ericka has heard from Nick's girlfriends, he is extravagantly generous with his money, but he never gives them gifts, no matter what the occasion is. He gives them money instead and tells them to pick out something they'll like; he doesn't care whether it's jewelery or furs or anything else. But he doesn't pick it out himself."

Lauren remembered the beautiful earrings he'd given her, and the way she'd contemptuously informed him that she didn't want them. Her heart turned over. "Why would his mother want to forget about him, to pretend he didn't exist?"

"I can only guess. She was from one of the most prominent families in Grosse Pointe. She was an acclaimed beauty, the queen of the debutante ball. To people like that, bloodlines mean everything. They all have money, so their social status is based on the prestige of their family connections. When she married Nick's father, she became a social outcast from her own class. These days, that's changed—money is its own prestige. Nick moves in her social circles now and completely eclipses her and her husband. Of course, being handsome in addition to being outrageously rich doesn't hurt him a bit.

"At any rate, in the early days Nick must have been a living reminder of her fall from social grace. She didn't want him around, and neither did his stepfather. You would have to know the woman in order to comprehend such coldhearted, utter selfishness. The only person who matters to her, other than herself, is Nick's half brother—she positively dotes on him."

"It must be painful for Nick to see her."

"I don't think it is. The day she gave his present to the maid, his love for her died. He killed it himself, carefully and completely. He was only five years old, but he had the strength and determination that enabled him to do it, even then."

Lauren had a simultaneous urge to strangle Nick's mother and to find Nick and lavish on him her own love, whether he wanted it or not.

Just then Tony materialized at the table and handed Mary a small piece of paper with a name on it. "You've had a phone call from this man. He says he needs some papers that are locked in your office."

Mary glanced at the note. "I guess I'll have to go back. Lauren, you stay and finish your lunch."

"Why did you not eat your pasta?" Tony frowned accusingly at both women. "Does it not taste good?"

"It isn't that, Tony," Mary said, putting her napkin on the table and reaching for her purse. "I was telling Lauren about Carol Whitworth, and it ruined our appetites."

The name roared in Lauren's ears and pounded in her brain. A silent scream of denial rose up in her throat, cutting off her breath when she tried to speak.

"Laurie?" Tony worriedly squeezed her shoulder as she continued to stare in paralyzed horror at Mary's retreating back.

"Who?" she whispered frantically. "Who did Mary say?"

"Carol Whitworth. Nick's mama."

Lauren raised her stricken blue eyes to his. "Oh God," she breathed hoarsely. "Oh God, no!"

Lauren took a cab back to the building. The shock had faded slightly, leaving in its place a cold numbness. She walked into the marble lobby and went over to the reception desk, where she asked to use the phone. "Mary?" she said when the other woman answered. "I'm not feeling well—I'm going home."

Wrapped in her robe that night, she sat staring into the empty fireplace in her apartment. She pulled the afghan she had knitted the previous year closer around her shoulders, trying to ward off the chill, but it was inside her. It shuddered through her every time she thought of her last visit to the Whitworths: Carol Whitworth serenely presiding over an intimate little gathering where three people were plotting against her own son. Her son. Her beautiful, magnificent son. Oh God, how could she do that to him!

Lauren shivered with impotent fury and clutched at the afghan with fingers that longed to scratch and claw at Carol Whitworth's regal face—that vain, unlined, haughty, lovely face.

If there was any spying being done, Lauren felt sure it was Philip, not Nick, who was doing it. But if it was Nick, if he really was paying someone to leak information on the Whitworth Enterprises bids, she wouldn't blame him. If it had been within her power at that moment, she would have brought Whitworth Enterprises crashing down around Philip's ears.

Nick might love her; Mary thought he did. But Lauren would never know. The moment he discovered she was related to the Whitworths, he would kill whatever feelings he had for her, exactly as he had killed his feelings for his mother. He would want to know why she had applied for a job at Sinco, and he would never believe it was coincidence, even if she lied to him.

Lauren cast a bitter, contemptuous glance around the silken love nest where she was ensconced. She'd been living like Philip Whitworth's pampered mistress. But no longer. She was going home. If she had to, she would get two jobs and teach piano too, to make up for the difference in salary. But she couldn't stay in Detroit.. She'd go insane watching for a glimpse of Nick everywhere she went, wondering if he ever thought of her.

* * *

"Feeling better?" Jim asked the next morning. Dryly, he added, "Mary said she was talking about Carol Whitworth, and it made you ill."

Lauren's face was pale but composed as she closed his office door and handed him the sheet of paper she'd just rolled out of her typewriter.

He unfolded it and scanned the four simple lines. "You're resigning for personal reasons—what the hell does that mean? What personal reasons?"

"Philip Whitworth is a distant relative of mine. I didn't know until yesterday that Carol Whitworth is Nick's mother."

Shock jerked him erect in his chair. He stared at her in angry confusion, then he said, "Why are you telling me this?"

"Because you asked why I was resigning."

He watched her silently, the rigidity slowly fading from his features. "So you're related to his mother's second husband," he said finally. "So what?"

Lauren hadn't expected an argument. Exhausted, she sank into a chair. "Jim, when is it going to occur to you that as Philip Whitworth's relative, I could be spying on you for him?"

Jim's amber eyes turned sharp and piercing. "Are you, Lauren?"

"No."

"Has Whitworth asked you to?"

"Yes."

"And you agreed?" he snapped.

Lauren didn't know it was possible to feel this miserable. "I thought about it, but on my way to be interviewed here, I decided I couldn't do it. I never expected to be hired, and I wouldn't have been. . . ." Briefly, she told him how she had met Nick that evening. "And the next day you interviewed me and offered me a job."

She leaned her head back and closed her eyes. "I wanted to be near Nick. I knew that he worked in this building, so I accepted your offer. But I have never relayed one bit of information to Philip."

"I can't believe this," Jim said shortly, rubbing his fingers over his forehead as if he was getting a splitting headache. The moments ticked away in silence. Lauren was too desolate to notice or to care. She simply sat there, waiting for him to pronounce sentence on her. "It doesn't matter," he said finally. "You aren't quitting. I won't let you."

Lauren gaped at him. "What are you talking about? Don't you care that I could be telling Philip everything I know?"

"You aren't."

"How can you be sure?" she challenged.

"Common sense. If you were going to spy on us, you wouldn't walk in here to resign and tell me you're related to Whitworth. Besides, you're in love with Nick, and I think he's in love with you."

"I don't think he is," Lauren said with quiet dignity. "And even if he is, the minute he discovers who I am related to, he won't want anything to do with me. He'll insist on knowing why I happened to apply for a job at Sinco, and he'll never believe it was coincidence, even if I was willing to lie to him, which I'm not. . . ."

"Lauren, a woman can confess almost anything to a man if she chooses the right time to do it. Wait until Nick comes back, and then——"

When Lauren refused with a firm shake of her head, he threatened, "If you resign without notice like this, I won't give you a good reference."

"I don't expect one."

Jim watched her leave his office. For several minutes he was very still, his brows drawn together in a thoughtful frown. Then he slowly reached out and picked up the telephone.

"Mr. Sinclair." The secretary bent down beside Nick, her voice lowered to avoid disturbing the seven other major U.S. industrialists seated around the conference table discussing an international trade agreement. "I'm sorry to disturb you, sir, but there's a Mr. James Williams on the phone for you. . . ."

Nick nodded, already sliding his chair back, his face betraying none of the alarm he felt over this emergency interruption. He couldn't imagine what disaster could have arisen that would warrant Mary's having Jim call him here. The secretary showed him to a private room, and Nick snatched up the telephone. "Jim, what's wrong?"

"Nothing, I just needed some guidance."

"Guidance?" Nick repeated in angry disbelief.

"I'm in the middle of an international trade meeting and—"

"I know, so I'll be quick. The new sales manager I hired can come to work for us three weeks from now, on November fifteenth."

Nick swore in irritation. "So what?" he snapped.

"Well, the reason I'm calling is because I wanted to know if it would be all right if he reports for work in November, or if you'd rather have him wait and start in January as we originally discussed. I—"

"I can't believe this!" Nick interrupted furiously. "I don't give a damn when he starts, and you know it. November fifteenth is fine. What else?"

"That's about all," Jim replied imperturbably. "How's Chicago?"

"Windy!" Nick snarled. "So help me, if you've gotten me out of this meeting just to ask me that—"

"Okay, I'm sorry. I'll let you go. Oh, by the way, Lauren resigned this morning."

The announcement hit Nick like a slap in the face. "I'll talk to her on Monday when I get back."

"You won't be able to—her resignation's effective immediately. I think she plans to leave for Missouri tomorrow."

"You must be losing your touch," Nick gritted sarcastically. "Usually they fall in love with you, and you have to transfer them to another division to get them out of your hair. Lauren saved you the trouble."

"She's not in love with me."

"That's your problem, not mine."

"The hell it is! You wanted to play bedtime games with her, and when she wouldn't, you worked her until she was pale and exhausted. She's in love with you, and you've made her take messages from other women, made her—"

"Lauren doesn't give a damn about me!" Nick snapped furiously, "and I haven't got time to discuss her with you."

He slammed the phone into the cradle and stalked back into the conference room. Seven men glanced up at him with a mixture of polite concern and accusation. By mutual agreement, none of them was taking calls except in extreme emergency. Nick sat down in his chair and curtly said, "I apologize for the interruption. My secretary overestimated the importance of a problem and had the call forwarded here."

Nick tried to concentrate on the business at hand and nothing else, but visions of Lauren kept floating through his mind. In the middle of a heated discussion over marketing rights, he saw Lauren laughing, her face turned up to the sun, her hair blowing around her shoulders as they sailed on Lake Michigan.

He remembered looking up into her enchanting face.

"What happens to me if this slipper fits?"

"I turn you into a handsome frog."

Instead she'd turned him into a raving maniac! Jealousy had been driving him insane for two weeks. Every time her phone rang, he wondered which lover was calling her. Every time a man looked at her in the office, he had a wild urge to smash the man's teeth down his throat.

Tomorrow she'd be gone. On Monday he wouldn't see her. It was best for both of them. It was best for the whole goddamned corporation; his own executives were sidling out of the way when they saw him coming!

The meeting adjourned at seven o'clock, and when dinner was over, Nick excused himself to go up to his suite. As he walked down the main corridor of the fashionable hotel toward the elevators, he passed the window of an exclusive jewelry shop. A magnificent ruby pendant surrounded by glittering diamonds caught his eye and he paused. He looked at the matching earrings. Perhaps if he bought Lauren the pendant. . . . Suddenly he felt like a small boy again, standing beside Mary, buying a little enameled pillbox.

He turned away and stalked down the corridor. Bribery, he reminded himself savagely, was the lowest form of begging. He would not beg Lauren to change her mind. He would not beg anyone for anything.

He spent an hour and a half on the telephone in his suite, returning calls and dealing with business matters that had arisen in his absence. When he hung up, it was nearly eleven. He walked over to the windows and gazed out at the twinkling Chicago skyline.

Lauren was leaving. Jim said she was pale and exhausted. What if she was ill? What if she was pregnant? Hell, what if she was? He couldn't even be certain if it was his child or someone else's.

Once he could have been certain. Once he had been the only man she'd ever known. Now she could probably teach *him* things, he thought bitterly.

He thought of the Sunday afternoon he'd gone to her apartment to give her the earrings. When he'd tried to get her into bed, she'd exploded at him. Most women would have been satisfied with what he was offering, but not Lauren. She had wanted him to care, to be involved emotionally with her as well as sexually. She had wanted some sort of commitment from him.

Nick stretched out on the bed. It was just as well that she was leaving, he decided furiously. She should go back home and find some small-town jerk who'd grovel at her feet, tell her he loved her and make any commitment she wanted.

The meeting reconvened at precisely ten o'clock the following morning. Because all the men present were industrial giants whose time was extremely valuable, everyone was punctual. The chairman of the committee looked at the six men seated around the conference table and said, "Nick Sinclair will not be here today. He asked me to explain that he was called back to Detroit this morning on an urgent matter."

"We all have urgent matters pending," one of the members growled. "What the hell is Nick's problem that he can't be here?"

"He said it's a labor relations problem."

"That's no excuse!" another member exploded. "We all have labor relations problems."

"I reminded Nick of that," the chairman replied.

"What did he say?"

"He said that *nobody* has a labor relations problem like his."

Lauren carried another armload of her belongings out to her car, then she paused to look up at the overcast October sky. It was either going to rain or snow, she decided dismally.

She walked back into the apartment, leaving the door slightly ajar so that she could nudge it open with her foot when she carried out the next load of her things. Her feet were damp from splashing through the little puddles on the sidewalk, and she mechanically bent down and took off her canvas sneakers. She was planning to wear them when she drove home, so she'd have to dry them quickly. She carried them to the kitchen, put them in the oven and turned it on to Warm, leaving the oven door open.

Upstairs she put on another pair of shoes and closed the last suitcase. All she had to do now was write a note to Philip Whitworth, then she could leave. Tears burned her eyes, and she brushed them away with impatient fingertips. Picking up her suitcase, she carried it downstairs.

Halfway across the living room she heard footsteps coming from the kitchen behind her. She swung around in surprise, then froze as Nick stalked out of the kitchen. She saw the reckless glitter in his eyes as he came toward her, and her mind screamed a warning; he knew about Philip Whitworth.

Panicked, she dropped the suitcase and started edging away. In her haste she caught the backs of her knees on the arm of the sofa, lost her balance and landed flat on her back on the cushions.

His eyes gleaming with amusement, Nick looked at the delectable beauty sprawled invitingly across the sofa. "I'm flattered, honey, but I'd like something to eat first. What are you serving—besides baked shoes?"

Warily Lauren scrambled to her feet. Despite his humorous tone, there was an iron grimness in the set of his jaw, and every powerful muscle of his body was tensed. She took a cautious step out of his reach.

"Stand still," he ordered softly.

Lauren froze again. "Why . . . why aren't you at the international trade meeting?"

"As a matter of fact," he drawled, "I've asked myself that same question several times this morning. I asked myself that question when I walked out on seven men who require my vote on vitally important issues. I asked myself that question on the way here, when the woman in the seat beside me on the plane threw up in a bag."

Lauren choked back a nervous giggle. He was tense, he was angry, but he wasn't furious. Therefore he didn't know about Philip.

"I asked myself that question," he continued, advancing a step, "when I practically jerked an old man out of the back seat of a taxi and took it myself, because I was afraid I'd get here too late,"

Lauren tried desperately to decipher his mood and couldn't. "Now that you're here," she said shakily, "what do you want?"

"I want you."

"I told you—"

"I know what you told me," Nick interrupted impatiently. "You told me I'm too old and too cynical for you. Right?"

She nodded.

"Lauren, I am only two months older than I was in Harbor Springs. Even though I *feel* a hell of a lot older than I did then. But the fact is you didn't think I was too old for you then, and you don't really think so today. Now, I'll unload your car and you can start unpacking your things."

"I'm going home, Nick," Lauren said with quiet determination.

"No, you're not," he said implacably. "You belong to me, and if you force me to, I'll carry you up to bed and make you admit it there."

Lauren knew he could do exactly that. She backed away another step. "All you would prove is that you can physically overpower me. Nothing I admitted there would count. What does matter is that I don't want to belong to you in any way!"

Nick smiled somberly. "I want to belong to you . . . in every way."

Lauren's heart flung itself against her ribs. What did he mean, belong? She knew instinctively he wasn't offering marriage, but at least he was offering himself. What would happen if she told him now about Philip Whitworth?

238

Nick spoke, his coaxing voice tinged with desperation. "Consider what an amoral, unprincipled cynic I am—think of all the improvements you could make to my character."

The simultaneous urge to laugh and weep snapped Lauren's control. Her hair tumbled forward in a heavy curtain as she bent her head and fought back tears. She was going to do it; she was going to let herself become that sordid cliché—the secretary in love with her boss, having a secret affair with him. She was going to gamble her pride and self-respect on the chance that she could make him love her. She was going to risk having him hate her when she eventually told him about Philip.

"Lauren," Nick said hoarsely, "I love you."

Her head shot up. Unable to believe her ears, she stared at him through tear-glazed eyes.

Nick saw her tears and his heart sank with bitter defeat. "Don't you dare cry," he warned tersely, "I have never said that to a woman before, and I. . . ." His words trailed off as Lauren unexpectedly flung herself into his arms, her shoulders shaking. Uncertainly, he tipped her chin up and gazed at her face. Her thick lashes were spiky with tears, and her blue eyes were drenched with them. She tried to speak and Nick tensed, braced for the rejection he had dreaded all the way from Chicago.

"I think you are so beautiful," she whispered brokenly. "I think you are the most beautiful—"

A low groan tore from Nick's chest, and he smothered her mouth with his. Devouring her lips with the insatiable hunger that had been torturing him for weeks, he crushed her melting, pliant body to the rigid, starved contours of his own. He kissed her fiercely, tempestuously, tenderly, and still he could not get enough of her. At last he dragged his mouth from hers, fighting down the rampaging demands of his body, and held her in his arms, pressed against his pounding heart.

When he didn't move for several minutes, Lauren leaned back in his arms and raised her face to his. He saw the question in her eyes and the willing acceptance of his decision. She would lie beside him here, or anywhere else he chose.

"No," he murmured tenderly. "Not like this. I'm not going to walk in here and rush you into bed. I did something like that in Harbor Springs."

The impudent beauty in his arms smiled one of her bewitching smiles. "Are you really hungry? I could fix you some sautéed stockings to go with the shoes. Or would you prefer something more conventional, like an omelette?"

Nick chuckled and brushed a kiss over her smooth forehead. "I'll have my housekeeper fix something for me while I shower. Then I'm going to get some sleep. I didn't get any last night," he added meaningfully.

Lauren gave him a look of sham sympathy, which earned her another kiss.

"I suggest you sleep too, because when we come back from the party tonight, we're going to bed, and I intend to keep you awake until morning."

In fifteen minutes he had unloaded her car. "I'll pick you up at nine," he said when he was ready to leave. "It's black tie; do you have something formal to wear?"

Lauren hated to wear the clothes that had belonged to Philip Whitworth's mistress, but for tonight she didn't have any choice. "Where are we going?"

"To the Children's Hospital Benefit Ball at the Westin Hotel. I'm one of the sponsors, so I have tickets every year."

"That doesn't sound very discreet," Lauren said uneasily. "Someone may see us together there."

"Everyone will see us together. It's one of the social highlights of the year, which is why I want to take you. What's wrong with that?"

If the benefit ball was an elaborate society function, none of the other employees at Global were likely to be there, which explained to Lauren why Nick wasn't worried about causing office gossip. "Nothing's wrong with it. I'd love to go," she said, raising on tiptoe to kiss him goodbye. "I'd go anywhere with you."

17

NICK LOOKED BREATHTAKINGLY ELEGANT IN HIS RAVEN black tuxedo, snowy ruffled shirt and formal black bow tie when Lauren answered her door that night. "You look wonderful," she said softly.

His own gaze moved with glinting admiration over her vivid features, over her shining hair caught up in intricate sophisticated twists at the back of her head, then froze for a moment at the tantalizing display of her creamy breasts swelling above the neckline of her black velvet sheath gown before sweeping over the straight skirt, which was slashed at the side from knee to heel. "Don't you like it?" Lauren asked, handing him a black velvet cape that was lined with white satin.

"I love them," he said, and Lauren blushed when she realized what he was referring to.

The Westin Hotel was located in downtown Detroit's magnificent Renaissance Center. In honor of the ball, a red carpet had been laid from the curb to the hotel's main entrance. Television cameras were positioned on both sides of it. As Nick's chauffeur pulled his limousine to a stop, newspaper photographers jostled their way to the front, their cameras raised.

A doorman stepped forward and opened Lauren's door. When Nick followed her out of the limousine and took her elbow, flashbulbs exploded on both sides, and television cameras tracked their progress up the red carpet.

The first person Lauren saw when they walked into the crowded ballroom was Jim. He saw them too, and he watched them approaching with a look of ill-concealed glee on his face. Yet when he put out his hand, Lauren noticed that Nick hesitated before acknowledging the greeting.

"You're back early from Chicago," Jim remarked, seemingly oblivious to his friend's cold reserve. "I wonder why?"

"You know damned well why," Nick retorted grimly.

Jim's brows lifted, but he turned his tawny, appreciative gaze on Lauren. "I'd tell you how gorgeous you look, but at the moment, Nick is already restraining the urge to knock my teeth down my throat."

"Why?" Lauren gasped, her own gaze flying to Nick's granite features.

Jim answered with a chuckle. "It has something to do with two dozen red roses and a kiss he witnessed. He's forgotten about a girl I was in love with once but couldn't quite get up the nerve to ask to marry me. He got tired of waiting for me to bolster my courage, so he sent Ericka two dozen—"

Nick's breath exploded in laughter. "You bastard," he said good-naturedly, and this time his handclasp was sincere.

For Lauren it was a night of magic, a night filled with the scent of flowers, of twinkling chandeliers and glorious music. A night of dancing in Nick's arms and standing by his side while he introduced her to the people he knew—and he seemed to know everyone. People surrounded them the moment they stepped off the dance floor or paused to have a glass of champagne. It was obvious to Lauren that Nick was greatly respected and well liked, and she felt absurdly proud of him. And he was equally proud of her—she could see it in his warm smile when he introduced her to his acquaintants, and in the possessive way he kept his arm around her waist.

"Lauren?"

It was well after midnight. She tipped her head back and smiled up at him as they danced. "Hmmm?"

"I would like to leave now." The desire in his gray eyes told Lauren why. She nodded, and without a protest let him lead her off the dance floor.

She had just decided that this was the most perfect night of her life when a familiar voice sent panic shooting through her entire nervous system. "Nick," Philip Whitworth said, his voice raised slightly, his face a mask of cordiality, "It's nice to see you."

Lauren's blood ran cold. *Oh no! Not here, not like this!* she prayed wildly.

"I don't believe we've met this young lady," Philip added, his brows lifted toward Lauren in a politely inquiring manner that made her feel dizzy with relief.

She dragged her eyes from Philip and looked at Carol Whitworth and then Nick. Mother and son faced each other like polite strangers; a slim, regal blond woman and a tall, darkly handsome man who had her gray eyes. With cool courtesy, Nick introduced them as "Philip Whitworth and his wife, Carol."

In the limousine a few minutes later, Lauren could feel Nick watching her. "What's wrong?" he finally asked.

She drew an unsteady breath. "Carol Whitworth is your mother. Mary told me a few days ago."

His expression didn't alter. "Yes, she is."

"If I were your mother," Lauren said in a suffocated whisper, turning her head away. "I would be so proud of you. Every time I looked at you, I would think, that handsome, elegant, powerful man is my—"

"Your lover," Nick whispered, dragging her into his arms and kissing her with fierce tenderness.

Lauren slid her fingers through his thick dark hair, holding his mouth to hers. "I love you," she whispered.

A sigh of relief seemed to go through Nick's body. "I was beginning to think you were never going to say that."

Lauren snuggled in his arms, but her contentment was short-lived. Her relief that Philip Whitworth hadn't exposed her slowly gave way to alarm. By pretending not to know Philip and Carol in front of Nick, Lauren had participated in a flagrant deception that in a way made a fool of him. Panic rose in her chest. She would tell him tonight, after they made love. She had to tell him before the web of her deception entangled her more than it already had.

When they reached her apartment, Nick lifted her satin cape off her shoulders and draped it over a chair. His hands went to the buttons on his tuxedo jacket, and as he started to take it off, Lauren experienced a thrill of excitement. Turning, she walked over to the windows, trying to steady herself. She heard Nick come up behind her. "Would you like a drink?" she asked in a trembling voice.

"No." His arm slid around her waist, drawing her back against him as he bent his head and pressed a tantalizing kiss against her temple. Lauren's breathing became shallow and rapid as his warm lips touched her ear, then her nape, and his hands began moving lazily over her midriff. One hand angled down over her stomach to curve around her hip, while the other slid up and gently closed over a velvet-covered breast. His touch was exquisite delight, and when his fingers slipped beneath her bodice to tease and possessively caress her sensitive breast, Lauren felt the demanding heat of his rising passion pressing boldly against her from behind.

By the time his hands went to her shoulders, turning her into his arms, quick, piercing stabs of desire were shooting through Lauren's entire body. His parted lips touched hers as his arms drew her gently to his hardened length. He kissed her with a slow, melting hunger, which deepened moment by moment to a burning insistence and then burst into a ravenous urgency. His tongue plunged into her mouth in a deep, raw kiss.

Driven by a mixture of love and the fear of losing him, Lauren arched upward in a fevered need to share and stimulate his burgeoning passion. She felt the gasp of his breath against her mouth as her tongue teased his warm lips, felt the reflexive clutching of his hands on her back and hips as she caressed the hard muscled flesh of his back and shoulders.

Somewhere in the recesses of his passion-drugged mind Nick was aware that Lauren was kissing him as she had never kissed him before, and that she was sensuously moving her hips against his rigid arousal, deliberately inciting the tidal waves of desire that were surging through him. But he didn't actually compare the uninhibited woman in his arms with the shyly uncertain girl she had been in Harbor Springs until Lauren pulled back and started to unfasten the studs from his shirtfront.

He looked down at her graceful hands, and his traitorous mind instantly replayed the same moment in Harbor Springs—except then he had had to put her hand on his shirt and urge her to unbutton it. That night she had been inexperienced and shy. She had obviously gained a great deal of experience since then.

Icy regret and disappointment poured through

him, and he covered her fingers with his hands, stopping her. "Fix me a drink, will you?" he said, hating himself for what he was thinking and the way he was feeling about her.

Taken aback by the tired, defeated bitterness in his voice, Lauren dropped her hands. She went over to the bar, fixed him a bourbon and water and gave it to him. She saw his lips twist in a humorless smile when he noted that she remembered exactly what he preferred to drink, but without commenting on it, he lifted it to his lips and drank.

Lauren was bewildered by his attitude, but she was utterly stunned by his next words. Lowering the glass, he said, "Let's get it over with, so I can stop wondering. How many have there been?"

Lauren stared at him. "How many what?"

"Lovers," he clarified bitterly.

She could hardly believe her ears. After treating her as if her standards of morality were childish, after acting as if promiscuity was a virtue, after telling her how men preferred experienced women, he was jealous. Because now he cared.

Lauren didn't know whether to hit him, burst out laughing or hug him. Instead she decided to exact just a tiny bit of revenge for all the misery and uncertainty he had put her through. Turning, she walked over to the bar and reached for a bottle of white wine. "Why should the number make any difference?" she asked innocently. "You told me in Harbor Springs that men don't prize virginity anymore, that they don't expect or want a woman to be inexperienced. Right?"

"Right," he said grimly, glowering at the ice cubes in his glass.

"You also said," she continued, biting back a smile, "that women have the same physical desires men have, and that we have the right to satisfy them with whomever we wish. You were very emphatic about that—"

"Lauren," he warned in a low voice, "I asked you a simple question. I don't care what the answer is, I just want an answer so I can stop wondering. Tell me how many there were. Tell me if you liked them, if you didn't give a damn about them, or if you did it to get even with me. Just tell me. I won't hold it against you."

Like hell you wouldn't! Lauren thought happily as she struggled to uncork the bottle of wine. "Of course you won't hold it against me," she said lightly. "You specifically said—"

"I know what I said," he snapped tersely. "Now, how many?"

She flicked a glance in his direction, implying that she was bewildered by his tone. "Only one."

Angry regret flared in his eyes, and his body tensed as if he had just felt a physical blow. "Did you . . . care about him?"

"I thought I loved him at the time," Lauren said brightly, twisting the corkscrew deeper into the cork.

"All right. Let's forget him," Nick said curtly. He finally noticed her efforts with the wine bottle and walked over to help her.

"Are you going to be able to forget him?" Lauren

asked, admiring the ease with which he managed the stubborn cork.

"I will . . . after a while."

"What do you mean, after a while? You said there was nothing promiscuous about a woman satisfying her biological—"

"I know what I said, dammit!"

"Then why do you look so angry? You didn't lie to me, did you?"

"I didn't lie," he said, slamming the bottle onto the bar and reaching for a glass from the cabinet. "I believed it at the time."

"Why?" she goaded.

"Because it was *convenient* to believe it," he bit out. "I was not in love with you then."

Lauren loved him more at that moment than ever. "Would you like me to tell you about him?"

"No," he said coldly.

Her eyes twinkled, but she backed a cautious step out of his reach. "You would have approved of him. He was tall, dark and handsome, like you. Very elegant, sophisticated and experienced. He wore down my resistence in two days, and—"

"Dammit, stop it!" Nick grated in genuine fury.

"His name is John."

Nick braced both hands on the liquor cabinet, his back to her. "I do not want to hear this!"

"John Nicholas Sinclair," Lauren clarified.

The relief Nick experienced was so intense that he hardly knew how to cope with it. He straightened and turned toward her. Lauren was standing in the center of the room, an angel in seductive black velvet, an exquisitely sensual young beauty with unconscious poise in every graceful line of her body. There was a fineness about her, a quiet pride in herself that had prevented her from becoming a convenient receptacle for the passions of boys and men.

She was in love with him.

He could make her his mistress, or he could make her his wife. In his heart he knew that she belonged at his side as his bride; anything less would destroy her pride and shame her. That beautiful body of hers had been offered only to him. He could not accept her gift and her love and in return offer her some obscure, tenuous thing called a "meaningful relationship." Although she was very young he loved her, and she was wise enough not to play games with his life. She was also stubborn, willful and courageously defiant, as he had learned to his intense fury and frustration during the past several weeks. . . .

He looked at her in silence, and then he drew a long deep breath. "Lauren," he began gravely, "I would like four daughters with wobbly blue eyes and studious horn-rimmed glasses on their little noses. Also, I've become very partial to your honey-colored hair, so if you could manage. . . ." He saw the tears of joyous disbelief filling her eyes, and he jerked her into his arms, crushing her against his heart, jarred by the same emotions that were shaking her. "Darling, please don't cry. Please don't," he whispered thickly, kissing her forehead, her cheek and finally her lips. Reminding himself that this was only Lauren's second experience with lovemaking, and that he was not going to rush her, Nick leaned down, swung her into his arms and carried her upstairs to the bedroom.

With his mouth still locked to hers, he slipped his hand from beneath her knees. The exquisite sensation of her legs sliding down his thighs made him catch his breath sharply. While he removed his clothes, Lauren undressed before his burning gaze. And when her lacy undergarments finally drifted to the floor, she lifted her face to his and stood before him unashamedly.

A shattering feeling of tenderness made Nick's hands shake as he cupped her face between his palms, his fingers trembling over her smooth features. After weeks of stubbornly defying him and coldly denying him, Lauren was looking at him now with unconcealed surrender. Love glowed in her eyes, a love so quietly intense that he felt both humbled and profoundly proud. "Lauren," he said, his deep voice raw with the new, unaccustomed emotions inside him, "I love you too."

In answer, she slid her hands up his bare chest, wrapped her arms around his neck and pressed herself against the full length of his naked, rigidly aroused body, sending flames of desire shooting uncontrollably through his bloodstream. Trying to restrain his exploding passion, he bent his head and kissed her. Her soft lips parted; his tongue slipped between them for one sweet arousing taste, withdrew . . . then hungrily, urgently, plunged again, and suddenly it was out of control. With a low groan he pulled her down onto the bed and rolled her onto her back, pressing her into the pillows, his hands and mouth fiercely urgent as he kissed and caressed her.

Somewhere in the tumult of her whirling senses, Lauren realized that Nick's lovemaking was different tonight. In Harbor Springs he had handled her body as a maestro handles a familiar instrument, his hands deft, skilled; tonight there was a tormenting gentleness, a subtle reverence in the way his hands caressed and excited her. In Harbor Springs his passion had been carefully controlled, restrained; tonight he was as desperate for her as she was for him.

His lips and tongue touched her breasts, circling her hardened nipples, and Lauren lost the ability to think at all. Her fingers clenched convulsively in his thick hair, holding his head to her breast, then glided over the bunched muscles of his shoulders and arms. "I want you," he whispered hoarsely. "I want you so much!"

His hoarse words of passion inflamed her, and his whispered endearments stirred her to her soul. Each touch of his seeking fingers, each brush of his lips and tongue sent her soaring higher and higher into a universe where nothing existed except the wild beauty of his lovemaking.

When his hands parted her thighs, Lauren moaned in her throat and arched her hips to him. Nick's restraint broke. His lips captured hers in a deep, raw kiss and he plunged into her incredible warmth. "Move with me, darling," he coaxed thickly, and when Lauren did, he groaned and drove full length into her. The fierce hunger of his deep strokes, the urgency of each thrust, sent waves of shivering ecstacy shooting through Lauren, an ecstacy that finally exploded with a force that tore a low scream from her throat. Nick tightened his arms around her, crushing her to him, and with one final plunge, he joined her in blissful oblivion.

Early the next morning she was jarred awake by the harsh ringing of the phone. Reaching across Nick's naked chest, she picked up the receiver and answered it. "It's Jim—for you," she said, handing him the phone.

After a brief conversation he hung up, then swung his legs off the bed and combed his hands through his hair. "I have to fly to Oklahoma today," he explained with a mixture of regret and resignation. "A few months ago I bought an oil company owned by a man who over the years had alienated all his employees. My people have been trying to negotiate with those same employees on their new contracts, but they're used to promises being made and not kept. They're demanding to talk to me, or else they're going on strike." He was already pulling on his trousers and shrugging into his shirt.

"I'll see you tomorrow at the office," he promised a few minutes later at the front door. He drew her into his arms for a long, drugging kiss, then reluctantly released her. "I may have to fly all night to get here, but I'll be back tomorrow. I promise."

18

DOZENS OF WATCHFUL, SPECULATIVE FACES TURNED TO watch Lauren's progress through the office Monday morning. Bewildered, she hung up her coat and cointinued to her desk, where she found Susan Brook and a half dozen other women gathered around it.

"What's up?" she asked. She felt radiantly happy; Nick had called her twice from Oklahoma, and sometime today she would see him again.

"You tell us," Susan said gaily. "Isn't that you?" She plunked the Sunday newspaper down on Lauren's desk and smoothed it out.

Lauren's eyes widened. An entire page had been devoted to the Children's Hospital Benefit Ball. In the center was a color picture of her—with Nick. They were dancing, and he was grinning down at her. Lauren's face was in profile, tilted up to his. The caption read, "Detroit industrialist J. Nicholas Sinclair and companion."

"It does look like me, doesn't it?" she hedged,

glancing at the excited, avidly curious faces surrounding her desk. "Isn't that an amazing coincidence?" She didn't want her relationship with Nick to be public knowledge until the time was right, and she certainly didn't want her co-workers to treat her any differently.

"You mean it isn't you?" one of the women said disappointedly. None of them noticed the sudden lull, the silence sweeping over the office as people stopped talking and typewriters went perfectly still. . . .

"Good morning, ladies," Nick's deep voice said behind Lauren. Six stunned women snapped to attention, staring in fascinated awe as Nick leaned over Lauren from behind and braced his hands on her desk. "Hi," he said, his lips so near her ear that Lauren was afraid to turn her head for fear he would kiss her in front of everyone. He glanced at the newspaper spread out on her desk. "You look beautiful, but who's that ugly guy you're dancing with?" Without waiting for an answer, he straightened, affectionately rumpled the hair on the top of her head and strolled into Jim's office, closing the door behind him.

Lauren felt like sinking through the floor in embarrassment. Susan Brook raised her brows. "What an amazing coincidence," she teased.

Nick came out of Jim's office a few minutes later and asked Lauren to come upstairs with him. Once they were in his office, he pulled her into his arms for a long, satisfying kiss. "I missed you," he whispered, then he sighed and reluctantly released her, linking his hands behind her back. "I'm going to miss you even more—I have to leave for Casano in an hour. Rossi couldn't reach me, so he called Horace Moran in New York. Apparently some Americans are snooping around the village, asking questions about him. I have a security team checking it out. In the meantime, Rossi's gone into hiding, and there's no phone where he is.

"I'm going to take Jim with me. Ericka's father panicked and sent Ericka to Casano to try to soothe Rossi. She speaks some Italian. I'll be back on Wednesday, or Thursday at the latest."

He frowned. "Lauren, I never explained to you about Ericka—"

"Mary did," she said, managing to look cheerful even though she felt miserable about his leaving. Besides missing him, she would also have another three or four days of anxiety, waiting to tell him about Philip. She definitely couldn't tell him now, when he was about to go away. His anger would ferment and simmer for days. She had to tell him when she could be with him to soothe it. "Why are you taking Jim?"

"When the president of Sinco retires next month, Jim is going to take over the position. By taking him with me, we can discuss immediate goals and long-range plans for Sinco." He grinned at her. "Also," he admitted, "I'm feeling very grateful to Jim for his interference in our lives, and I've decided to interfere with his. By taking him to Italy, where Ericka is . . . I see you understand my thinking," he said when she started to smile.

With a final hug he let her go, then he went over to his desk and began shoving papers into his briefcase. "If Rossi calls again, I've told Mary to transfer his call to you wherever you are. Assure him that I'm on my way and that there's nothing to worry about.

"We have four labs testing samples of Rossi's formula right now. Within two weeks we should know whether he's a genius or a fake, and until we know which he is, we'll assume he's not a fake and pamper him."

Lauren listened to his rapid-fire monologue with an inward smile of admiration. Being married to Nick was going to be like living on the fringe of a tornado, and she was going to be caught up in the whirl.

"By the way," he said, so casually that Lauren was instantly on guard, "a magazine reporter called me this morning. They know who you are and they know we're getting married. When the story breaks, I'm afraid the press will start hounding you."

"How did they find out?" Lauren gasped.

He shot her a glinting smile. "I told them."

Everything was happening so quickly that Lauren felt dazed. "Did you happen to tell them when and where we're getting married?" she chided.

"I told them soon." He closed his briefcase and drew her out of the chair in which she had just sat down. "Do you want a big church wedding with a cast of hundreds—or could you settle for me in a little chapel somewhere, with just your family and a few friends? When we come back from our honeymoon we could throw a huge party, and that would satisfy our social obligations to everyone else we know."

Lauren quickly considered the burden a big church wedding would place on her father's health and nonexistent finances, and the highly desirable alternative of becoming Nick's wife right away. "You and a chapel," she said.

"Good." He grinned. "Because I would go quietly insane waiting to make you mine. I'm not a patient man."

"Really?" She straightened the knot in his tie so that she'd have an excuse to touch him. "I never noticed that."

"Brat," he said affectionately, then he added, "I've written a check and given it to Mary. Put it in your bank, take a few days off and use it to buy your trousseau while I'm gone. It's rather a large check. You won't be able to spend it all on clothes. Use the rest of it to buy something special as a memento of our engagement. Jewelry," he said, "or a fur."

When he left, Lauren leaned back against his desk, her smile tinged with wistful sadness as she remembered Mary's words at lunch. "From that day forward Nick has never bought a gift for a woman. . . . He gives them money instead and tells them to pick out something they'll like . . . he doesn't care if it's jewelry or furs. . . ."

She shoved the gloomy thought aside. Someday, perhaps, Nick would change. In the meantime she had more to be thankful for than any woman alive.

She glanced at her wristwatch. It was ten-fifteen, and she still hadn't done any work.

Jack Collins stared dazedly at the big round clock on the wall across from his hospital bed, fighting the grogginess he always got from the hypodermics they gave him before they took him down for tests. He tried to focus, to concentrate. The clock said ten-thirty. It was Monday. Rudy was supposed to call with the results of the investigation on the bilingual secretary who'd been assigned to Nick Sinclair.

As if he had conjured up the call, the phone beside his bed began to ring. He groped for it and missed, then brought the receiver to his ear.

"Jack," the voice said, "this is Rudy."

Jack slowly composed a mental image of Rudy's round face, his beady eyes. "Did you check out the Danner woman?" he asked.

"Yeah," Rudy said. "I checked her out, just like you said. She's livin' in a fancy condo in Bloomfield Hills, and some old guy is payin' her rent. I talked to the gatekeeper, and he said this old guy keeps the place for his mistresses. The last dame who lived there was a redhead. Old man Whitworth came calling on her one night and found her entertaining another man, and he threw her out.

"The gatekeeper says Danner lives nice and quiet —he can see her condo from his gate." Rudy's chuckle was lewd. "The gatekeeper said Whitworth isn't getting his money's worth out of her, because he's only been there once since she moved in. The way I figure it, Whitworth's gettin' old and. . . ."

Jack struggled against the fog that seemed to cloud his senses. "Who?"

"Whitworth," Rudy said. "Philip A. Whitworth. I figure he's lost the urge and—"

"Listen to me, and shut up!" Jack rasped. "They're taking me downstairs for tests, and they gave me a shot that's putting me to sleep. Go to Nick Sinclair and tell him what you've told me. Have you got that? Tell Nick—" dizziness washed over Jack in waves "—tell him I think she's the leak in the Rossi deal."

"She's what? She is? You gotta be kidding! That broad is . . ." Rudy's tone changed from scorn to military self-importance. "I'll take care of it Jack, you leave everything to—"

"Shut up, damn you, and listen to me!" Jack rasped. "If Nick Sinclair is away, go to Mike Walsh, the corporation's chief attorney, and tell him what I said. Don't talk to anyone else about it. Then I want you to watch her. I want her office calls monitored. I want you to keep track of every move she makes. Get another man to help you. . . ."

Lauren was staring dreamily into space when the phone rang on Tuesday morning. She was so happy and so excited that she could hardly concentrate on the mundane tasks of her job. Even if she had wanted to get Nick off her mind, which she didn't, it would have been impossible to stop thinking of him, because the office staff was teasing her constantly. She answered the telephone and absently noted the tiny click that had occurred every time she'd picked it up since yesterday. "Lauren, my dear," Philip Whitworth said smoothly, "I think we ought to have lunch together today."

It wasn't an invitation, it was an order. With every fiber of her being, Lauren longed to tell Philip Whitworth off and hang up on him, but she didn't dare. If she angered him, there was always the chance that Philip might tell Nick who and what she was before she had a chance to tell him herself. Then, too, she was living in Philip's apartment, and she couldn't move away while Nick was gone because he wouldn't be able to call her. If he called her at the office, she could tell him she was moving into a motel, but she'd have to invent a reason, and she didn't want to add an outright lie to her deceit. "All right," she agreed unenthusiastically. "But I can't be away from the office for very long."

"We can hardly dine in your building, Lauren," Philip reminded her sarcastically.

A frisson of alarm tingled over her at his tone. She felt uneasy about being alone with him, uneasy about what he wanted to say to her. Then she remembered Tony's and felt better. "I'll meet you at Tony's restaurant at noon. Do you know where it is?"

"Yes, but forget it. You can't get a table there unless—"

"I'll make the reservation," Lauren said briskly.

The restaurant was jammed with people waiting to be seated when she got there. Tony saw her and managed a harassed smile from across the room, but it was Dominic who took her to her table. The young man blushed furiously at Lauren's wan smile of greeting. "Your table is not so good, Lauren. I am sorry. If you will call sooner next time, you will have a better one."

Lauren understood what he meant when he led her toward the tables at the back of the dining room that adjoined the cocktail lounge. The dimly lit lounge was separated from the room by nothing more substantial than stained-wood trelises covered with climbing plants. A steady din of conversation punctuated with laughter was coming from the crowded cocktail lounge, and waiters rushed back and forth to the coffeepots that were kept in an alcove beside the table.

Philip Whitworth was already seated, idly swirling the ice cubes in his glass, when Lauren walked up to the table. He stood politely, waited until Dominic had seated her, and then offered her a glass of wine. He looked very calm, very composed, very . . . pleased, she thought, as she noted his expression. "Now then," he said, "suppose you tell me how things really stand between you and our mutual friend. . . ."

"You mean your stepson!" Lauren corrected bitterly, angered that he still intended to deceive her.

"Yes, my dear," he responded quickly, "but let's not use his name in this very public place."

Recollections of the way he and his wife had treated Nick ripped through Lauren until she was seething inside. She tried to remember that Philip had not actually mistreated her, however, and her voice was carefully tempered. "Within the next day or two you're going to read it in the papers, so I'll tell you now that we're going to be married."

"Congratulations," he said pleasantly. "Have you told him yet about your . . . relationship with me? He obviously knew nothing about it when we encountered you two at the charity ball."

"I'm going to tell him very soon."

"I don't think that's a good idea, Lauren. He feels a certain animosity toward my wife and me—"

"With very good reason!" Lauren said before she could stop herself.

"Ah, I see you already know the story. Since you do, consider how he will then react when he discovers you've been living as my mistress, wearing clothes I purchased for you."

"Don't be ridiculous! I'm not your mistress—"

"*We* know that, but will *he* believe it?"

"I will make him believe it," Lauren said in a low, taut voice.

Philip's smile was coolly shrewd, calculating. "I'm afraid you'll find it impossible to convince him if he also thinks you told me about his little project in Casano."

Panic was streaking through Lauren in paralyzing waves, and alarm bells were clanging in her stricken mind. "I told you nothing about Casano, absolutely nothing! I've never told you anything confidential."

"He will believe you told me about Casano."

She clasped her hands on the table to still their trembling. Slowly, relentlessly, fear was uncoiling its silky tendrils in her stomach. "Philip, are you

. . . threatening to tell him I was your mistress, to tell him those other lies?"

"Not threatening you, exactly," he replied smoothly. "We're about to strike a bargain, you and I, and I merely want you to understand that you are not in a position to argue with my terms."

"What bargain?" Lauren said, but God help her, she already knew.

"In return for my silence, I will occasionally ask you for information."

"And you think I'll give it to you?" she said with tearful scorn. "You honestly believe that?" Tears burned behind her eyes and choked her voice. "I would die before I'd do anything to hurt him, do you understand me?"

"You're overreacting," he said sharply, leaning forward. "I don't want to put the man out of business—I'm only trying to save my own company. It's faltering badly because of Sinco's competition."

"That's just too bad!" Lauren hissed.

"It may mean nothing to you, but Whitworth Enterprises is Carter's birthright, his inheritance, and that's very important to my wife. Now, let's stop arguing about whether or not you're going to help, because you have no choice. Friday is the deadline for getting bids in on four major contracts. I want to know the amount Sinco is bidding." He produced a small piece of paper with the names of four projects written on it, uncurled Lauren's fingers, placed it in her hand and squeezed her fingers around it. Then he gave her hand a friendly, paternal pat. "I'm afraid I have to get back to the office," he said, shoving his chair back.

Lauren looked at him, so immersed in rage that she felt nothing else, not even fear. "These bids are very important to you?" she asked.

"Very."

"Because your wife wants to preserve the company for her son? That's very important to her?"

"More important than you can imagine. Among other things, if I tried to sell the company now, which is my only alternative, our finances would become a matter of public record. It would be most embarrassing."

"I see," Lauren said with deadly calm. To convince him for the time being that she intended to cooperate, she added carefully, "And you promise not to tell any of those lies to Nick if I help you?"

"My word of honor," he said.

Lauren walked into the office still in a state of cold, murderous rage. Carol Whitworth wanted to purchase her beloved second son's "inheritance" by destroying what her first son had built. They actually expected Lauren to help. She was being blackmailed, and the blackmail would never end, she knew. The Whitworths were greedy, ruthless and unscrupulous. Before they were finished, Global Industries would become another part of Carter's inheritance.

A few minutes later, the phone on her desk rang. Automatically she picked it up. "I hate to rush you, my dear," Philip's voice said smoothly, "but I want that information today. You'll find the bids that you need somewhere in the engineering department. If I could have the cover sheet it would help us immensely."

"I'll do my best," Lauren said tonelessly.

"Excellent. Very sensible. I'll meet you down in front of the building at four o'clock. Just run down to the lobby, and I'll be waiting in the car. The entire matter will take you only ten minutes."

Lauren hung up and walked through the offices to the engineering department. For the present, she had no concern about acting suspiciously. As soon as Jim returned, she herself would tell him what had happened. Perhaps he would even help her tell Nick.

"Mr. Williams would like the files on these four jobs," she told the secretary in engineering.

In a matter of moments Lauren had all four files. She took them back to her desk. In the front of each file was a cover sheet showing the name of the job, a summary of the technical equipment that would be provided if Sinco was awarded the contract and the amount Sinco was bidding.

Lauren removed the sheets and went over to the copy machine, then she took the copies and the originals back to her desk. She put the originals back in the files, removed some correction fluid from her desk drawer, and very carefully, very calmly changed the amounts Sinco was bidding, increasing each figure by several million dollars. The correction fluid was visible on the copy she was working with, but when she ran duplicates of it, the fluid was invisible and the changes impossible to detect. She was just turning away from the copy machine when a young man with a round face stepped forward. "Excuse me, miss," he said, "I'm from the company who services this photocopy machine, and it's been having problems all day. Would you mind running those originals through the machine again so I can see if it's working properly?"

A vague uneasiness stirred in Lauren, but the machine had been breaking down regularly, so she complied. He removed the copies produced from the tray, glanced at them, and nodded. "Looks like its really fixed this time," he said.

Lauren saw him drop the copies in the wastebasket as she turned away.

She did not see him stoop to retrieve them a moment later.

As she walked across the lobby, a Cadillac pulled up at the curb. The window on her side moved down electronically, and Lauren leaned into the car and handed Philip the envelope.

"I hope you understand how important this is to us," he began "and—"

Fury roared through Lauren, screaming in her ears. She turned on her heel and ran back into the building. She almost knocked over the young man with the round face, who hastily concealed a camera behind his back.

19

"THANK GOD YOU'RE BACK!" MARY BURST OUT LATE Wednesday afternoon when Nick strode swiftly into his office, followed by Ericka and Jim. "Mike Walsh needs to talk to you immediately. He says it's an emergency."

"Have him come up," Nick said, shrugging out of his suit jacket. "And then come and join us in a toast. I'm about to whisk Lauren off to Las Vegas to get married. The plane is being refueled and checked out right now."

"Does Lauren know about this?" Mary said, frowning. "She's downstairs in Jim's office, hard at work."

"I'll convince her of the wisdom of the plan."

"When the plane is airborne and she has no choice," Ericka put in with a knowing smile.

"Exactly." Nick grinned in high good spirits. He had missed her so much that he'd called her three times a day, every day, like a lovesick schoolboy. "Make yourselves comfortable," he added over his shoulder. Reaching into a wide closet that held several changes of clothing, he took out a fresh shirt.

Five minutes later, he walked out of the bathroom, freshly shaven, and glanced at Mike Walsh and the round-faced man who were standing near the couch where Jim and Ericka were seated. "What's up, Mike?" he asked, going over to the bar and removing a bottle of champagne, his back to the others.

"There's a security leak in the Rossi project," the attorney began cautiously.

"Right. I told *you* that."

"The men in Casano trying to find out about Rossi were Whitworth's men."

Only a momentary stillness in Nick's hand as he unwound the wire from the plastic champagne cork betrayed his tension at the mention of Whitworth's name. "Go on," he urged evenly.

"Evidently," the attorney continued, "there's a woman on our payroll who appears to have been spying for Whitworth. I arranged for Rudy here to listen in on the extension of her office telephone and to keep her under surveillance."

Nick took down four champagne glasses from the bar, his mind dwelling on Lauren's smile, her beautiful face. Tonight was going to be their wedding night. After tonight he and he alone would have the right to take her in his arms, to join his starved body with hers, to kiss and caress her. . . . "I'm listening," he lied. "Go on."

"Yesterday she was photographed passing him copies of four of Sinco's bids. We have in our possession a set of the copies she passed to Whitworth to use as proof in court."

"That son of a—" Nick fought down his blaze of fury, trying not to let his animosity for Philip Whitworth spoil his mood. This was his wedding day. Coolly he said, "Jim, I'm going to do what I should have done five years ago. I'm going to put him out of business. From now on, I want Sinco to bid on every job he bids on, and I want you to bid below our cost. Is that clear? I want that bastard out of our hair!"

When Jim murmured agreement, Mike continued. "We can swear out a warrant for the young woman's arrest. I've already discussed the matter with Judge Spath, and he is ready to do so as soon as you give the word."

"Who is she?" Jim demanded when Nick seemed more interested in pouring champagne into his glasses.

"Whitworth's mistress!" Rudy burst out eagerly, his voice ringing with pompous self-importance. "I checked her out personally. The dame is living like a queen in a fancy Bloomfield Hills condo that Whitworth's paying for. She dresses like a model, and. . . ."

Dread exploded in Nick's chest, and his whole body tensed against the agonizing certainty already pounding in his brain. His mind formed the question, but before he could force the words out, he had to brace his hands on the bar for support. With his back still to them, he whispered, "Who is she?"

"Lauren Danner," the attorney said, cutting off a further descriptive outpouring from the eager security man. "Nick, I know she's been working for you personally and that she's the girl who practically fell at our feet that night. The publicity involved in her arrest will definitely help discourage anyone else who might consider spying on us, but I waited to talk to you before we pressed charges against her. Shall I—"

Nick's voice was strangled with fury and pain. "Go back to your office," he ordered, "and wait there. I'll call you." Without turning, he jerked his head in Rudy's direction. "Get him out of my sight, and keep him out—permanently!"

"Nick—" Jim spoke to Nick's back.

"Get out!" Nick's voice lashed like a whip crack, then became dangerously controlled. "Mary, call Lauren and have her come up here in ten minutes. Then you go home. It's nearly five."

In the tomblike silence that followed their departure, Nick straightened from the bar and tossed down the champagne he had poured to celebrate his marriage to an angel. A princess with laughing blue eyes who had walked into his life and turned it upside down. Lauren was spying on him, betraying him to Whitworth. Lauren was Whitworth's mistress.

His heart shouted a denial, but his mind knew it was true. It explained the way she lived, the clothes she wore.

He recalled introducing her to Whitworth on Saturday night, and as he remembered the way she'd pretended not to know him, he felt as if he was shattering into a million pieces. Fury and anguish poured through his veins like acid. He wanted to crush her in his arms and make her say it wasn't true; he wanted to pour his love into her until there was no room for anyone in her heart or her body but him.

He wanted to strangle her for her treachery, to murder her with his own hands.

He wanted to die.

Lauren glanced at the three security guards who were standing in Nick's private reception area as she hurried toward his office. They watched her, their expressions strangely alert, wary. She smiled slightly as she passed them, but only one of them responded —he nodded, a curt unfriendly inclination of his head.

At Nick's office door she paused to smooth her hair. Her hand trembled with a mixture of delight at seeing him again and fear over how he was going to react when she told him of her involvement with Philip. She had intended to tell him tonight, after he'd had time to relax, but now that Philip was blackmailing her she had to tell him right away. "Welcome back," she said, walking into his suite.

Nick was standing at the window with his back to her, one hand braced high against the frame, staring out across the city. The drapes were drawn over the remainder of the glass wall, and none of the lights had been turned on to dispel the gloom of a prematurely dark and rainy night.

"Close the door," he said softly. His voice sounded strange, but his back was toward her as she walked to him and she couldn't see his face.

"Did you miss me, Lauren?" he asked, still without turning.

Lauren smiled at the question he always asked her when he had been away from her. "Yes," she admitted, boldly sliding her arms around his waist from behind. His body seemed to tense at her touch, and when she rubbed her cheek against his broad, muscular back, it felt as hard as iron.

"How much did you miss me?" he whispered silkily.

"Turn around and I'll show you," she teased.

His hand came down from the window, and he turned. Without looking at her he walked over to the sofas and sat down. "Come over here," he invited smoothly.

Lauren obediently went over to the sofa and stood looking down into his handsome, shadowed face, trying to read his strange mood. His expression was impassive, almost aloof, but when she started to sit beside him, he caught her wrist and pulled her onto his lap.

"Show me how much you want me," he urged.

There was an odd note in his voice that sent unexplainable alarm dancing down Lauren's spine, but it was promptly squelched by the commanding insistence of his mouth on hers. He kissed her thoroughly, expertly, and Lauren helplessly surrendered to the torrid demands of his lips. He had missed her. His fingers were already unfastening her silk blouse, pulling her bra down to expose her breasts as he lowered her onto the sofa and covered her half-naked body with his. His mouth skillfully aroused her swelling breasts and hardened nipples, while his hand insinuated itself beneath her skirt and pulled down the lace band of her underpants. "Do you want me now?"

"Yes," Lauren gasped, writhing beneath him.

His free hand shoved into the hair at her scalp and tightened. "Then open your eyes, honey," he ordered softly. "I want to be sure you know it's me who's on top of you and not Whitworth."

"Nick . . . !" Lauren's frantic scream was strangled as Nick lunged to his feet, twisted his hand in her hair and cruelly jerked her up with him.

"Listen to me. Please!" Lauren cried out, terrified by the black rage, the virulent hatred blazing in his eyes. "I can explain everything, I—" A low scream tore from her throat as he tightened his grip in her hair, wrenching her head around and down.

"Explain that," he ordered in a terrifying whisper.

Lauren's gaze froze in terror on the papers scattered across the coffee table: copies of the four bids she had given Philip; enlarged black-and-white photographs showing her leaning into his car; the license plate on the back of his Cadillac, and the State of Michigan registration showing Philip A. Whitworth as the owner of the vehicle. "Please, I love you! I—"

"Lauren," he interrupted in a menacingly soft voice. "Will you still love me five years from now when you and your lover get out of prison?"

"Oh Nick, please listen to me," she implored

brokenly. "Philip isn't my lover, he's a relative. He sent me to Sinco to apply for a job, but I swear I've never told him anything." The rage drained from Nick's face, replaced by a terrible contempt that alarmed Lauren so much her words tumbled out in a disjointed frenzy. "Until . . . until he saw us at the dance, he let me alone, but now he's trying to blackmail me. He threatened to tell you lies if I didn't—"

"Your relative," Nick repeated with freezing sarcasm. "Your relative is trying to blackmail you."

"Yes!" Lauren feverishly tried to explain. "Philip thought you were paying someone to spy on him, so he sent me here to find out who, and—"

"Whitworth is the only one paying a spy," Nick jeered scathingly. "And the only spy is you!" He released her and tried to push her away, but Lauren clung to him.

"Please listen to me," she begged wildly. "Don't do this to us!"

Nick jerked her arms loose, and she crumpled to the floor, her shoulders racked with deep choking sobs. "I love you so much," she wept hysterically. "Why won't you listen to me? Why? I'm *begging* you to just listen to me."

"Get up!" he snapped. "And button your blouse." He had already started toward the door. Her chest heaving with convulsive, silent sobs, Lauren straightened her clothing, braced a hand on the coffee table and slowly pushed herself to her feet.

Nick wrenched the door open and the security

guards stepped forward. "Get her out of here," he ordered icily.

Lauren stared in paralyzed terror at the men coming purposefully toward her. They were taking her to jail. Her gaze flew to Nick, silently imploring him for the last time to listen, to believe, to stop this.

With his hands in his pockets, he returned her gaze without flinching, his chiseled features a mask of stone, his eyes like chips of gray ice. Only the muscle jerking in his tightly clenched jaw betrayed the fact that he was feeling any emotion at all.

The three armed guards surrounded her, and one of them took her by the elbow. Lauren yanked free, her blue eyes deep pools of pain. "Don't touch me." Without looking back, she walked with them out of his office and across the silent, deserted reception area.

When the door closed behind her, Nick went over to the sofa. Sitting down with his forearms resting on his knees, he stared at the enlarged black-and-white photo of Lauren handing Whitworth the stolen copies of the bids.

She was very photogenic, he thought with a stab of bittersweet pain. The day had been windy, and she had not bothered with a coat. The photograph had captured her delicate features in profile with the wind whipping her hair into glorious abandon.

It was a picture of Lauren betraying him.

A muscle moved convulsively in Nick's throat as he swallowed over the constriction there. The photograph should have been taken in color, he decided.

Mere black and white couldn't capture her glowing skin, the gold highlights in her beautiful hair or the sparkle of her vivid turquoise eyes.

He covered his face with his hands.

The silent guards escorted Lauren across the marble lobby, which was crowded with late-departing employees. In the press of so many people, Lauren was spared the humiliation of curious onlookers. Everyone else was rushing home, absorbed with individual thoughts. Not that she particularly cared who witnessed her shame; at the moment, she cared about nothing.

It was dark outside and raining, but Lauren hardly felt the icy sting of the rain pelting against her thin silk blouse. She looked disinterestedly for the police car that she expected to see waiting at the curb, but there was none. The guard on her left and the one behind her stepped back. The guard on her right also turned to leave, then he hesitated and said with curt compassion, "Do you have a coat, miss?"

Lauren looked at him with pain-dazed eyes. "Yes," she said inanely. She did have a coat; it was with her purse in Jim's office.

The guard glanced uncertainly at the curb, as if he expected someone to pull over and offer her a ride. "I'll get it for you," he said, and walked back into the building with his companions.

Lauren stood on the sidewalk, rain glazing her hair and pelting her face like a million icy hypodermic needles. Apparently she wasn't going to be taken to jail, after all. She didn't know where to go, or how to get there without money or keys. In a kind of trance she turned and started to walk down Jefferson Avenue, just as a familiar figure strode swiftly out of the building toward her. For a moment hope flared and burned painfully bright. "Jim!" she called when he and Ericka were about to pass without seeing her.

Jim turned sharply, and Lauren's stomach clenched at the bitter, accusing fury in the single scathing glance he passed over her. "I have nothing to say to you," he snapped.

All hope died inside of Lauren and with its death came a blessed numbness. She turned on her heel, shoved her frozen hands into the pockets of her tweed skirt and started walking down the street. Six steps later, Jim's hand grasped her arm, turning her around. "Here," he said, his expression just as hostile as before. "Take my coat."

Lauren carefully pulled her arm from his grasp. "Don't touch me," she said calmly. "I don't ever want to be touched."

Alarm flickered in his gaze before he extinguished it. "Take my coat," he repeated tersely, already starting to remove it. "You'll freeze to death."

Lauren found nothing unpleasant about the prospect of freezing to death. Ignoring his outstretched coat, she lifted her gaze to his. "Do you believe what Nick believes?"

"Every single word," he averred.

With her hair plastered to her head and the rain driving into her upturned face, Lauren said with great dignity, "In that case, I don't want your coat."

She started to turn, then stopped. "But you can give Nick a message for me when he finally discovers the truth." Her teeth chattered as she said, "T-tell him not to ever come near me again. T-tell him to stay away from me!"

Without thinking about where she was going, Lauren automatically walked the eight blocks to the only people who would take her in without being paid. She went to Tony's restaurant.

With frozen knuckles she rapped on the back entrance. The door opened and Tony was staring at her, his black tuxedo a discordant contrast to the noise and steam of the kitchen behind him. "Laurie?" he said. "Laurie! *Dio mio!* Dominic, Joe," he shouted, "come quick!"

Lauren awoke in a warm comfortable bed and opened her eyes to a charmingly quaint but unfamiliar room. Her head was pounding ferociously as she struggled to her elbows and looked around. She was in the house above the restaurant, and Joe's young wife had put her to bed after a hot bath and a warm meal. She had not died of exposure, she realized. How disappointing—how anticlimactic, she decided morbidly. Her body ached as if she'd been beaten.

She wondered when Nick would discover that she'd changed the figures on the bids. If any of the four contracts were awarded to Sinco, Nick would surely wonder how that could have happened. He would wonder why Whitworth hadn't bid less than Sinco had, and he might compare the copies of the bids Lauren had given Philip with the originals.

Then again, there was also the possibility that other companies besides Sinco and Whitworth would be awarded the contracts, in which case Nick would always believe she'd betrayed him.

Lauren threw back the heavy quilts and climbed slowly out of bed. She felt too sick to care what happened.

She felt even worse a few minutes later, when she walked into the family kitchen and heard Tony on the telephone. His sons were all seated at the table. "Mary," Tony was saying, his face furrowed into stern lines, "this is Tony. Let me talk to Nick."

Lauren's heart thumped, but it was too late to stop him because he was already launching into a nonstop monologue. "Nick, this is Tony," he said. "You better come over here. Something happened to Laurie. She came here last night almost frozen. She had no coat, no purse, no nothing. She wouldn't say what was wrong. She wouldn't let any of us touch her except for—What?" His face turned angry. "Don't you use that tone of voice with me, Nick! I—" He was perfectly still for a moment, listening to whatever Nick was saying, then he took the receiver away from his ear and looked at it as if it had just grown teeth. "Nick hung up on me," he told his sons.

His amazed gaze encountered Lauren standing uncertainly in the doorway. "Nick said you stole information from him, that you're his stepfather's mistress," he told her. "He said he never wants to hear your name, and if I try to speak to him about you again, he will have his bank foreclose on the loan they made for improvements to my restaurant. Nick said that to me—he talked to me like that!" he repeated disbelievingly.

Lauren started forward, her face pale with remorse. "Tony, you don't know what's happened. You don't understand."

"I understand the way he spoke to me," Tony said, his jaw clenched. Ignoring her, he turned back to the phone and dialed with furious intent. "Mary," he said into the phone, "you put Nick back on the line right now." He paused while Mary apparently asked him a question. "Yes," he replied, "you bet your life it's about Lauren. What? Yes, she's here."

Tony handed the phone to Lauren, his expression so angry and hurt that she felt ill. "Nick won't talk to me," Tony said, "but Mary wants to talk to you."

With a mixture of hope and fear, Lauren said, "Hello, Mary?"

Mary's voice was like an icicle. "Lauren, you have done enough damage to those of us here who were foolish enough to trust you. If you have any decency at all, you'll keep Tony out of this. Nick is not making idle threats—he meant what he said to Tony. Is that clear?"

Lauren swallowed the lump of desolation in her throat. "Perfectly clear."

"Good. Then I suggest you stay where you are for the next hour. Our corporate attorney will deliver your possessions to you and explain your legal situation. We were going to notify you through Philip Whitworth, but this will be vastly preferable. Goodbye, Lauren."

Lauren sank into a chair at the table, too ashamed to look at the men who would now be watching her with the same bitter condemnation that Jim and Mary had shown her.

Tony's hand clamped reassuringly on her shoulder, and Lauren drew a long, unsteady breath. "I'll leave as soon as the attorney arrives with my purse." She dragged her gaze upward. Instead of despising her, the boys and Tony were looking at her with helpless sympathy.

After everything that had happened to her, Lauren felt better able to cope with animosity than kindness, and their compassion wrenched her heart, weakening the dam that was holding back her emotions. "Don't ask me to explain," she whispered. "If I did you wouldn't believe me."

"We would believe you," Dominic said with blushing fierceness. "I was standing behind the screen where the coffeepots are kept, and I heard every word that . . . that pig said to you at lunch, but I did not know his name. Papa recognized him and he came to stand with me, because he wondered why you would be eating with someone Nick hates."

Lauren's composure slipped another notch toward tears, but she blinked them back and said with a tremulous smile, "The service must have been terrible that day, with both of you standing guard over me." She hadn't cried in years until she'd met Nick. After last night there would be no more tears. Ever. She had wept at his feet, begging him to listen to her. Just thinking of it made her cringe with mortification and fury.

"I tried to call Nick after you left that day," Tony said, "to tell him that Whitworth was threatening you and that you were in trouble, but Nick was in Italy. I told Mary to have him call me as soon as he came back, but I did not ever believe you would really give Nick's stepfather the information."

Lauren heard the reproof in Tony's voice at that, and she lifted her shoulders in a weary shrug. "I didn't give him what he wanted. Nick only thinks I did."

Half an hour later Tony and Dominic escorted her downstairs to the restaurant, which wasn't open for business yet, and stood protectively behind her chair. Lauren instantly recognized Mike Walsh as the man who had been with Nick the night she'd literally fallen at their feet. He introduced the man who was with him as Jack Collins, the head of Global's security division in Detroit. Then both men sat down across from her.

"Your purse," Mike said, handing it to her. "Would you like to check the contents?"

Lauren kept her face carefully expressionless. "No."

"Very well," he said curtly. "I'll come directly to the point. Miss Danner, Global Industries has sufficient evidence against you to charge you with theft, conspiring to defraud and several other serious crimes. At this time, the corporation is not going to insist on your arrest. However, if you are ever again seen on the premises of Global Industries, or any of its subsidiaries, the corporation can and will press charges against you for the crimes I just mentioned.

A warrant for your arrest has already been prepared. If you are seen on our premises, the warrant will be signed, and you will be arrested. If you are in another state, we will insist on extradition."

He opened a large manila envelope and withdrew several sheets of paper. "This is a letter stating the terms I have just set out." He handed her a copy of the letter, along with an official-looking legal document. "This—" he indicated the document "—is an injunction, signed by the court, which now makes it illegal for you to set so much as one foot on Global property. Do you understand?"

"Perfectly," Lauren said, lifting her chin in silent rebellion.

"Do you have any questions?"

"Yes, I have two of them." Lauren rose, then turned to press a fond kiss to Tony's cheek and another to Dominic's smooth one. She knew she would break down under the strain of an emotional goodbye; she was saying farewell to her two friends now, when it was easier. She turned back to the attorney and asked, "Where is my car?"

The attorney inclined his head toward the door of the restaurant. "Mr. Collins here drove it over. It's parked right outside. What is the other question?"

Lauren ignored the attorney and asked Jack Collins, "Are you the one who discovered all this 'proof' against me?"

Despite his pallor, Jack Collins's eyes were inquisitive and sharp. "A man who works for me conducted the investigation while I was in the hospital.

Why do you ask, Miss Danner?" he inquired, watching her closely.

Lauren picked up her purse from the table. "Because whoever did it was not very good at his job."

She pulled her gaze from Jack Collins and managed a brief teary smile at Tony and Dominic. "Goodbye," she said softly. "And thank you."

She walked out of the restaurant and never looked back.

Both of the men from Global Industries watched her leave. "Stunning young woman, isn't she?" the attorney said.

"Beautiful," Jack Collins agreed, his brows knitted thoughtfully together.

"But treacherous and deceitful as they come."

Jack Collins's frown deepened. "I wonder if she is. I kept watching her eyes. She looked angry and she looked hurt. She didn't look guilty."

Mike Walsh heaved himself impatiently out of his chair. "She's guilty. If you don't think so, go look at the file your assistant put together on her."

"I think I will," Jack said.

"You do that!" Tony said angrily, shamelessly eavesdropping. "Then you come talk to me, and *I'll* tell you the truth. Whitworth made her do it!"

20

NICK LEANED BACK IN HIS CHAIR, WATCHING WHILE Jack Collins, Mary, Jim and Tony filed into his office. He had agreed to this meeting about Lauren only because Jack had insisted that it was vitally necessary for the corporation's sake, in case she should decide to sue them.

Sue them for what, Nick thought bitterly. He wished to God he were somewhere else right now. Anywhere else. They were going to talk about her, and he was going to have to listen. She had been gone for a month, and he still hadn't been able to tear her out of his mind.

He kept expecting to look up and see her walking into his office, her shorthand notebook and pen in hand, ready to write down his instructions.

Last week he had been deeply engrossed in the corporation's new financial statement, and suddenly a woman in the reception room had laughed. It had sounded like Lauren's soft, musical laugh, and he had leaped out of his chair, telling himself that he intended to drag her into his office and warn her for the last time to stay away. But when he strode into the reception area and saw that it was some other woman, his heart had sunk.

He needed a rest, he told himself—some relaxation and the right sort of diversion. He had been pushing himself too hard, trying to drive her out of his thoughts by working until he was mentally and physically exhausted. All that was going to change now. In a few hours he was leaving for Chicago to attend the international trade committee meeting—the meeting he had walked out on to go rushing after Lauren, and which had now been rescheduled so that the committee could conclude the business they'd been unable to resolve without his vote. On Sunday, three days from now, when the meeting adjourned, Vicky was joining him in Chicago, and they were flying to Switzerland for three weeks. Three consecutive weeks of skiing during the day and making love at night should solve all his problems very nicely. Spending Christmas in Switzerland again, as he had three years ago, was also a vastly appealing idea.

Whom had he spent it with three years ago? He tried to remember.

"Nick," Jack Collins said, "may I begin?"

"Yes," he said shortly, turning his head toward the windows. How long would it take before he could blot out the memory of Lauren weeping at his feet? "Please don't do this to us," she had sobbed. "I love you so much."

He rolled his gold pen idly between his fingertips,

aware that Tony was watching him angrily, just waiting for the slightest opportunity to plead Lauren's defense.

Her defense, Nick thought sarcastically. What defense? Because Lauren was Italian, Tony was automatically biased in her favor. Because she was so heartbreakingly beautiful, Tony was blind to her treacherous nature. He couldn't blame Tony, because he himself had been just as blind, just as stupid. Lauren had captivated him, fascinated and enchanted him. From the very first, he had been enthralled by her, rendered senseless by his uncontrollable, fiery desire for her. . . .

"I realize," Jack Collins was saying, "that Lauren Danner is a very unpleasant topic to all of you, but the five of us in this room have all known each other for many years, and there's no reason we can't speak openly among ourselves, is there?"

When no one replied, Jack sighed with frustration. "Well, she's a damned difficult subject for me to discuss too. The investigation on her was technically my responsibility, and I'm going to tell you now that it was done very poorly. The young man who handled the security check while I was in the hospital was inexperienced and overeager, and that's putting it politely. If I hadn't been back in the hospital twice since then, I'd have looked into this before.

"Now that I have," he continued doggedly, "I'll admit that I still can't figure the woman out—at least not completely. I've already talked to each of you separately. Now I'm hoping that by bringing all of us together we can resolve some of the contradictions that keep bothering me. Perhaps each of us has a part of the puzzle, and now we can fit them all together. Tony, for the time being I'm going to address myself only to Nick, Mary and Jim. I'd like you not to comment until the end."

Tony's black eyes narrowed with impatience, but he clamped his mouth shut and sat back on one of the green sofas.

"Now then," Jack said, directing his attention to Nick, Jim and Mary. "All three of you have told me that you believe Lauren Danner applied for a job here because she wanted to spy on us for Philip Whitworth. And all three of you have indicated that she was an extremely intelligent young woman with superior typing and shorthand skills. Right?"

Mary and Jim said yes. Nick nodded curtly.

"Then the next question I would ask is, why would an intelligent, skilled secretary fail every single clerical test she was given and claim that she had never been to college when in fact she has a master's degree from a university, which tells us she's a gifted pianist?" When everyone remained silent, he continued, "And why would an intelligent, educated woman who wants a job so that she can spy, do one of the silliest damned things I've ever seen—write on her application under positions desired the jobs of president and personnel manager?"

Jack looked around at the withdrawn expressions of his audience. "The obvious answer is that she did *not* want to get the job. In fact, she did everything in her power to make certain she wouldn't be offered one, didn't she?" No one answered and he sighed, "As I understand it, she was on her way back to her car from the interview when she met Nick, who interceded on her behalf that same night. The next day Jim interviewed her, and in a complete about-face, Miss Danner decided to work for Sinco and accepted Jim's job offer. Why?"

Jim leaned his head back against the sofa. "I've already told you and Nick what Lauren told me. She said she met Nick that night, and she accepted the job because she wanted to work near him. She said she thought he was an ordinary engineer who worked for Global."

"And you believed her?" Jack asked.

"Why wouldn't I?" Jim sighed disgustedly. "I saw her crying when she found out who he really was. I'm the same idiot who also believed that Whitworth was a relative of hers, and that even though he had asked her to spy on us, she wouldn't do it."

"Actually," Jack said, his mouth twisting with grim amusement, "Whitworth *is* her relative. I checked it out, and according to the Whitworth family tree, which was traced about thirteen years ago and recorded in a book used mostly by society snobs, the Danners are seventh or eighth cousins of the Whitworths."

The uncontrollable spurt of joy that Nick experienced was instantly quashed. Cousins or not, Lauren was still his stepfather's mistress.

"I understand," Jack said, massaging his temple as if he had a headache, "that Miss Danner did not request to be assigned to you, Nick. In fact, I understand from Weatherby that she was adamantly opposed to the idea."

"She was," Nick gritted. He couldn't stand much more of this. Talking about her was twisting his gut into knots.

"If she truly wanted to spy for Whitworth," Jack persisted, "why would she argue against being assigned to you, when working for you would have given her much better access to confidential information?"

Nick picked up a file on his desk and began reading it. "She didn't want to work for me because we'd quarreled about a personal matter." *She didn't want to sleep with me,* Nick added silently.

"That doesn't make sense," Jack said firmly. "If you'd quarreled, she should have relished the opportunity to retaliate by coming up here and spying on you."

"Nothing about that girl makes sense," Mary said hesitantly. "When I told her about Nick's mother, she turned as white as a—"

"I don't have the time for this!" Nick cut in curtly. "I'm leaving for Chicago. Jack, I can clear this up in a few sentences. Lauren Danner came to Sinco to spy. She's Whitworth's mistress. She is a consummate liar and a magnificent actress."

Tony opened his mouth to argue, and Nick said in a low, thunderous voice, "Don't defend her to me, dammit! She let me introduce her to my own mother and stepfather! She stood there letting me make an ass of myself by introducing her to her accomplices, one of whom is her lover! She betrayed all of us; not just me. She told Whitworth about Rossi and had Whitworth's people swarming all over Casano looking for him. She provided bidding information to Whitworth that is going to cost Sinco a fortune in profits. She—"

"She wasn't Whitworth's mistress," Jack interrupted when Tony leaped to his feet to protest. "I know that's what my investigator told you, but the truth is that, although Whitworth does own the apartment, he only visited her there once, on the night she arrived, for perhaps thirty minutes."

"My stepfather's age must be impairing his—"

"You stop talking about Laurie like this!" Tony spat out furiously. "I—"

"Save your breath, Tony," Nick snapped.

"I got plenty of breath to spare, and now I'm going to have my say! Dominic and I heard what Whitworth said to her the day they had lunch at my place. Laurie told him right off that you and her were getting married, and she told him that she was going to tell you she was related to him. As soon as she said that, Whitworth started talking about how you might think she was his mistress and that you might think she told him about this Casano. Laurie got upset and told him she didn't say nothing about Casano, and she wasn't his mistress. Then she asked him right out if he was trying to blackmail her. He said he was bargaining with her. He said he'd keep quiet if she would give him information—"

"Which she did," Nick snapped. "Within an hour! She did it because she intended to keep right on lying to me until Whitworth finally put us out of business."

"No!" Tony shouted. "She told him she would die before she'd do anything to hurt you. She—"

Nick's hand slammed down on the desk as he surged to his feet. "She's a treacherous bitch and she's a liar. That's all I need to know. Now all of you get out of here!"

"I'm going!" Tony almost shouted, stomping across the office. "But there's one more thing you need to know. What you did to her hurt her worse than I've ever seen anybody hurt. You threw her out with no coat, no money, no nothing, and does she call Whitworth? No, she walks eight blocks in the cold and rain to collapse in my arms. So I'm tellin' you now—" Tony drew himself up to his most impressive height and slapped his hat on his head "—from now on you're off my list, Nick. If you wanna eat in my restaurant, you better bring Laurie with you!"

21

"MR. SINCLAIR." THE SECRETARY IN CHICAGO BENT down beside Nick, her voice lowered to a whisper to avoid disturbing the seven other major U.S. industrialists seated around the conference table discussing the final details of an international trade agreement. "I'm sorry to disturb you, sir, but there's a Mr. James Williams on the phone for you. . . ."

Nick nodded and slid his chair back. Seven men glanced up and looked at him with irritated accusation. Except in matters of extreme emergency, none of them was taking calls. During the last meeting and now this one, only Nick had received an urgent call, and the last time the meeting had to be aborted and rescheduled because he had abruptly walked out on them.

Nick strode from the conference room, gripped by the memory of the last time Jim's call had interrupted him in this meeting. That time Jim had fabricated some silly damned excuse for calling, so that he could say that Lauren had resigned. "Yes, what is it?" Nick said, angry at the memory of her, angry at the pain that thinking of her always evoked.

"There's quite a celebration going on over in the engineering department," Jim began, his voice hesitant and confused. "Nick, even though Lauren gave Whitworth copies of our four bids, we have just been awarded two of the four contracts. The low bidders on the other two contracts still haven't been announced." He paused, evidently waiting for Nick to answer. "I can't figure it out—what do you think?"

"I think," Nick snarled, "that the stupid bastard isn't smart enough to win a poker hand with a deck of marked cards."

"Whitworth is conniving and wily and anything but stupid," Jim argued. "I think I'll get the file from Jack Collins in security and go over the figures that Lauren—"

"I told you what I wanted you to do," Nick interrupted in a low, deadly voice. "Regardless of who gets the remaining two contracts, I want Sinco to bid on every job that Whitworth bids on, and I want you to bid it below our cost if necessary. I want that bastard out of business in one year!"

Nick slammed the phone down and stalked back into the conference room. The chairman looked at him with ill-concealed reproof for the interruption. "Now, may we resume?"

Nick nodded curtly. He voted carefully on the next three issues, but as the morning drifted into afternoon, and afternoon darkened into early evening, it became more and more impossible to think of anything but Lauren. Snow fell outside the windows of the Chicago skyscraper as the meeting continued, and Tony's outraged voice played through his mind. . . . "You threw her out with no coat, no money, no nothing, and does she call Whitworth? No! She walks eight blocks in the cold and rain, to collapse in my arms."

Eight blocks! Why hadn't the guards let her stop to get her coat? He remembered the thin blouse she'd been wearing, because he had unbuttoned it himself with every intention of exposing and degrading her, exactly as he had. He remembered the sheer perfection of her creamy breasts; the incredible silkiness of her skin; the exquisite taste of her lips; the way she had kissed him and held him to her. . . .

"Nick," the chairman said sharply, "I assume you are in favor of this proposal?"

Nick dragged his gaze from the windows. He had no idea what proposal was being discussed. "I'd like to hear more about it before I decide," he prevaricated.

Seven surprised faces turned toward him. "It's your proposal, Nick," the chairman scowled. "You wrote it."

"Then naturally I'm in favor of it," he informed them coolly.

The committee dined as a group in one of Chicago's most elegant restaurants. The moment their meal was over, Nick abruptly excused himself to return to his hotel. Snow fell in thick flakes, dusting his tan cashmere overcoat and clinging to his bare head as he strolled down Chicago's Michigan Avenue, glancing disinterestedly into exclusive shops whose brightly lit windows were decorated for Christmas.

He shoved his hands into his coat pockets, mentally cursing Jim for calling him this morning about Lauren, and cursing Lauren for walking into his life. Why hadn't she called Whitworth to come and get her when the guards forcibly removed her from the Global building? Why in God's name had she walked eight blocks in freezing weather to go to Tony?

After he had hurt and degraded her, why had she wept at his feet like a heartbroken angel? Nick paused to take a cigarette out of his pack and put it in his mouth. Bending his head, he cupped his hands over the flame and lit it. Lauren's voice drifted through his mind, choked with racking sobs. "I love you so much," she had wept. "Please listen to me. . . . Please don't do this to us. . . ."

Fury and pain blazed through him. He could not take Lauren back, he reminded himself forcefully. He would never take her back.

He was willing to believe that Whitworth had blackmailed her into giving him the bids. He was even willing to believe that Lauren hadn't told Whitworth about the Rossi project. After all, if she had, Whitworth's men wouldn't have been swarming all over the village asking questions about Nick's activities—they'd have been asking about Rossi. Apparently they didn't even know the chemist's name. Even if they found out, it wouldn't matter.

The lab tests had proved Rossi's formula to be only a fraction as effective as he'd claimed it was, besides being a skin and eye irritant.

Nick stopped at the light on the corner, where a man in a bright red Santa Claus costume was standing beside a black iron pot and ringing a bell. Christmas had never been particularly pleasant to Nick. It was a holiday that invariably called to mind the visit he had paid to his mother as a boy; in fact, he never thought of her except at Christmas time.

Cars glided past him, their tires crunching in the fresh snow. This Christmas could have been different; it could have been a beginning. He would have taken Lauren to Switzerland. No—he would have spent it at home with her. He would have built a roaring fire in the fireplace, and they could have started their own traditions. He would have made love to her in front of the fire, with the lights from the Christmas tree glowing on her satin skin. . . .

Nick angrily jerked his mind away from those thoughts and stalked across the street, ignoring the horns that blared their protest and the headlights flying toward him. There would be no Christmases with Lauren. He wanted her badly enough to forgive her for almost anything, but he could not, would not, forgive or forget the fact that she had betrayed him to his mother and stepfather. Perhaps in time he could have forgiven her for conspiring against him, but not with the Whitworths. Never with them.

Nick inserted his key into the double doors of his penthouse suite. "Where the hell have you been?"

Jim Williams demanded from the Queen Anne sofa where he was lounging with his feet propped on an antique coffee table. "I've come to talk about the bids Lauren gave Whitworth."

Nick jerked off his coat, furious at having his suite invaded, his privacy infringed upon and particularly at being forced—even for the moment it was going to take to get Jim out of here—to talk about Lauren again. "I told you," he said in a low, deadly voice, "that I wanted Whitworth out of business and I told you how I wanted it done. When you explained your part in Lauren's complicity, I excused it, but I will not—"

"You don't have to put Whitworth out of business," Jim interrupted quietly as Nick stalked toward him. "Lauren is doing it for you." From the sofa beside him, Jim picked up copies of the original bids and the altered copies that Lauren had made to give Whitworth. "She changed the figures, Nick," he said somberly.

The meeting of the committee on international trade reconvened at precisely nine o'clock the following morning. The chairman of the committee looked at the six men seated around the conference table. "Nick Sinclair will not be present today," he informed the thunderous-looking group. "He asked me to express his regrets and to explain that he was called away on an urgent matter."

In unison, six outraged faces turned to glare with impotent hostility at the vacant chair of their missing member. "Last time it was a labor relations problem. What the hell is Sinclair's problem this time?" a jowly man demanded unsympathetically.

"A merger," the chairman answered. "He said he is going to try to negotiate the most important merger of his life."

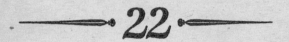

22

FENSTER, MISSOURI, WAS BLANKETED WITH A FRESH carpet of snow. With Christmas decorations hanging at all the town's intersections, Fenster had a Norman Rockwell quaintness about it that reminded Nick rather poignantly of Lauren's initial primness about sex.

Aided by the directions a taciturn old man had given him a few minutes before, Nick had no trouble finding the quiet little street where Lauren had grown up. He pulled to a stop in front of a modest white frame house with a swing on the porch and an enormous oak tree in the front yard, and turned off the ignition of the car he'd rented at the airport five long hours ago.

The slow, treacherous drive across snow-covered roads had been the easy part; facing Lauren was going to be the difficult part.

His knock was answered immediately by a wiry young man in his mid-twenties. Nick's heart sank.

Never in his worst imaginings during the drive down here had he considered the possibility that Lauren might have another man with her. "My name is Nick Sinclair," he said, and watched the young man's curious smile change to open animosity. "I would like to see Lauren."

"I'm Lauren's brother," the young man retorted, "and she doesn't want to see you."

Her brother! Nick's momentary relief was followed by an absurd impulse to smash the younger man's face for stealing Lauren's allowances when she was a little girl. "I've come to see her," Nick stated implacably, "and if I have to walk over you to get to her, I will."

"I believe he means it, Leonard," Lauren's father said, stepping into the hallway, his finger in a closed book he had been reading.

For a long moment, Robert Danner studied the tall, indomitable man in the doorway, his penetrating blue eyes observing the lines of strain and tension etched deeply into his visitor's features. A faint, unwilling smile softened the stern line of Mr. Danner's mouth. "Leonard," he said quietly, "why don't we give Mr. Sinclair five minutes with Lauren to see if he can change her mind. She's in the living room," he added, inclining his head over his shoulder in the direction of the Christmas carols playing on the stereo.

"Five minutes, and that's all," Leonard grumbled, following right on Nick's heels.

Nick turned to him. "Alone," he said determinedly.

Leonard opened his mouth to argue, but his father intervened. "Alone, Leonard."

Nick silently closed the door to the cheerful little living room, took two steps forward and stopped, his heart hammering uncontrollably in his chest.

Lauren was standing on a stepladder, hanging tinsel on the upper branches of a Christmas tree. She looked heartbreakingly young in her trim jeans and bright green sweater and poignantly, vulnerably beautiful with her hair tumbling in burnished honey waves over her shoulders and back.

He ached to pull her off the ladder and into his arms, to carry her over to the sofa and lose himself in her, to kiss and hold and caress her, to heal her pain with his body and hands and mouth.

Stepping down off the ladder, Lauren knelt to pull more tinsel from the box lying beside the gaily wrapped packages beneth the tree. From the corner of her eye she glimpsed a pair of gleaming brown men's loafers. "Lenny, your timing is terrific," she teased softly. "I've already finished. Does the star look all right on the top, or should I go to the attic and bring down the angel?"

"Leave the star on top," said an achingly gentle, deep voice. "There's already one angel in the room."

Lauren's head jerked around, her gaze riveted on the tall, solemn man standing a few feet away from her. The color drained from her face as her mind registered the determination carved into every masculine feature, from his straight dark brows to the tough jut of his chin and jaw. Every line of his well-remembered body was emanating wealth, power and the same forceful magnetism that she ran from in her dreams at night.

His features had been seared into her brain; she remembered him perfectly. She also remembered the last time she had seen him: she had been on her knees then too—weeping at his feet. Humiliation and fury sent her surging upright. "Get out of here!" she blazed, too blinded by her own torment to see the tortured regret, the sorrow that darkened his gray eyes.

Instead of leaving, he came toward her.

Lauren backed away one step and then held her ground, her whole body shaking with exploding violence. He reached for her, and she swung, slapping him full force on his face. "I said get out!" she hissed. When he didn't move Lauren lifted her hand in an incensed threat, "Damn you! Get out!"

Nick's gaze shifted to her raised palm. "Go ahead," he said gently.

Trembling with thwarted rage, Lauren jerked her hand down and wrapped her arms around her stomach, moving sideways to escape him, trying to sidle around the tree, away from him, out of the room.

"Lauren, wait—" He stepped into her path and reached for her.

"Don't touch me!" Lauren almost screamed, recoiling wildly from his hand. She moved sideways to take the remaining three steps that would enable her to circle past him and out of the room.

Nick was willing to let her do anything, *anything* to him, except to leave him. That he could not let her do. "Lauren, please let me—"

"No!" she cried hysterically. "Stay away from me!"

She tried to run, and Nick caught her by the arms. She turned on him like a demented weeping wildcat, struggling wildly, striking out at him. "You bastard!" she screamed in hysterical, maddened pain, pounding on his chest, his shoulders. "You bastard! I begged you on my knees!"

It took all of Nick's strength to hold her until her fury was finally sent and she collapsed against him, her slim body racked with wrenching sobs. "You made me beg—" she wept brokenly in his arms "—you made me beg."

Her tears tore at his heart, and her words slashed him like knives. He held her, staring blindly ahead, remembering the beautiful, laughing girl who had walked into his life and turned it upside down with her glowing smile.

"What happens to me if this slipper fits?"

"I turn you into a handsome frog."

His eyes stung with remorse and he closed them. "I'm sorry," he whispered hoarsely. "I'm so sorry."

Lauren heard the raw ache in his voice, and she felt the wall of icy numbness she'd built around herself begin to melt. She fought to blank out the exquisite beauty of being in his arms again, of being pressed against his big, strong body.

In the lonely weeks of sleepless nights and angry desolate days, she'd come to the quiet conclusion that Nick was incurably cynical and hard. His mother's desertion had made him that way, and nothing she herself could do would ever change him. He would always be capable of shutting her out of his life and coldly walking away from her, because he would never really love her.

He had learned at five that a woman was not to be entrusted with his heart. He would offer Lauren his body, his affection—but nothing else. He would never let himself be completely vulnerable again.

His hands were moving up and down her back in a gesture of helpless comfort, spreading warmth wherever they touched her. Summoning the last vestiges of her self-control, Lauren firmly pushed away from him. "I'm fine now. Really." She dragged her gaze to his fathomless gray eyes and said quietly, "I want you to leave now, Nick."

His jaw tightened and his whole body tensed at the calm, deathly finality in her voice, but instead of leaving, he seemed to block her words from his mind, as if she had spoken in a language he didn't understand. With his eyes still holding hers, he reached into his jacket pocket and took out a flat box wrapped in silver paper. "I've brought you a present," he said.

Lauren stared at him. "What?"

"Here," he said, lifting her hand and putting the box in it. "It's a Christmas present. It's for you—go ahead and open it."

Mary's words suddenly rang through Lauren's mind, and her whole body began to tremble. "He intended to bribe his mother into coming back to him. . . . He gave her the present . . . and insisted she open it right then. . . ."

"Open it now, Lauren," he said. His face was carefully blank, but Lauren saw the desperation in his eyes and the rigid tension in his powerful shoulders, and she knew that he expected her to reject his gift. And him.

She pulled her gaze from his and shakily removed the silver paper from the flat velvet box, which was discreetly embossed with the name of a Chicago jeweler, followed by the name of a Chicago hotel. She opened the catch. On a bed of white velvet was a spectacular ruby pendant surrounded by a row of dazzling diamonds. The magnificent pendant was easily the size of a pillbox.

It was a bribe.

For the second time in his life, Nick was trying to bribe a woman he loved to come back to him. Tears of tenderness filled Lauren's eyes, and sweetness pierced her heart.

Her voice was hoarse and tight, as if the words were being wrenched from him. "Please," he whispered. "Please . . . " He jerked her into his arms, crushing her to his lean, hard length, burying his face in her hair. "Oh please, darling . . ."

Lauren's defenses crumbled completely. "I love you!" she said brokenly, winding her arms tightly around his neck, running her hands over the bunched muscles of his shoulders, smoothing his thick, dark hair.

"I bought you earrings too," he coaxed hoarsely,

urgently. "I'll buy you a piano—your college said you were a gifted pianist. Would you like a grand piano or would you rather have—"

"Don't!" Lauren cried in anguish as she rose up on her toes and silenced him with her lips. A shudder ran through his body and he wrapped his arms around her, his mouth opening on hers with hungry desperation, his hands moving over her back and the sides of her breasts, then sweeping lower, pulling her hips to his as if he wanted to absorb her body into his.

"I've missed you so much," he whispered, trying to gentle his kiss, his mouth moving on her parted lips with tender, melting hunger as his hand sank slowly into the thick hair at her nape. But his control snapped almost instantly and with a groan, he tightened his hand, his tongue driving into her mouth with fierce, compulsive urgency.

Lauren kissed him back with all the bursting, aching love in her heart, arching closer to him, holding him tightly to her.

An endless time later, she surfaced to reality, her arms still wrapped around him, her cheek pressed against the violent pounding of his heart. "I love you," he whispered, and before Lauren could answer he continued in a husky voice that was part pleading, part teasing, "You have to marry me. I think I've just been voted off the committee on international trade—they think I'm unstable. And Tony took me off his list. Mary says she'll quit if I don't bring you back. Ericka found your earrings, and she gave them to Jim. He said to tell you that you can't have them unless you come back for them. . . ."

Tiny colored lights twinkled on the Christmas tree in the immense sunken living room. Stretched out on the carpet in front of the fireplace, Nick held his sleeping wife cradled in the crook of his arm, watching the firelight dancing on the tumbled waves of her hair spread over his bare chest. They had been married for three days.

Lauren stirred, moving closer to him for warmth. Careful not to disturb her, he drew the satin quilt up around her shoulders. Reverently he touched her cheek, tracing its elegant curve. Lauren had brought joy to his life and laughter to his home. She thought he was beautiful. When she looked at him, he *felt* beautiful.

Somewhere in another part of the big house a clock began chiming the hour of midnight. Lauren's lashes slowly flickered open, and he looked into her enchanting blue eyes. "It's Christmas," he whispered.

His wife smiled up at him, and her answer made his throat tighten. "No," she said softly, laying her fingers against his jaw. "Christmas came three days ago."

The enchanting new novel from the
author of the *New York Times*
bestseller *Until You*

JUDITH MCNAUGHT

REMEMBER WHEN

Judith McNaught creates an unforgettable world
filled with her "very special brand of dazzling wit,
passion, and tender sensuality."—*Romantic Times*

COMING SOON IN HARDCOVER!

POCKET
B O O K S

1131-01

The Entrancing Novel
from the
New York Times
Bestselling
Author of *Perfect*

Until You

by

Judith McNaught

**Now Available in
Paperback from**

POCKET
STAR
BOOKS

1032-01

Pocket Books
Proudly Presents

UNTIL YOU
Judith McNaught

Available
from Pocket Books

The following is a preview of
Until You . . .

Leaning heavily on his cane, the ancient butler stood in the shabby drawing room and listened in respectful silence as his illustrious visitor imparted the news that the butler's employer had just met an untimely demise. Not until Lord Westmoreland finished his tale did the servant permit himself to show any reaction and, even then, Hodgkins sought only to placate and reassure. "How very distressing, my lord, for poor Baron Burleton, and for you as well. But then—accidents do happen, don't they, and you should not blame yourself. Mishaps are mishaps, and that's why we call them that."

"I'd hardly call running a man down and killing him a 'mishap,'" Stephen Westmoreland retorted with a bitterness that was directed at himself, not at the servant. Although this evening's accident had been much the fault of the drunken young baron who'd bounded across the street in front of Stephen's carriage, the fact was that Stephen had been holding the reins, and he was alive and unharmed, while young Burleton was dead. Furthermore, it now seemed that no one was going to mourn Burleton's passing and, at the moment, that seemed a final injustice to Stephen. "Surely your employer must have some family somewhere—someone to whom I could explain personally about the accident?"

Hodgkins merely shook his head, distracted by the dire realization that he was suddenly unemployed again and likely to remain so for the rest of his life. He'd only obtained this position because no one else had been willing to work as butler, valet, footman, and cook—and for the absurdly small wages Burleton was able to pay. Embarrassed by his temporary lapse into self-pity and his lack of proper decorum, Hodgkins cleared his throat and hastily added, "Baron Burleton had no close living relatives, as I said. And since I've been in the baron's employ for only three weeks, his acquaintances aren't really known to—" He broke off, a look of horror on his face. "In my shock, I forgot about his fiancée! The nuptials were to take place this week."

A fresh wave of guilt washed over Stephen, but he nodded, and his voice became brisk and purposeful. "Who is she and where can I find her?"

"All I know is that she's an American heiress the baron met when he was abroad, and that she's to arrive tomorrow on a ship from the Colonies. Her father was too ill to make the voyage, so I presume she's either traveling alone or, more likely, with a female companion. Last night, the baron was commemorating the end of his bachelorhood. That's all I know."

"You must know her name! What did Burleton call her?"

Caught between nervousness at Lord Westmoreland's terse impatience and shame because his own memory had been deteriorating with age, Hodgkins said, a little defensively, "As I said, I was new to the baron's employ, and not taken into his confidence.

In my presence, he . . . he called her 'my fiancée,' or else 'my heiress.'"

"Think, man! You must have heard him refer to her name at some time!"

"No . . . I . . . Wait, yes! I do recall something . . . I recall that her name made me remember how very much I used to enjoy visiting Lancashire as a boy. Lancaster!" Hodgkins exclaimed in delight. "Her surname is Lancaster, and her given name is Sharon . . . No, that's not it. Charise! Charise Lancaster!"

Hodgkins was rewarded for his efforts with a slight nod of approval accompanied by yet another rapid-fire question: "What about the name of her ship?"

Hodgkins was so encouraged and so proud that he actually banged his cane upon the floor with glee as the answer popped into his mind. "The *Windsong!*" he crowed, then flushed with embarrassment at his boisterous tone and unseemly behavior.

"Anything else? Every detail could be helpful when I deal with her."

"I do recall some other trifles, but I shouldn't like to indulge in idle gossip."

"Let's hear it," Stephen said with unintended curtness.

"The lady is young and very beautiful, the baron said. A real 'looker' he called her. I also gathered that she was rather madly in love with him and wanted the union, while it was the baron's title that was of primary interest to her father."

Stephen's last hope that this marriage was simply one of convenience had died at the news that the girl was "madly in love" with her fiancé. "What about Burleton?" he asked as he pulled on his gloves. "Why did he want the marriage?"

"I can only speculate, but he seemed to share the young lady's feelings."

"Wonderful," Stephen murmured grimly, turning toward the door.

Not until Lord Westmoreland left did Hodgkins permit himself to give in to despair at his own predicament. He was unemployed and virtually penniless again. A moment ago, he'd almost considered asking, even begging, Lord Westmoreland to recommend him to someone, but that would have been not only inexcusably presumptuous, but futile. As Hodgkins had discovered during the two years it had taken him to finally obtain a position with Baron Burleton, no one wanted a butler, valet, or footman whose hands were spotted with age and whose body was so old and stooped that he could neither straighten it nor force it to a brisk walk.

His thin shoulders drooping with despair, his joints beginning to ache dreadfully, Hodgkins turned and shuffled toward his room at the back of the shabby apartment. He was halfway there when the earl's sharp, impatient knock forced him to make his slow way back to the front door. "Yes, my lord?" he said.

"It occurred to me as I was leaving," Lord Westmoreland said in a curt, businesslike voice, "that Burleton's death will deprive you of whatever wages he owed you. My secretary, Mr. Hargrove, will see that you're compensated." As he turned to leave, he added, "My households are always in need of competent staff. If you aren't longing for retirement right now, you might consider contacting Mr. Hargrove about that as well. He'll handle the details." And then he was gone.

Hodgkins closed the door and turned, staring in stunned disbelief at the dingy room, while vigor and youth began to surge and rush warmly through his veins. Not only did he have a position to go to, but a position in a household belonging to one of the most admired, influential noblemen in all of Europe!

The position hadn't been offered out of pity, of that

Hodgkins was almost certain, for Lord Westmoreland wasn't known as the sort of man to coddle servants, or anyone else. In fact, rumor had it that ever since that "unfortunate incident" several years ago, the earl had become a distant, exacting, quite unapproachable man even among his peers. Still, the humiliating idea that the earl might have pitied him lingered until Hodgkins suddenly remembered something else the earl had said—something that filled him with exquisite pleasure and pride: Lord Westmoreland had specifically implied that he regarded Hodgkins as *competent*. He'd used that very word!

Competent!

Slowly, Hodgkins turned toward the hall mirror and, with his hand upon the handle of his black cane, he gazed at his reflection. Competent . . .

He straightened his spine, though the effort was a bit painful, then squared his narrow shoulders. With his free hand he reached down and carefully smoothed the front of his faded black jacket. Why, he didn't look so very old, Hodgkins decided—not a day over three-and-seventy! Lord Westmoreland certainly hadn't thought him decrepit or useless. No indeed! He'd thought Albert Hodgkins would be a worthy addition to one of his magnificent households!

Hodgkins tipped his head to the side, trying to imagine how he would look wearing the elegant Westmoreland livery of maroon and gold, but his vision seemed to blur and waver. He lifted his hand, his long, thin fingers touching, feeling at the corner of his eye where there was an unfamiliar wetness.

He brushed the tear away along with the sudden, crazy impulse to wave his cane in the air and dance a little jig. Dignity, he very strongly felt, was far more appropriate in a man who was about to join the household staff of Lord Stephen Westmoreland.

* * *

The sun was a fiery disc sliding into the horizon by the time a seaman walked down the dock to the coach that had been waiting there since morning. "There she is—the *Windsong*," he told Stephen, who'd been leaning against the door of the vehicle, idly watching a drunken brawl taking place outside a nearby pub. Before raising his arm to point out the ship, the seaman cast a cautious glance at the two coachmen, who both held pistols in clear view and were obviously not as indifferent as their master to the dangers lurking everywhere on the wharf. "That's her, right there," he said to Stephen, indicating a small ship just gliding into port, its sails dim silhouettes in the deepening twilight. "And she's only a bit late."

Straightening, Stephen nodded to one of the coachmen, who tossed the seaman a coin for his trouble. Then he walked slowly down the dock, wishing that his mother or his sister-in-law could have been there with him when Burleton's bride disembarked. The presence of concerned females might have helped soften the blow when he delivered the tragic news to the girl, news that was going to shatter her dreams.

"This is a nightmare!" Sheridan cried at the astonished cabin boy who'd come to tell her for the second time that "a gentleman" was waiting for her on the pier—a gentleman she naturally assumed was Lord Burleton. "Tell him to wait. Tell him I *died*. No, tell him we're still indisposed." She shoved the door closed, shot the bolt, then pressed her back to the panel, her gaze darting to the frightened maid who was perched on the edge of the narrow cot in the cabin they'd shared, twisting a handkerchief in her plump hands. "It's a nightmare, and when I wake up in the morning, it will all be over, won't it, Meg?"

Meg shook her head so vigorously that it set the ribbons on her white cap bobbing. "It's no dream. You'll have to talk to the baron and tell him something—something that won't vex him, and something he'll believe."

"Well that certainly eliminates the truth," Sheridan said bitterly. "I mean, he's bound to be just a trifle miffed if I tell him I've managed to misplace his fiancée somewhere along the English coastline. The *truth* is I *lost* her!"

"You didn't lose her—she eloped! She ran off with Mr. Morrison when we stopped in the last port."

"Either way, what matters is that she was entrusted to my care, and I failed in my duty to her father and to the baron. There's nothing to do but go out there and tell the baron that."

"You mustn't!" Meg cried. "He'll have us thrown straight into a dungeon! Besides, you have to make him feel kindly toward us because we have no one else to turn to, nowhere to go. Miss Charise took all the money with her, and there isn't a shilling to buy passage home."

"I'll find some sort of work." Despite her confident words, Sherry's voice trembled with strain, and she looked about the tiny cabin, unconsciously longing for somewhere to hide.

"You don't have any references," Meg argued, her voice filling with tears. "And we don't have anywhere to sleep tonight and no money for lodgings. We're going to land in the gutter. Or worse!"

"What could be worse?" Sheridan said, but when Meg opened her mouth to answer, Sherry held up a hand and said with a trace of her normal humor and spirit, "No, don't, I beg you. Don't even consider 'white slavery.'"

Meg paled and her mouth fell open, her voice dropping to a dazed whisper. "White . . . slavery."

"Meg! For heaven's sake, I meant it as a . . . a joke. A bad joke."

"If you go out there and tell him the truth, they'll toss both of us straight into a dungeon."

"Why," Sherry burst out, closer to hysterics than she'd ever been in her life, "do you keep talking about a dungeon?"

"Because there's laws here, miss, and you—we—we've broken some. Not apurpose, of course, but they won't care. Here, they toss you into a dungeon—no questions asked nor answers heard. Here, there's only one sort of people who matter, and they're the Quality. What if he thinks we killed her, or stole her money, or sold her, or something evil like that? It would be his word against yours, and you aren't nobody, so the law will be on his side."

Sheridan tried to say something reassuring or humorous, but her wit and courage had both suffered from weeks of unabated tension and stress, compounded by a long bout of illness during the voyage, followed by Charise's disappearance two days ago. After a lifetime of determined optimism and robust health, she suddenly felt weak, terrified, and alarmingly dizzy. The room began to revolve and she clutched at the back of a chair for support. Then she forced herself erect, smoothed her hair back into it's stern chignon, and reached for her cloak. "It's time to meet the baron and face my fate," she said. "You stay here, out of sight. If I don't come back for you right away, wait for a few hours and then leave as quietly as you can. Better yet, stay aboard. With luck, no one will discover you until the ship is already under way in the morning. There's no point in both of us being arrested and hauled away, if that's what he decides to do."

After the relative quiet of their tiny, dim cabin, the noise and bustle on the torch-lit deck was jarring.

Stevedores with trunks and crates on their shoulders were swarming up and down the gangplank, unloading cargo and taking on new provisions for the *Windsong*'s voyage in the morning. Winches creaked overhead as cargo nets were slung over the side of the vessel and lowered onto the pier. Sherry picked her way carefully down the gangplank, jostled by seamen and stevedores, searching among the throng for a man who looked like an English nobleman—a thin, pale, pompous male who she was certain would be decked out in satin knee breeches and dripping with fobs and seals to impress his bride.

And then she saw the tall, dark man standing on the pier, impatiently slapping his gloves against his thigh, and she knew it was him. Even though he wasn't foppish, pale, or overbred, everything about him set him apart and marked him as "privileged." Confidence, strength, and purpose emanated from every inch of his dark-clad figure as he watched her approach, and Sherry's fear promptly escalated to panic. For the past two days she'd secretly counted on her own ability to calm and cajole the affronted bridegroom into seeing reason, but the man whose dark brows were drawing together in a deep frown looked about as malleable as stone. He was doubtlessly wondering where the devil his fiancée was and why Sheridan Bromleigh, not Charise Lancaster, was walking down the gangplank. And he was clearly annoyed.

Stephen wasn't annoyed, he was stunned. He'd expected Miss Lancaster to be a giddy seventeen- or eighteen-year-old with bouncing curls and rosy cheeks, decked out in ruffles and lace. What he saw standing before him was a composed, pale young woman of perhaps twenty with high cheekbones, wide gray eyes, and light hair pulled back in a spinsterish bun. Instead of ruffles, she was wearing a sensible, but unattractive brown cloak, and his first thought as he held out his hand was that Burleton must have been truly besotted to think her a raving beauty.

Despite her outward composure, Stephen sensed that she was tense, frightened—as if she had some sort of premonition, and so he changed his mind and decided the best course for both of them was probably the most direct one. "Miss Lancaster," he said after quickly introducing himself, "I'm afraid there's been an accident." Guilt tore at him as he added tightly, "Baron Burleton was killed yesterday."

For a moment, she simply stared at him in shocked incomprehension.

"Accident? Killed? He isn't here?"

Stephen had expected her to dissolve into tears, at the very least, or even to have hysterics. He had not expected her to withdraw her cold hand from his and say in an odd, quiet voice, "How very sad. Please give my condolences to his family." She'd turned and taken several steps down the pier before he realized she was obviously in complete shock. "Miss Lancaster," he called, but his voice was drowned out by an alarmed shout from above as a cargo net swung wide from its winch.

"STEP ASIDE! LOOK OUT!"

Stephen saw the danger and lunged for her, but he wasn't in time—the cargo net swung wide, striking her in the back of the head and sending her flying onto the pier on her face. Already shouting to his coachmen, Stephen crouched down and turned her over in his arms. Her head fell back limply and blood began to run from the huge bump at the back of her scalp.

"She's still very weak, but I think she's going to make it," Dr. Whitticomb said as he walked into the earl's study. "Yesterday I wouldn't have given a farthing for her chances, but she's young and strong. She was even able to speak a few words to me just now." His smile faded as the younger man looked up and he noted the deeply etched lines of fatigue and strain at his eyes and mouth. "You, however, look like the very devil, my lord," he added with the blunt familiarity of a longtime family friend. "I was going to suggest we go up to see her together after supper—providing you invite me to stay for supper, of course—but the sight of you might frighten her into a relapse if you don't have some sleep and a shave first."

"I don't need any sleep," Stephen said, so relieved that he felt positively energized as he walked over to a silver tray and pulled the stopper out of a crystal decanter. "I won't argue about the shave, however," he said with a slight smile as he poured brandy into two glasses and held one of them out to the physician. Lifting his own glass in the gesture of a toast, he said, "To your skill in bringing about her recovery."

"It wasn't my skill, it was more like a miracle," the physician said, hesitating to drink the toast.

"To miraculous recoveries, then," Stephen said, raising his glass to his lips. Then he stopped again as Whitticomb negated the second toast with another shake of his head.

"I didn't say she was recovered, I said she probably wasn't going to die, and that she's able to speak." The earl's gaze narrowed, and he hesitated before saying cautiously, "Even if she recovers, there's a . . . a complication."

"What the hell does that mean?"

"It means she has no memory."

"She what?" he demanded.

"She doesn't remember anything that took place before she opened her eyes in the bedchamber upstairs. When you see her tonight, it's imperative that you not say or do anything to upset her. Head wounds are very unpredictable, and neither of us would want to lose her. Try to make her feel calm and reassured."

Sheridan sensed the presence of people in the darkened room as she floated in a comforting gray mist, drifting in and out of sleep, her mind registering neither fear nor concern, only mild confusion. She clung to that blissful state because it allowed her to escape the nameless fears and haunting questions nagging at the back of her mind.

"Miss Lancaster?"

The voice was very near her ear, kind but insistent, and vaguely familiar.

Reluctantly, she opened her eyes and blinked, trying to focus, but her vision was strangely blurry and she saw two of everything, each object superimposed over the other.

"Miss Lancaster?"

She blinked again, and the images separated into two men, one of them middle-aged and gray-haired with spectacles. Kindly and confident. The other man was much younger. Handsome. Not so kindly. Not so confident, either. Worried.

The kindly, older man was speaking. "Do you remember me, Miss Lancaster?"

Sheridan started to nod, but it made her head pound horribly. "Doctor," she whispered, and then her own questions began to rush in on her. "Where am I?"

"You're safe."

"Where?" she persisted stubbornly.

"You're in England."

For some reason, that depressed her. "Why?"

The two men exchanged a startled glance.

". . . Want to know," she whispered insistently.

"You came here to join your fiancé . . ."

A fiancé. So that was it—she was engaged. The younger man was evidently her fiancé, which explained why he looked so worried and weary. She lifted her eyes to his and managed a wan, reassuring smile which had a very odd effect: He frowned and his gaze snapped to the physician, who shook his head as if in warning. The frown bothered her for some reason, and so did the physician's warning look, but she didn't know why. It was incongruous, but at that moment, not knowing who she was or where she'd been or how she came to be there, the only thing she *did* seem to know for certain was that one must always apologize for causing unhappiness to another. She knew that rule of courtesy as if it were deeply ingrained in her. Instinctive. Imperative. Urgent.

Sherry surrendered to the overwhelming compulsion, and in a faint, thready voice she finally managed to look at him and say, "I'm sorry."

Her fiancé winced as if her words had hurt him, and then, for the first time in her recollection, she heard his voice—deep, gentle, incredibly reassuring. "Don't apologize," he said. "Get some sleep."

Exhausted and bewildered, Sherry turned her head away. "Talk . . . to me. Please," she managed, and then she framed into one whispered word all the thoughts and emotions that were warring inside her. "Afraid."

Her eyes were already drifting closed when she heard the sharp scrape of chair legs on the polished wood floor as a heavy chair was pulled up beside the bed, and her hand was enfolded in a strong, warm grip.

"Hate . . . being . . . afraid," she mumbled.

A knot of fear and admiration made Stephen's chest ache as he watched her drifting deeper and deeper into sleep. Her head was swathed in bandages and her face was ghostly pale, but what struck him forcibly was how *small* she looked in that bed, swallowed up by pillows and bedcovers. Small and frail and fragile.

She had apologized, though he was entirely to blame, not only for her injury, but for the death of her fiancé and her dreams. If she died as well, he knew he'd never be able to live with that on his conscience. He already carried more burdens, more memories, than he could endure.

Look for
Until You